SELECTED SHORT STORIES OF
JOHN O'HARA

SELECTED SHORT STORIES OF JOHN O'HARA

Introduction by Louis Begley

THE MODERN LIBRARY

NEW YORK

2003 Modern Library Paperback Edition
Biographical note © 1994 by Random House, Inc.
Introduction © 2003 by Louis Begley

LIBRARY OF CONGRESS CATALOGING-IN-PUBLICATION DATA

O'Hara, John, 1905–1970.
[Short stories. Selections]
Selected short stories of John O'Hara / introduction by Louis Begley.
p. cm.
ISBN 0-8129-6697-X
1. United States—Social life and customs—20th century—Fiction. I. Title.

PS3529.H29 A6 2003
813'.52—dc21
2002026423

Modern Library website address: www.modernlibrary.com

Printed in the United States of America

2 4 6 8 9 7 5 3 1

John O'Hara

John O'Hara was born in Pottsville, Pennsylvania, on January 31, 1905, the eldest of eight children. Even though his father, Patrick Henry O'Hara, was a prominent and relatively wealthy surgeon, the town's elaborate caste system pegged him as "the Irish doctor." Indeed John O'Hara, an Irish-Catholic outsider in WASP-dominated Pottsville, was a rebellious adolescent: he was thrown out of several boarding schools, and a drunken spree prevented his graduation as valedictorian from Niagara Preparatory School in 1924. The following year, O'Hara's world changed completely when his father's death plunged the family into poverty. Gone forever were the young man's hopes of attending Yale; instead he continued working as a cub reporter for the *Pottsville Journal* until chronic lateness (and frequent debilitating hangovers) eventually cost him his job.

Determined to escape Pottsville, O'Hara shipped out as a steward on a liner to Europe in 1927. (At various times in his youth he had found employment working as a soda jerk, running an amusement park, and reading gas meters.) Upon his return he hitchhiked to Chicago; finally, in 1928, O'Hara headed for New York City, where he covered everything from sports to religion on a succession of newspapers and magazines, including the *Herald Tribune,* the *Morning Telegraph,* and *Time.* In addition, he worked briefly as a press agent in the publicity department of RKO-Radio Pictures. A lone distinction marked O'Hara's early hand-to-mouth years in New York: in May 1928 *The New Yorker* published his first piece, beginning an association that would continue stormily for four decades. O'Hara, who would produce more than four hundred short stories in his lifetime, later took great pride in having published more fiction in *The New Yorker* than any other author. An ill-fated, two-year marriage to Helen ("Pet") Petit, a young Wellesley-educated actress from a well-to-do Episcopalian family, ended in divorce in 1933. This, followed by a wretched stint as managing editor of a magazine in Pittsburgh, left him in near-suicidal despair.

Finally resolving to concentrate only on fiction, O'Hara sequestered himself in a Manhattan hotel to write a series of integrated short stories that became, instead, *Appointment in Samarra.* An instant success when it was published by Harcourt, Brace in 1934, O'Hara's first novel was praised by Ernest Hemingway, F. Scott Fitzgerald, and Dorothy Parker. As John Updike has observed: "*Appointment in Samarra* is, among other things, an Irishman's revenge on the Protestants who had snubbed him, a book in which O'Hara had taken his own advice to his fellow Pottsville scribe Walter Farquhar: 'If you're going to get out of that God awful town, for God's sake write something that will *make* you get out of it. Write something that automatically will sever your connection with the town, that will help you get rid of the bitterness you must have stored up against all those patronizing cheap bastards.'"

The success of *Appointment in Samarra* made O'Hara attractive to Paramount Studios as a screenwriter, and he began the first of a sequence of jobs with major Hollywood film companies that continued into the 1950s. *BUtterfield 8,* another popular novel, followed quickly in 1935, along with *The Doctor's Son and Other Stories,* his first collection of short fiction. Yet the 1930s remained a restless time for O'Hara, until in 1937 he married Belle Wylie, the daughter of a socially prominent Manhattan physician descended from an old

Southern family; thus began the writer's lifelong connection with the Episcopalian enclave of Quogue, Long Island, where the Wylies maintained a summer residence. The couple's only child, their daughter, Wylie, was born in 1945. Although O'Hara's next novel, *Hope of Heaven* (1938), was a failure, he quickly rebounded with *Files on Parade* (1939), a volume of short fiction that solidified his reputation as a master of *The New Yorker* short story. *Pal Joey,* his 1940 collection of epistolary tales about a New York nightclub entertainer, served as the basis of the Rodgers and Hart hit Broadway musical, for which O'Hara supplied the libretto. Two more volumes of stories—*Pipe Night* (1945) and *Hellbox* (1947)—ensued before he returned to longer fiction.

A Rage to Live (1949), O'Hara's first "Pennsylvania novel" since *Appointment in Samarra,* was a bona fide bestseller, yet its success carried a price. A devastating review of the book in *The New Yorker* by Brendan Gill caused O'Hara to sever ties with the magazine—and abandon writing stories—for more than a decade. During the 1950s he published two minor novellas—*The Farmers Hotel* (1951) and *A Family Party* (1956)—as well as two major novels: National Book Award winner *Ten North Frederick* (1955) and blockbuster bestseller *From the Terrace* (1958), which O'Hara regarded as his major achievement as a writer. Although devastated by his wife's death in 1954, O'Hara married Katharine ("Sister") Barnes Bryan the following year and soon moved to the countryside near Princeton, New Jersey.

In 1960 O'Hara returned to *The New Yorker* with the novella "Imagine Kissing Pete," which became part of the trilogy *Sermons and Soda-Water* (1960). Over the next ten years, O'Hara's output of short fiction was prodigious and established him as one of the finest short-story writers of modern times. Six popular collections of his new stories appeared: *Assembly* (1961), *The Cape Cod Lighter* (1962), *The Hat on the Bed* (1963), *The Horse Knows the Way* (1964), *Waiting for Winter* (1966), and *And Other Stories* (1968). Many critics felt that the mainspring of O'Hara's genius was his unerring precision in capturing the speech and the milieus of his characters, whether the setting was Pennsylvania, Hollywood, or New York. "The work of no other writer," Lionel Trilling once wrote, "tells us so precisely, and with such a sense of the importance of communication, how people look and how they want to look, where they buy their clothes and where they wish they could buy their clothes, how they speak and how they think they ought to speak." Less memorable, however, were O'Hara's novels written during the 1960s: *Ourselves to Know* (1960), *The Big Laugh* (1962), *Elizabeth Appleton* (1963), *The Lockwood Concern* (1965), *The Instrument* (1967), and *Lovey Childs: A Philadelphian's Story* (1969).

When John O'Hara died on April 11, 1970, he left behind some fifty unpublished stories that were brought out posthumously in two volumes: *The Time Element and Other Stories* (1972) and *Good Samaritan and Other Stories* (1974). Likewise, *The Ewings,* the novel O'Hara finished shortly before his death, came out in 1972.

CONTENTS

INTRODUCTION

Louis Begley

Never one to mince words, John O'Hara said about short stories, "No one writes them better than I do." That is the truth, if one compares his oeuvre as a whole with any other corpus of short fiction written in the twentieth century in English. The corpus of his work is prodigious. Eleven volumes of O'Hara's collected stories appeared during his lifetime, and more than four hundred stories were published in magazines—principally *The New Yorker*. Some fifty were published after his death. Certainly, there are short stories by Hemingway and a small number of other writers that some may find are better than O'Hara's, but overall O'Hara, in my opinion, stands unequaled.

The stories in this volume show O'Hara's wide range of interests and his ability to treat with a virtuoso's ease characters and situations from any place on America's geographic and sociological spectrum. One novella-length piece, "The Doctor's Son," is set in what O'Hara called his Pennsylvania Protectorate, consisting of the small town of Pottsville in Schuylkill County, where he was born, and which, in his fiction, he referred to as Gibbsville, and the surrounding anthracite mining region of northeastern Pennsylvania. In this nostalgic tale of first love and rapid coming-of-age during the Spanish flu epidemic that struck directly after World War I, we encounter Jim Malloy, then fifteen years old, the narrator of this story and many others. Like O'Hara, Jim was the son of the town's leading Catholic surgeon, and like O'Hara he had extensive, though often vicarious, knowledge of the middle and upper spheres of his town. Because of his parents' social position in Pottsville, O'Hara had an insider's knowledge, but he was an insider equipped with a keen outsider's vision. The first half of the twentieth century was a time when anti-Irish and anti-Catholic prejudice was as endemic in the United States as prejudice against Jews, and was especially virulent among the sort of provincial families of English, German, and Pennsylvania Dutch descent that dominated Pottsville and Gibbsville. Having grown up in this corrosive atmosphere, O'Hara had an innate sense of the precariousness of his place in the world, and a preternatural sensitivity to fine distinctions of class. Both O'Hara and Malloy learned about the lower depths of the town and of the mining region the way sons of small town doctors then did: accompanying the old man on his rounds of house calls to patients. Over the course of his career, O'Hara analyzed and chronicled the social and moral landscape of the Protectorate with the same kind of attention and genius that Trollope and Balzac devoted to the protectorates they created, Barsetshire and its Church of England clergy, and the moneyed classes of Restoration France.

In the other stories included here, O'Hara drew on the rich experience of America he acquired after leaving Pottsville as a very young man. This is how he described the relationship between him and his material in the Introduction to *Sermons and Soda-Water*, a collection of three novellas:

> I have lived with as well as in the Twentieth Century from its earliest days. The United States in this Century is what I know, and it is my business to write about it to the best of my ability, with the sometimes special knowledge I have. . . . I want to record the way

people talked and thought and felt, and to do it with complete honesty and variety.

There were many layers of this knowledge. Before the success of his brilliant first novel, *Appointment in Samarra*—set in mythical Gibbsville and published in 1934, before he turned thirty—O'Hara passed through a period of severe poverty. He worked variously as a steward on a cruise ship, a hand-to-mouth journalist for newspapers in Pottsville, Philadelphia, and New York, and a night clerk in a cheap Broadway hotel. *Appointment in Samarra* brought the first significant earnings from his literary work, as well as the opportunity to do profitable stints in Hollywood as a screenplay writer and repairer of scripts written by others. Thereafter, he could be a full-time writer, except for a brief period during World War II, reflected in the story "War Aims," when he served as a correspondent with the Navy. Real money came with *Pal Joey*, the Rodgers and Hart Broadway musical, for which O'Hara wrote the book based on his own *New Yorker* stories, and then the novels *A Rage to Live* and *Ten North Frederick*. It made possible seeking membership in the best clubs to which he could get elected, a succession of apartments on Manhattan's Upper East Side, summer houses in Quogue, and, eventually, a fine year-round house in Princeton. Quogue is a village on the south shore of eastern Long Island. In O'Hara's day it was a resort of choice for predominantly Protestant, pure white lawyers, brokers, and bankers. It had a suitably exclusive club for golf, tennis, and beach duty that O'Hara joined. A population of locals made their living in the service of the summer people. We find Quogue, without its ever being named, in several of these stories, including notably "The Decision," "Doctor and Mrs. Parsons," "Too Young," "Summer's Day," and "Price's Always Open."

O'Hara had been drinking since adolescence—he was thrown out of boarding school for going on a binge the night before graduation, at which he was to have performed as valedictorian and class poet—and continued to drink so heavily that, even at a time when many of America's best writers were drowning themselves and their talent in liquor, he stood out as an egregious and unpleasant drunk. By the time he was in his forties, his health had been so severely undermined that his life was literally at stake. He decided to put work and survival first, and went permanently on the wagon. Until then he had been an inveterate habitué of bars and nightclubs. In Pottsville, that had meant saloons and their clientele of miners, mill workers, prostitutes, derelicts and roughs, as well as clubs where a trusted customer could rent a room for an assignation. With Prohibition, the age of the speakeasy began. The speakeasies O'Hara frequented in New York and in Los Angeles ran the gamut from the lowest to the most chic, "21," El Morocco, and the Stork Club being his preferred New York hangouts. "Everything Satisfactory," "A Phase of Life," and "Where's the Game?" record observations he made in his life as a barfly. The success of O'Hara's fiction—he received the National Book Award for *Ten North Frederick* and was elected to the National Institute of Arts and Letters—and his second and third marriages to well-liked and well-connected women, Belle Wylie and, after Belle's premature death, Katharine Barnes Bryan, made him respectable. He came to know important politicians, and men and women who were not writers or in show business but had family money and moved in what O'Hara considered good society. That later phase of O'Hara's life is reflected in stories like the remarkable "Graven Image," "The Cold House," and "Over the River and Through the Wood."

The first sentence or two or the short opening paragraph of any of the stories in this volume should be enough to make the reader want to devour its contents from cover to cover in one sitting, and to go on to read every other piece of O'Hara's short fiction. It does not take more to make us know that we are in the hands of a master who will not allow our attention to flag or disappoint us. The means O'Hara uses to cast his spell can be disarmingly—and deceptively—simple. Take, for instance, the first sentence of "Price's Always Open": "The place where everybody would end up before going home was Price's." Or, " 'What do you do?' I said to him. 'Do you just sit around and drink coffee all night long till daylight?'" These being the first two sentences of "I Could Have Had a Yacht." Or "Matty Wall was getting a little old, and for that reason if for no other he preferred to keep a respectable place," the first sentence of "A Respectable Place." The trick, which is quite obvious, but, as anyone who has tried knows, difficult to pull off, is to write a few words that arouse in the reader an irresistible curiosity. Why does one stop at Price's, what is the occupation of the coffee drinker, why wouldn't Matty's place be respectable without his positively wanting to keep it as such?

In other stories, O'Hara hooks the reader by a flash evocation of a setting, or a mood, or the protagonist's character or place in the world. I have chosen almost at random the openings of three stories, starting with "The Decision" and its sense of stasis, artificiality, and impending spooky terror:

> The home of Francis Townsend could have been taken for the birthplace of a nineteenth-century American poet, one of those little white houses by the side of the road that are regarded by the interested as national shrines. In front of the house there was a mounting block and hitching post, iron, with the head of a horse holding an iron ring, instead of a bit, in its mouth. These, of course, had not been used in the last thirty years, but use did not govern the removal of many objects about the Townsend place. Things were added, after due consideration, but very little was ever taken away.

In "Everything Satisfactory" we are told that "The status of Dan Schecter was such that he was as welcome, or was made as welcome, in a Hollywood night club when he came in alone as when he brought with him a party of twenty." A surprising amount of information is crammed in the most casual way possible into these thirty-seven words, including the sly distinction between being welcome and being "made welcome" that is like a mark left by the swift swipe of a big cat's paw. In "In the Morning Sun," we are drawn into a sense of summer languor and mystery about to be confronted:

The door between the kitchen and the dining room swung back and forth, wung-wung, wung-wung, behind Mrs. Demarest. She stopped, without seeming to stop, to straighten the centerpiece on the dining room table, and continued through the dining room to the side porch, which ran along that side of the house. . . . The porch was cool, almost as cool as the interior of the house, but she went out through the screen door to where her son was sitting under the tree.

O'Hara wrote effortlessly. His style is efficient and spare. It does not call attention to itself. The purpose, from which he never strays, is to get the story across to the reader with the maximum of accuracy and conviction, without a possibility of misunderstanding. In his fiction, O'Hara never showed off, and never allowed an effect of style to call attention to the writing and distract the reader from the narrative. He avoided equally the oversimplification of language that in Hemingway's fiction sometimes lends itself to parody, and the flights into poetry in F. Scott Fitzgerald's fiction, although he admired deeply both writers and counted them among his friends. There are no attempts in O'Hara's work to mystify or impress the reader by erudition, word play, or obscurity. For his lightning-fast, incisive descriptions of people, he drew on his encyclopedic knowledge of how Americans identify themselves to each other and determine their place in the local and national pecking order. Stored up in his prodigious memory were the myriad coded signals emitted by clothes and shoes, hats, college rings and fraternity pins, and how one wears them, as well as the specific significance of such clues to gradations in status as the school and college one has attended, membership in certain clubs, speech patterns and nuances of courtesy and rudeness, where one lives or spends vacations, and how long one has been at a particular address or owned a particular house. As one might expect from the author of the *Pal Joey* stories, O'Hara had a special talent for revealing character through speech. Its versatility and devastating, deadpan precision are on display in such stories as "A Phase of Life," "Pardner," "Where's the

Game?" and, most notably, "I Could Have Had a Yacht," which is a long monologue.

O'Hara did not go to college. There wasn't enough money for it after his father the doctor died, leaving an estate that amounted to almost nothing. Since the doctor's practice had been very successful, and he had lived like a rich man, O'Hara's expectations of the sort of start in life he might be given had to be radically altered. He felt poor and, he feared, he was déclassé; certainly his dream of going to Yale—the college of choice among Pottsville swells of his acquaintance—had become unattainable. The social pressures of Pottsville were soon behind him, but with his growing reputation as a short-story writer published regularly by *The New Yorker,* and the breakthrough of *Appointment in Samarra,* he found himself increasingly living in a milieu of writers and editors, a number of whom had been to Ivy League colleges and the right prep schools. Some belonged, it seemed practically as a matter of right, to exclusive men's clubs, and dressed like gentlemen to the manner born. A man as powerfully ambitious and gifted as O'Hara, who feels that he has been cheated by fate, may make a show of looking down on advantages of privilege. That was not O'Hara's way. He admired unabashedly the style and folkways of East Coast society, and set about acquiring its accoutrements as soon as he could afford them, with more than a touch of exaggeration and defiance. Along the way, he was tagged as a snob—unfairly, because there is no evidence that O'Hara had ever fawned, or curried favor with, real or imagined social superiors, and there was no place in his character for that other odious hallmark of a snob, which is contempt for people who stand lower on the social ladder. Nor can his work be used to indict him of snobbery. While many of the protagonists of O'Hara's short fiction belong to the middle or upper middle class, many do not: in the stories in this volume, which are in this regard representative of his work, one finds as central characters a bartender, a counterman in a diner, a black man who washes cars in a Manhattan garage, young women whom one might have once referred to as B-girls, lowly office employees, and part-time criminals. The middle-class world of O'Hara's novels is not hermetic like, for instance, Wharton's. Its population is variegated, constituting a generous cross section of American society. O'Hara's moral judgment of his personages is rigorous and unaffected by social status; there is no element of condescension in his treatment of any of them.

Nevertheless, in the post-Depression age of the proletarian novel, the predominance of middle-class settings in O'Hara's work did not serve him well, and the amplitude and steely realism of his portrayal of the American scene were out of tune in the last decades of the twentieth century with the taste of many of those who make *ex cathedra* judgments about the reputations of writers. It is said that somehow O'Hara lacks relevance. Why that should be so, why the travails and afflictions of the middle or upper middle class should be presumed to hold less interest than the adventures of truck drivers, drifters, and past or present addicts, and why clarity of plot and dialogue and accuracy of description are less artistic than minimalist anomie or a novelist's concentrating attention on the writing of a novel rather than on plot and character depiction, may remain an unsolved mystery. O'Hara's short fiction, as it becomes well known again, may bring about a reappraisal. Curiously, the charge of snobbery has stuck to O'Hara, fed by anecdotes of his arrogance, hot temper, passion for clubs and club insignia and showy automobiles, with lasting and unfair harm to his reputation. He has been a victim of the bizarre view, which has surprising vigor, that the good or bad behavior of a writer of fiction in his personal life, and the writer's being free or not free of undesirable character traits, have a bearing on the quality of the work, that a good writer should be a "good person" as we understand that today. A great part of this fallacy derives from the vogue for intimate biographies of writers. No such biography of Shakespeare is available, but the lack of anything beyond meager scraps of information about his life has not interfered with our appreciation of his work on stage or in print. Certainly, the scabrous aspects of Proust's sadistic proclivities or Dostoevsky's anti-Semitism, which have been aired in multi-thousand-page biographies, do not impugn the standing of their novels as masterpieces.

O'Hara was not the first great writer to have been seduced by the way the rich and the wellborn live. The trail has been blazed by others. In fact, O'Hara comes off as possibly less starstruck than— to choose just three examples—Honoré de Balzac, who was insistent on having the prized "de," to which he was not entitled, inserted between his name and surname, and was fixated on a vision of a secret world of dukes and duchesses of his invention, about which he wrote in some of the best volumes of his *Human Comedy*; Proust, who shared Balzac's infatuation with high aristocracy and devoted a great part of *In Search of Lost Time* to the dissection of its mores; and even Trollope, with his Irish hunters that he transported in a freight wagon while crisscrossing England by rail as a postal inspector so that he could, whenever possible, unload his horse and ride to hounds, and his magnificent creations who reign over the parliamentary novels: the Duke of Omnium, the greatest nobleman of the realm; his heir, Mr. Plantagenet Palliser, conceived by Trollope as the epitome of the perfect English gentleman; and Mr. Palliser's wife, the beautiful and admirable Lady Glencora. Trollope's satisfaction at having become successful enough to be elected to the Cosmopolitan and later the Athenaeum and Garrick clubs in London was immense—and touching! None of these predilections and foibles detract from Balzac's, Proust's, or Trollope's novels; on the contrary, they provided the nourishment necessary for their creation, just as O'Hara's passionate study of the American caste system, and the deadly precision of the symbols and distinctions that sustain it, was indispensable in the conception of the Pennsylvania Protectorate and the other loci of his fiction—New York, Los Angeles, as well as small towns in which we may recognize Quogue—and the legion of their unforgettable denizens.

—

LOUIS BEGLEY is the author of six novels, the most recent of which is *Schmidt Delivered*. He lives in New York City.

SELECTED SHORT STORIES OF
JOHN O'HARA

THE DECISION

The home of Francis Townsend could have been taken for the birthplace of a nineteenth-century American poet, one of those little white houses by the side of the road that are regarded by the interested as national shrines. In front of the house there was a mounting block and a hitching post, iron, with the head of a horse holding an iron ring, instead of a bit, in its mouth. These, of course, had not been used in the last thirty years, but use did not govern the removal of many objects about the Townsend place. Things were added, after due consideration, but very little was ever taken away.

The Townsend place was on the outskirts of the seacoast village, out of the zone where the sidewalks were paved. In the fall of the year and in the spring, the sidewalk was liable to be rather muddy, and Francis Townsend several times had considered bricking the path—not that he minded the mud, but out of consideration for the female pedestrians. This project he had dismissed after studying the situation every afternoon for a week. He sat by the window in the front room and came to the conclusion that (a) there were not really many pedestrians during the muddy seasons, since there were few summer people around in spring or fall, and (b) the few natives who did use the sidewalk in front of his place were people who had sense enough to be properly shod in muddy weather. Another and very satisfying discovery that Francis Townsend made was that few people—men, women, or children—came near his house at all. For a long, long time he had entertained the belief that the street outside was a busy thoroughfare, more or less choked with foot and vehicular traffic. "I am really quite alone out here," he remarked to himself. This allowed for the fact that he had made his study of the muddy-sidewalk problem in the afternoon, when traffic was presumably lighter than in the morning, when, for instance, housewives would be doing their shopping. The housewives and others could not have made *that* much difference; even if the morning traffic were double that of the afternoon, it still was not considerable. It was, of course, impossible for Francis Townsend to make his study in the morning, except Sunday morning, for Francis Townsend's mornings were, in a manner of speaking, spoken for.

Every morning, Francis Townsend would rise at six-thirty, shave and have his bath, and himself prepare first breakfast, which consisted of two cups of coffee and a doughnut. In the winter he would have this meal in the kitchen, cheerful with its many windows and warm because of the huge range. In the summer he would take the coffee and doughnut to the front room, where it was dark and cool all day. He would run water into the dirty cup and saucer and put them in the sink for the further attention of Mrs. Dayton, his housekeeper, who usually made her appearance at eight-thirty. By the time she arrived, Francis Townsend would have changed from his sneakers and khaki pants and cardigan to a more suitable costume—his black suit, high black kid shoes, starched collar, and black four-in-hand tie. He would smoke a cigarette while he listened to Mrs. Dayton stirring about in the kitchen, and pretty soon would come the sound of the knocker and he would go to the front door. That would be Jerry Bradford, the letter carrier.

"Good morning, Jerry."

"Good morning, Francis. Three letters an-n-nd the New York paper."

"Three letters and the paper, thank you."

"Fresh this morning. Wind's from the east. Might have a little rain later in the day."

"Oh, you think *so*?"

"Well, I might be wrong. See you tomorrow, in all likelihood." Jerry would go away and Francis would stand at the open doorway until Jerry had passed the Townsend property line. Then sometimes Francis would look at the brass nameplate, with its smooth patina and barely distinguishable name: "F. T. Townsend, M.D." The plate was small, hardly any larger than the plate for a man's calling card, not a proper physician's shingle at all, but there it was and had been from the day of his return from medical school.

He would go back to his chair in the front room and wait for Mrs. Dayton to announce breakfast, which she did in her own way. She would say, "Morning," as greeting, and nod slowly, indicating that breakfast was on the table. Francis then would take his paper and letters to the dining room and partake of second breakfast— oatmeal, ham and eggs, toast that was toasted over a flame, and a pot of coffee. Mrs. Dayton appeared only once during breakfast, when she brought in the eggs and took away the cereal dishes.

Francis Townsend's mail rarely was worth the pleasure of anticipation. That did not keep him from anticipating Jerry Bradford's knock on the door or from continuing to hope for some surprise when he slit the envelopes with his butter knife. The reading of his mail did, in fact, give him pleasure, even though it might be no more than an alumni-association plea, a list of candidates for membership in his New York club, or an advertisement from a drug or instrument company. Francis Townsend would read them all, all the way through, propping them against the tall silver salt-cellar, and then he would take them with him to the front room, so that Mrs. Dayton could not see them, and there he would toss them in the fire or, in warm weather, put a match to them.

Then, every day but Sunday, Francis Townsend would take his walk. For the first thirty of the last forty years, Francis Townsend had had a companion on his walk. The companion always had been a collie; not always the same collie, but always a collie. But about ten years ago, when the last Dollie (all of Francis Townsend's dogs had been called Dollie) died, Francis Townsend read somewhere or heard somewhere that it took too much out of you to have dogs; you no sooner grew to love them, and they you, than they died and you had to start all over again with a new one. This bit of dog lore came at a time when Francis Townsend had just lost a Dollie and was suffering a slight nosebleed. It was not a proper hemorrhage, but it was not exactly reassuring as to Francis Townsend's life expectancy, and he did not want to take on the responsibility of another Dollie if Dollie were to be left without anyone to take care of her, any more than he wanted to go through the pain of losing another dog. Therefore, for the last ten years or so, Francis Townsend had taken his walk alone.

Although he would not have known it, Francis Townsend's daily—except Sunday—walk was as much a part of the life of the village as it was of his own life. The older merchants and their older children and older employees took for granted that around a certain hour every morning Francis Townsend would be along. Harris, the clothing-store man; McFetridge, the hardware-store man; Blanchard, the jeweler; Bradford, brother of Jerry Bradford, who had the Ford-Lincoln-Mercury agency—among others—took for granted that Francis Townsend would be along around a certain hour every morning. He had to pass their places on his way to the bank, and when they saw him, they would say, "Hello, Francis," and would usually say something about the weather, and Francis would nod and smile, and, without coming to a full stop, he would indicate that the comment or the prediction was acceptable to him.

His first full stop always was the bank. There he would go to Eben Townsend's desk and Eben would push toward him a filled-in check. "Morning, Francis," "Good morning, Eben," they would say, and Francis would put "F. T. Townsend, M.D.," on the check, and his cousin would give Francis three five-dollar bills. Francis would thank him and resume his walk.

At his next stop, Francis would sometimes have to wait longer than at the bank. Eventually, though, the barkeep would come to wait on Francis. "Hyuh, Francis," he would say, and place a quart of rye whiskey and a pitcher of water on the bar.

"Hyuh, Jimmy," Francis would say, and pour himself a rye-and-water. "Well, well, well."

"Ixcuse me, Francis, I got a salesman here," Jimmy might say. "Be with you in two shakes of a ram's tail."

"That's all right, Jimmy. Take your time. I'll be here for a while."

This conversational opening, or something very like it, had been fairly constant for forty years, inasmuch as the barkeep's name always had been Jimmy, since a father and a son had owned the business, or at least tended bar, during the forty mature years of Francis Townsend's life. Jimmy the father had discovered long, long ago that, as he put it, Francis was good for the entire bloody morning and didn't take offense if you left him a minute to transact your business. Francis was indeed good for the entire morning. If it happened to be one of Jimmy's busy days, he would remember to put four toofers—two-for-a-quarter cigars—on the bar in front of Francis before he left him, and Francis would smoke them slowly, holding them in his tiny, even teeth, looking up at the ceiling with one of them in his mouth, as though William Howard Taft or Harry Truman had just asked his advice on whom to appoint to the Court of St. James's. Francis never bothered anybody, not even during the years of two World Wars. He never tried to buy drinks for the Coast Guard or the Army Air Forces, and he was not a man whose appearance welcomed invitations on the part of strangers. Among the villagers—the few who would drink in the morning out of habit or temporary necessity—none would bother Francis or expect to be bothered by him. Francis had his place at the bar, at the far corner, and it was his so long as he was present. First-generation Jimmy and second-generation Jimmy had seen to that.

Each day, Monday through Saturday, January through December, Francis Townsend would sip his drinks and smoke his cigars until the noon Angelus from St. Joseph's Church. If he happened to be the only customer in the bar, Francis would say to Jimmy, "Ahem. The angel of the Lord declared, if I may say so."

"Correct, Francis."

Francis would take two of the three five-dollar bills from a lower vest pocket, and Jimmy would size up the rye bottle and pick up the money and return the estimated and invariably honest change. The tradition then was for Jimmy to say, "Now the house breaks down and turns Cath'lic."

"A rye, then," would be Francis Townsend's answer, in Francis Townsend's weak attempt at brogue. Whereupon Jimmy would hand Francis Townsend a wrapped bottle of rye and Francis would go home and eat the nice lunch Mrs. Dayton had prepared and take a good nap till time for supper, and after supper, when Mrs. Dayton had gone home, he would sit and read some of the fine books, like *Dombey and Son*, the Waverley Novels, Bacon's *Essays*—the fine books in the front room—till it was time to bank the kitchen fire for the next morning and finish off the last of the wrapped bottle of rye.

That was about the way it had been with Francis Townsend from the time he finished medical school. That year, soon after his graduation, his uncle, who had raised him, said to him one day, "What are your plans, Francis?"

"First, I thought I'd interne at a hospital in Pittsburgh. A great many mines and factories out there and a man can learn a lot. Then, of course, I'll come back here and hang out my shingle. And I have an understanding with a girl in Philadelphia, Uncle. We're not engaged, but—we have an understanding."

His uncle got up and filled his pipe from the humidor on the mantelpiece in the front room. "No, boy," he said. "I'm sorry to say you can't have any of those things. You can never practice medicine, and you can't marry."

"Why, I can do both. I'm accepted at the hospital out in Pittsburgh, and the girl said she'd wait."

"Not when I tell you what I have to tell you. Do you know that both your father and your mother died in an institution? No, of course you don't know. There aren't many people in this village know. Most of the people my age think your father and mother died of consumption, but it wasn't consumption, France. It was mental."

"I see," said Francis. He stood up and filled his own pipe, with his class numerals in silver on the bowl. "Well, then, of course you're right." He took his time lighting up. "I guess there's no way out of that, is there, Uncle?"

"I don't know. I don't know enough about such things, putting to one side that I do know you shouldn't marry or you shouldn't doctor people."

"Oh, I agree with you, Uncle. I agree with you." Francis sat down again, trying to assume the manner of one Deke talking to another Deke in the fraternity house. "I wonder what I ought to do? I don't think I ought to just sit here and wait till I begin to get loony myself. There ought to be some kind of work where I couldn't do anybody any harm."

"You won't have to worry about money. I've fixed that at the bank. Give yourself plenty of time to pick and choose. You'll decide on something."

"Oh, very likely I will," Francis said. "I won't just stay on here in the village." But that, it turned out, was what he did decide to do.

EVERYTHING SATISFACTORY

The status of Dan Schecter was such that he was as welcome, or was made as welcome, in a Hollywood night club when he came in alone as when he brought with him a party of twenty. Not that he ever had brought a party of twenty to the Klub Kilocycle. The Klub, which has been called the little club without charm, is a late spot chiefly inhabited by musicians and radio characters, and visited by picture people only when broadcasts draw them to the vicinity of Sunset and Vine. No such thing had brought Dan to the Klub initially. He dropped in that first night without quite knowing where he was; it was during the time when he was carrying that torch for Sandra Sardou, and he'd been drinking.

"Good evening, Mr. Schecter," the headwaiter said.

"Good evening," said Dan. "Why, it's Paul. Where the hell've you been, Paul?"

"Right here, Mr. Schecter. Five years. I own a little piece of the joint. You alone, sir?"

"Uh-huh. Didn't you use to be at the Troc?"

"No, sir. The Victor Hugo and Lamaze, remember?"

"That's right. Paul, I wanta sit down."

"Yes, sir." Paul took Dan to a table, transmitted the drink order—double brandy and soda—to a waiter, and, with his native tact, left Dan before either man got bored with the other. When Dan woke up the next morning he was in his own bed, alone, and his car was in the driveway, intact. This latter was a pleasant discovery, for he was fully clothed, and it was a matter of fairly common knowledge that when Dan woke up with his clothes on there was usually a wrinkled car downstairs, or no car at all. His lawyer had told him that it was becoming more and more difficult to square these motoring lapses. He examined the match books in his pockets, which vaguely recalled to him his visit, or the early part of his visit, to the Klub Kilocycle, and he remembered Paul.

Later that day he telephoned Paul, who told him that one of the boys had driven him home on orders from Paul. "You always used to take care of me, Mr. Schecter. It was nothing. Glad to do it, Mr. Schecter."

"How much do I owe you?"

"You signed a small tab, sir. Eleven or twelve dollars," said Paul. "And I gave the waiter five dollars to take you home. You understand I had to take the waiter off his station, so I had to give him something."

"I'll be in tonight or tomorrow, Paul. That was very decent of you."

It was three or four nights later that Dan went to the Klub for the second time, again alone. Sandra still would not leave the little nobody she was married to, although Isabel Schecter had walked out on Dan. Never had Dan managed such things so badly, and he was in the paradoxical situation of carrying a torch and losing his grip. He began to think of Paul as his only friend. He shook hands with him and in his hand was a fifty-dollar bill, which Paul glanced at as he led Dan to a table.

At that time the entertainment at the Klub was rather special but of a kind that Dan, who had owned a four-hundred-dollar set of drums in college, could appreciate. The eight-piece combination was for your listening pleasure and not intended to be danced to;

the guitar, double-bass, and piano trio had made several recondite records; the blonde who sang with the band was known to every habitué, and Dan, watching her go to work, became aware that she was also known to him. He realized he must have been too drunk to notice her during his first visit.

"Paul," he said, summoning Paul. "Isn't that Mimi Walker?"

"That's right," said Paul, smiling.

"She looks wonderful," said Dan. "Tell her I'd like to buy her a drink."

Paul nodded, and when Mimi finished her songs he spoke to her. She turned in Dan's general direction and nodded, and in about five minutes she presented herself at Dan's table.

"Hello," she said. She seemed not to see that he had offered his hand and that his whole manner was of the friendliest. She sat beside him. "I'll have a bourbon and ginger ale."

"I didn't know you were here," said Dan.

"Come on, Dan. You didn't know I was anywhere. How phony can you get?"

"Do you think I'm a phony? I don't. A lot of things, but not a phony."

"Then don't start out as if you'd been—as if you had the Missing Persons Bureau out looking for me. I see where Sandra's still with her husband."

"Do you know her?"

"I was in a show with her. Oh, she's a lot younger than I am, but I used to know her, all right. She was always a lot smarter than I am. In fact, she still owes me some money on the Louis-Schmeling fight, and you know how long ago that was."

"She told me she was twenty-six."

"She could have been," said Mimi. "I mean she could have been sixteen when I knew her. That would make me thirty. O.K. I'm thirty. But you know better if you stop to think."

"You look wonderful," said Dan.

"Thanks."

"How long have you been here?"

"Five years," she said. "Since it opened."

"Oh."

"What do you mean, 'oh'?"

"I seem to remember Paul told me he's been here five years and owns a piece of the place. Is that how it is, Mimi?"

"For your information, I own a little piece of the joint myself. *Now* where are you?"

"Nowhere," said Dan.

"And that's exactly where you're going to get, Dan, so if you like the way I look, O.K., but just don't start thinking of a return engagement."

"You're a little ahead of me, but I guess that's what I *was* thinking."

"No!" She called the waiter. "Now I'll buy *you* a drink so you won't worry about the eighty cents it cost you to find out what you just found out. Give Mr. Schecter a double whatever he's having."

The waiter bowed respectfully. "The party on Five asked if you'll come over and have a drink with them, Miss Walker," said the waiter. "The one fella said he's a friend of Nat Wolff's."

"I'll be over," said Mimi.

"I know Nat, too, so don't go right away," said Dan, trying to be pleasant.

"Terribly sorry, chum, but I have to do another number."

"So soon? Well, I'll wait," said Dan.

She started to sing, "It'll be a long, long time." She got up and went to Table Five and spoke to the people but did not sit down. She went to the bandstand and sang a number and when she finished she went back and sat with the people on Five. Dan had a few drinks. He became aware of Paul standing near his table. How long Paul had been there, Dan had no way of knowing; he had been staring at the back of Mimi's head.

"Everything satisfactory, sir?" said Paul.

"I wouldn't go so far as to say that, Paul." He was on the point of asking Paul a question or two but decided against it for the time being. "We'll see how things work out."

Paul smiled. "Yes, sir."

The time passed. Dan clocked Mimi for six minutes at Table Five, and then when he thought it was six minutes more, it was over an hour more. Mimi would get up now and then and do a number and always rejoin the people at Five, and Paul would come around to Dan's table and smile and ask if everything was satisfactory. Dan's answers varied with the readiness of his wit. Somewhere along the line his drinks were being served in coffee cups, which, Paul felt he had to explain, was on account of The Law. The drinks went just as fast from coffee cups as they did from highball glasses, and they didn't have as much soda in them. On returning from a trip to the men's room, Dan hovered over his table unsteadily, glancing at the empty chairs and then at Mimi, laughing and talking at Table Five. Dan started to sit down, and if it had not been for Paul's help he would have missed the chair. "Thanks, Paul," said Dan.

"Everything satisfactory, Mr. Schecter?"

Dan laughed. "Goddam *un*satisfactory, but I said I'd wait and that's what I'm gonna do."

"Yes, sir," said Paul. "Tom, bring Mr. Schecter another drink." Dan and Paul grinned at each other.

The music stopped, had stopped without Dan's noticing, or noticing that he was the only customer in the place. He studied his watch without succeeding in concentrating on the position of the hands. "Paul!"

"Yes, sir."

"Am I the last one here? Where's Miss Walker?"

"She went home, sir," said Paul.

"Where does she live? Foolish question number five thousand two hundred and eighty." He gulped his drink and reached in his pocket and took out a money clip. He put two twenties on the table. "I'll give you twenty dollars more if you tell me where—no, *you* wouldn't tell me, you son of a bitch." He stood up and staggered to the street. Paul came up behind him and said to the doorman, "Mr. Schecter's car."

In a moment or two a boy drove the car around from the parking lot, and Paul went back inside the Klub and leaned against the bar. Mimi was standing there, and they both watched Dan getting into the driver's seat. She was frowning.

"I can't let him go like that," she said.

"You stay where you are," said Paul. "We'll read about him in the papers." The car roared away.

THE MOCCASINS

About twenty people were sitting in the half darkness of the living room and the even darker screened-in porch, but the people were in twos and fours, conversing quietly or not at all, so it did not seem like a party. The gathering lacked the unity of noise that often goes with a much smaller group. It did have something else, which could have been an air of unified expectancy, or simple languorousness, or the two combined. Mary thought she sensed both, as though the people were just sitting around, lying around, waiting for something, but nothing in particular, to happen. It was late at night. The people were all—except for one woman—deeply tanned, and half of them could have got their tan from sports, which would account for their being tired. None of the men got up when Mary and her brother followed the Negro houseman into the living room. A portly man in an unbuttoned Hawaiian printed shirt was playing drums, using the wire brushes softly and expertly to the recorded music of the Dorsey brothers on the radio-phonograph. He was one of the brownest of all, down his chest to the khaki shorts and then again down his legs to his short socks. He flashed a smile and waved a wire brush in greeting, but went on playing without interruption, more interested in the tune, "Blue Lou," than in the arrival of Mary and her brother.

A stout, golden-haired woman, the only person not burned by the sun, came up to greet Mary and Jack. Her smile was quick and polite and no more, implying that that would be all until the visitors identified themselves—and that if the identification were not satisfactory, the newcomers would be thrown right out.

"Mrs. Fothergill, I'm Jack Tracy, and this is my sister Mary."

The smile immediately warmed. "Oh, yes. Why, yes! I'm very *pleased*. Carl *Shepherd*."

"That's right," said Jack. He looked around, but in the dim light he could not recognize anyone. "He here?"

"No, he isn't. He isn't here *yet*, but he phoned from Hobe Sound. He's coming all right, and we're expecting you—my husband and I. Doc!" she called to the man at the drums.

He nodded in time with the music and spoke on the beat: "Com-eeng, Moth-thurr." The record ended and he joined the three. He moved quickly and with power that would not be good to run up against, but his gait was feminine. He waddled. Then immediately there was another contradiction—his hands were large and his grip was strong. He probably had been a capable guard in the late Hugo Bezdek or early Rockne era. His thin gray hair was parted in the middle and he looked as though he ought to be wearing a fraternity pin. His wife introduced the Tracys, and he put one hand on Jack's shoulder and the other on Mary's, which was bare.

"Carl'll be scooting in here any minute, but what's to keep us from a little libation? You name it, and we have it," he said. "There's a little thing of mine own called a Crusher." He grinned.

"Now, Doc," said Mrs. Fothergill.

"What's a Crusher?" Mary asked.

"You wouldn't want to try it and see, would you?"

"Maybe I'd just better have a Scotch," said Mary.

"Aw, no clients?" said Doc.

"Well . . ." said Mary.

"That's more like it," said Doc. "How about you, Mr. Tracy?"

"I think I'd better stick to bourbon-and-soda, sir," said Jack.

"Maybe you're right, if you've been drinking bourbon," said Doc. He chuckled. "I thought you were starting from scratch."

"*I* am," said Mary.

"Then, you come right along with Dr. Fothergill and learn how to make a Crusher. Mr. Tracy, you go along with *Mother*gill and give the ladies a treat." He put his arm around Mary and took her to a bar, which was on the porch.

"Fothergill and Mothergill, that's cute," said Mary.

He laughed. "I don't know who thought that up—at least, not in this generation. It's an old family joke, of course, back in West Virginia, where I come from, but they started calling us that, when we got married, in New York, too. Cannes. California. Down here. Whenever we meet a new crowd, sooner or later somebody'll get the idea of calling us Fothergill and Mothergill. Shanghai. India. Nairobi."

"You've lived everywhere," said Mary.

"Pretty near. Just about approximately everywhere—everywhere they'll have us," he said. He automatically but precisely mixed the drink during his chatter.

"This is a darling house," said Mary.

"It is that, all right. Frank and Hazel *really* know how to live."

"Who?"

"Oh, don't you know Frank and Hazel—the Blaylocks? You don't suppose this house belongs to us! No, child. We happen to know these friends of ours, and Hazel Blaylock broke her leg skiing up in the Laurentians, so they asked Mothergill and I to come down and open it for them, hold the fort till—now a little dash of Pernod. There. Yes, we keep it open for them till Hazel's leg heals, and, of course, much as we adore Hazel and much as I admire a pretty leg—well, we hope she takes good care of that leg for another month. Up north. That'll bring us right up to when we want to go to Palm Springs. There, take a sip of that and hold onto the top of your head."

Mary tasted the drink, putting a hand on her head. She smiled. "No effect so far."

"Of course not. I exaggerate a little, but it does have a wallop. Now your brother's, and one for Dr. Fothergill, and then you come over and sit with me." He made two highballs. As he was about finished, a man and a woman who had been talking earnestly in a far corner of the porch started for the door, which opened, Mary now could see, out onto a boat landing. A speedboat was tied up there.

"Hey, Buzz, don't go out there without a flashlight," Doc said.

"We know our way around," said the woman.

"Around each other," said Doc. "No, seriously—take a flashlight."

"Why?" said Buzz.

"Moccasins," said Doc. He reached under the bar.

The man looked at the woman and frowned. She shrugged, whereupon the man took the torch from Doc and they went out to the speedboat.

"If she feels that way about it, it must be love," said Doc. "Come on."

"Love could never get me to go out there," said Mary.

"Not at your age," said Doc.

Doc paused to give one of the highballs to Jack, who was sitting with Mrs. Fothergill and a couple—a young girl whom Mary had seen in New York and a second-rate movie actor, whom she had not noticed before. Then she and Doc went on inside to chairs near the drums.

"If you want to play, go ahead," said Mary.

"I will later. Just now I'd rather fan the breeze with you."

"All right," said Mary. "What did you mean about not at my age?"

They lit cigarettes before he answered. "At your age, love comes to *you*, and plenty of it, I imagine. You don't have to walk through moccasins for it."

"No?"

He studied her, then shook his head. "No." He waited a moment and then decided not to say what he might have been going to say. He swallowed half his highball before going on, and when he did, he returned to the chit-chat form. "Where do you usually go for the winter?"

"I've usually been in school."

"Good Lord, I knew you were young, but not that young. You probably came out this year."

"Last summer," she said.

"Last summer. Are you from Long Island?"

"Yes," she said.

"I smell money," he said. "Oh, sure. Your father is probably Herman Tracy."

"Yes," she said.

"Well, you've got nothing to worry about, except taxes, your head on a pikestaff, and stuff. Where does Carl Shepherd fit in? If I'm asking too many questions, it's because I always do. You're not related to Carl?"

"No," she said.

"That answers a *lot* of questions," he said.

"Does it? That's good," she said.

He smiled. "Don't be haughty with old Doc Fothergill. If I have your age right, I knew Carl before you were born, and if I haven't got it right, I'm only wrong by a year or so."

"Really?"

"Really," he said. "Now, I don't figure where your brother comes in." He looked out to the porch. "Well, now, maybe I do. In just this short space of time, he seems to be moving in on little Emily. Got that hambo from Hollywood talking to himself. I hope your brother can handle a sneak punch."

"How do you mean?"

"Well, our actor friend was doing all right with Emily before your brother got here," he said. "That's what I meant by a sneak punch. Mr. Hollywood's a bad actor, and I can say that again."

"Jack's a good fighter."

"Then that's settled. Maybe he belongs here," said Doc.

"Well, I should hope so."

"No, you shouldn't hope so," said Doc. The houseman took Doc's empty glass and Mary shook her head. Somebody got up and turned on the phonograph, which filled in the silence between Mary and Doc. She turned and saw that he was watching her. He smiled.

"Just beautiful, that's all."

"Thank you," she said.

"Not quite all. There's a lot of other things I'd like to know about you."

"Ask," she said.

"No. The things I want to know, you don't ask. You find out, but you don't ask. And it wouldn't do me any good to know anyway."

"No?"

The houseman handed Doc his drink. "No," said Doc. He drank deeply again, and looked slowly around the room and out to the porch. Two couples were dancing, the partners holding close to each other, and the conversations in the two rooms remained as subdued as when Mary had arrived at the party. Doc leaned forward and turned his head so that he faced Mary.

"Well?" she said.

"I'd give a year of my life to kiss you. Not a future year, mind you. One of the good ones."

"Would you?" she said.

"However, that's out of the question, for sixteen thousand reasons, so will you do me another favor?"

"I won't kiss you," she said.

"I have another favor. Will you please go home? Will you do me a favor and do yourself a favor and get out of here?"

"All right," she said, and started to rise. He reached out and touched her hand, but she pulled it away and went out to her brother. It took a minute to persuade him to leave, and Doc could not hear what words she used in doing it. When they came to the living room, Doc got up.

"I'll show you the way," he said.

"Thanks, we can find it," Mary said.

He walked with them to their car. "Tracy, I'd like to say one thing to your sister."

"My guess is you've said too much already. I probably ought to punch you in the nose, if I knew what this was all about."

"You don't, and anyway don't try it," said Doc. He spoke to Mary. "Just remember one thing. You don't have to walk through moccasins for it."

"What's he talking about?" said Jack.

"Oh, who cares?" said Mary.

DOCTOR AND MRS. PARSONS

For a few weeks last summer, when the population of the village was trebled by the presence of the summer people, Doctor Parsons had been able to get a few hours' rest after evening office hours by calling on Joe Peck. Joe had a house near the beach, nowhere near the club, and he was a bachelor who lived with his sister. He lived there the year round, and the Pecks were not people to encourage casual dropping in by anyone they had not known thirty or more years. Doctor Parsons would stretch out on the sofa, unmolested by the telephone. That lasted until one night a desperate mother with a sick child took her car and drove along every street and lane until she spotted Doctor Parsons' car. After that the word got around quickly that if Doctor Parsons was not in his office in the evening you might find him at Joe Peck's house. The doctor's next scheme was to steal a nap in his car by parking behind the stable on the old Medbury property, which was practically abandoned and in disrepair. That was a good scheme for a while, and then one night Doctor Parsons was shaken gently by Harry Rossini, one of the village policemen. "Doc, we got a pretty bad accident. Three cars smashed up. One kid dead already."

"How'd you know where to find me?"

"Doc, I knew you been coming here over three weeks. I'd be for letting you sleep, but..."

"O.K., Harry." This time Doctor Parsons wanted to cry.

"I wouldn't of wakened you for a case of sunburn, Doc, you know that. But here we got two kids they're still pinned under one of the cars."

"I understand, Harry."

"One of them is my sister's kid. You know, Thelma."

"Oh, God," said Doctor Parsons. "Well, let's go. . . . Say, Harry, maybe you could fix up a place in the lockup for me two or three nights a week."

"I can do it. That's what I'll do. We got a cell."

September came, but the population did not thin out so much as in normal years. Many of the summer people had been unable to solve the apartment situation in town, and many others were waiting for husbands and sons to get out of the Army and have a real rest at their summer places. Quite a few talked about staying down all winter, and quite a few actually stayed: the Indian summer was extremely mild, and it was kind of fun to live in the partly closed houses, wear old clothes all the time, and have impromptu parties. It gave the young fathers a chance to get acquainted with offspring whom many of them were seeing for the first time but whom Doctor Parsons knew by heart. He was not very good about the babies' names or even the names of their parents unless he had known *their* parents. He would come back to his office with his pockets stuffed with prescription blanks on which he had written such notations as "Fat girl, about 24, living in Ed Rogers house. Child 16 months. Diphtheritic croup." It had long since ceased to embarrass him when he would call at a house and ask how the little boy was today and find that in this house it had been the cook who was his patient. It no longer bothered him in cases like that to read the expression in the eyes of the lady of the house (likely to be a modern young woman, medically knowledgeable), which accused him of drunkenness or at best senile incompetence. If they didn't like it, they could get another doctor. Of course, there was no other doctor; Jess Williamson had been in the Army for three years, and so had all the other doctors within a radius of twenty miles.

Doctor Parsons had a practice that thirty years ago would have been his dreams come true, but last summer and last fall and the winter before and the summer before that, he had tried to sell, with no takers. He had not been in a duck blind since the fall of '42, or to a lodge meeting, or a bank directors' meeting, or the get-togethers of the county medical society, where a man could get drunk without shocking the populace. He had had to fire the high-school kid whom he had hired as chauffeur; the kid wanted to take the Buick home nights. Mrs. Doctor Parsons, as everyone called his wife, told people that she was downright thankful when Rhoda, the cook, quit to work in a defense plant, even though it meant she had to do the cooking and the housework. At least, that gave her something to do besides try to keep the books straight with the doctor's pocket records. It occupied her hands during those many, many hours when she was completely out of touch with the only man in the world who had ever touched her.

She knew about the cell in the lockup which Harry Rossini had fixed up for Doctor Parsons. Harry had kept his promise, although his niece, Thelma's kid, never was unpinned from that mess last summer. The hideaway was no Waldorf-Astoria, but it was pretty nice: it was the lone cell for female lawbreakers in a community where no cell had ever been required for female lawbreakers. So far, the cell had been occupied only by a few favored drunks and by Doctor Parsons. The idea of her husband's sleeping in a cell did not appeal to Mrs. Parsons, but she reminded herself, as she had many times in the past thirty years, that a finicky woman ought not to marry a doctor.

You got finicky about things, but never *very* finicky. Never about things like his being shaved by the barber every single day but getting a haircut about the time the hair made him resemble Benjamin Franklin walking in Philadelphia, Pennsylvania, with a loaf of bread under his arm. Like his fancying up with a white linen weskit for a lawn party and then not changing the weskit because it was too much trouble to remove watch and chain, thermometer and chain, fountain pen, pencil, and other stuff that Doctor Parsons considered essential weskit equipment. Like his not getting a new pair of spectacles to take the place of a pair with one badly chipped lens. Like his not stopping just for one minute, sixty seconds, and writing down the actual name of the fat young woman whose sixteen-months-old baby needed twenty thousand units of antitoxin. If you had no children to worry about, wasn't it all right to worry about Doctor?

Doctor Parsons came home one day all beaming, all smiles. This was one day around Christmas time. He came in the kitchen door, which was unusual for him, because he usually came in through the side door, which gave entrance to the waiting room of his office. It was shortly after noon, and Mrs. Parsons had some vegetable soup on the stove and was reading the weekly paper. "Well," she said.

"Well, well, well," he said. "Three holes in the ground."

"What are you so full of beans for, all of a sudden?"

"Any calls?" he said, taking off his hat and overcoat.

"Any calls. What's the matter? You think you're losing your popularity? Seven or eight calls. They're all in on your desk. What on earth's the matter with you?"

"I may be losing my popularity any minute," he said. He sat on a kitchen chair and removed his arctics. "Jess Williamson's home."

"Jess Williamson?"

"He's home and out of the Army. He isn't even wearing his uniform. He looks fine, feels fine. Ready to go to work."

"*He* can't go to work so soon. Does he realize?"

"Now, now. He took final—I mean terminal leave and went to visit with his wife's family in North Carolina. Took it easy, played golf, et cetera, and now he wants to start making some money."

"Well, now, that's wonderful. When does he want to start all this?"

"Right away. I'm taking him around on my calls this afternoon. I told him he could have my office till he got established again. I even told him he could live in this house till he and his wife got settled. You and I could go away next week if we knew where to go."

"Personally I don't care where we go just so we go."

"That's the way I feel about it," said Doctor Parsons.

They went away, Doctor and Mrs. Parsons, to a New England city where the second-best hotel was managed by a cousin of Mrs. Parsons. They would sleep until nine or ten in the morning and have breakfast in their room. They saw a few old friends they had there when they wanted to, went to the movies in the afternoon when they felt like it, and when they were good and ready they packed up and went home.

When they got home, the first thing, naturally, that they did was to call the Williamsons, who by that time were back in their own house. Mrs. Williamson had seen to it that there were flowers to greet the Parsonses, and Mrs. Parsons called up to thank the younger woman. Doctor Parsons called Doctor Williamson to ask if everything was under control. Everything was, and Doctor Williamson was enjoying his practice. It was a bank-meeting day and Doctor Parsons felt free enough, for once, to go, and was pleased by the compliments of his fellow-directors on his healthy appearance. The second night home he went to a lodge meeting, where there were some irreverent remarks as to his not knowing the inside password (which of course he knew). By the end of the first week he had seen quite a few friends and acquaintances but he had not had more than ten or twelve patients. He wondered about this, and then discovered the explanation. Everybody thought he was still away. He thereupon got them to put an ad in the weekly paper: "Dr. L. W. Parsons has returned from out-of-town and has resumed his practice." The paper came out the following Friday afternoon, and Doctor Parsons was in his office early Friday evening. Although his evening office hours normally were from six to eight, he was there that night from six to nine, without a single patient.

He went back to the sitting room, where his wife was listening to the radio and sewing. "Quiet tonight," he said.

"Yes. What a relief!" she said.

"Quietest since—back before the war." He lit a cigar. "I think I'll take it easy from now on. With Williamson here, I'm not going to take any new patients."

"I was going to suggest that," said Mrs. Parsons. "I don't see why you should."

"I wouldn't like to put the whole load on Williamson's shoulders, but I don't see why I can't do a few more things I'd like to do. For instance, go to New York every two or three weeks, just overnight, and watch some of the good men operate."

"We could both go. Every other week you could go to a clinic and I could—shop, or take in a matinée. I think that'd be nice."

"The more I think of it the more it sounds like a good idea," said Doctor Parsons.

"I think it's a *very* excellent idea."

"Mm-hmm." Doctor Parsons picked up that week's *Time* and turned the pages for a few minutes. "Say, I was wondering. Don't you think we ought to have Williamson and his wife over for Sunday-night supper soon? He knows all the young people, but people like Reverend McKittridge and his wife, and Lawyer Muldoon and *his* wife—he ought to get to know those people better."

"Mm-hmm."

He returned to his magazine and read an article, or most of it, then closed the magazine. "Want to play some cards?"

"All right," she said. "You get the table. By that time I'll be done with my sewing."

He brought out the table and set it up and put the straight-backed chairs in place. They sat down and he spread the cards for the cut. She picked her card; he picked his and held it out for her to see. He looked at her and saw that she was not looking at his card but at him, and there was worry in her eyes—worry, and almost pain. There was nothing for him to do but to laugh.

"Who do I think I'm fooling, huh?" he asked. He laughed, and now she smiled, too.

PARDNER

The dashboard clock told him it was too late to stop for something to eat at the Bond, but Malloy recalled from long before the war that there was a good diner just before you came into Hartford. It was a favorite spot of truckmen and served a good beef stew and the apple pie was good, too. But either he passed it while concentrating on his driving or the place no longer existed. In any case, he did not see it, and he decided to stop at the first place on the right-hand side of the road, eat a sandwich, and be on his way. He could get a good meal in New York, and a sandwich and cup of coffee were probably a better idea now, anyway; enough to keep him awake, not so much that he would get drowsy on the Parkway.

The place he chose turned out to be a real restaurant, not de-luxe, but it had a small bar as well as tables and the inevitable juke box. There was room to park right in front of the entrance. When he went in, a party of four were sitting in the rear of the room; the only other persons in evidence were the barkeep, two waitresses, and a boy who appeared to be of high-school age. As Malloy went to a table, the boy went to the front door and stared out at Malloy's car. Malloy gave his order to a waitress and the boy came to Malloy's table.

"I see you got a Doozy," said the boy.

"That's right," said Malloy.

"What year is it?"

"Built in thirty-two," said Malloy.

"Thirty-*two*? Fifteen years ago!"

"That's the way it adds up. Or subtracts," said Malloy.

"What is it, sixteen cylinders?"

"Eight," said Malloy.

"All right if I sit down a minute?" said the boy.

It was not all right, but there was no use making a point of it, and Malloy told the boy to sit down if he liked. The boy was not a standard type, but Malloy foresaw ten minutes of boredom while he answered the same old questions about the Duesenberg. The kid was rather short and very pale, and made Malloy think of the old term, momma's boy. His clothes were awful: a dark-brown double-breasted suit, brown leather-and-suede shoes, chocolate-colored shirt, and plain white four-in-hand tie. He wore a wristwatch with large, square, gold-looking links for a band and on the little finger of his left hand a ring with a large black stone surmounted by a large gold letter "C." On the little finger of the right hand, he wore some kind of school ring. His tie clasp, which he wore high, contained an ornament that may have been inspired by those Longhorn heads with which Frederic Remington used to clutter up his drawings. Finally, he wore a dark-brown hat, which he kept shifting, but which he at no time removed. He could probably run fifty balls in a game of straight pool.

"Can I buy you a drink?" the boy asked.

Malloy controlled the instinct to slap the kid's face. "No, thanks," he said.

"That makes sense," said the kid. "Driving a load of power like that there, a person's better off without any booze in him."

"Right," said Malloy. He realized that the kid was not patronizing him, only treating him as an equal, and he nodded solemnly.

"What's the fastest you ever had it up to?"

"A hundred and five."

The kid nodded approvingly, and Malloy was sorry he had not made it a hundred and twenty, just to see what the reaction would be.

"How many carburetors you got on her?"

"One," said Malloy.

"One. Did you ever stop to think of what you could do with three more?"

"No. A hundred and five's good enough for me."

The kid nodded, like saying, "Yes, at your age."

The waitress brought the sandwich and coffee.

"The usual, M'rie," the kid said. "You sure you won't have something?"

"Positive," said Malloy, and began to eat. The waitress, who obviously loathed the kid, brought the usual.

"Bourbon and 7-Up," said the kid. "You'd like it, or maybe you never heard of it."

"Heard of it," said Malloy, chewing. "You must have a drag here."

"Why? Because I can get a drink at my age?"

"Uh-huh."

"Christ, man, I own the joint."

"You what?"

"You heard me. It was left to me by my old man. My mother's trustee, and I don't get the full control of it till I'm twenty-one, but her and the bank do what I tell them to. The bank knows I know how to make a beautiful buck out of the joint, and they don't bother me, either. Hey, M'rie, bring me a fistful of nickels outa the till." This she did and he held out his hand for them without looking at her. She poured them in his hand instead of throwing them in his face. "Give the party on Four drinks on me, and then you can go home."

"Thanks," said M'rie.

"We'll have a little music," said the kid. "They say it promotes the digestive juices. I happen to like Spike Cooley, the King of Western Swing. Ever hear of him?"

"I don't think so," said Malloy. "The King of *Western* Swing? Where does that leave Benny Goodman?"

"B.G. went out with the horse and carriage for my dough. I don't have one of The Eye's platters in my joint. I turned them over to the U.S.O." He took a gulp of his usual. He nodded in agreement with himself. "Yes sir, Western swing's the coming thing. Say!"

"What?"

"I just gave them a slogan—Western swing's the coming thing. Well, it is. I like it. I like it. Have you ever been out West?"

"Uh-huh."

"Ranching?"

"In a way." Malloy had done his ranching in the writers' annex at Paramount.

"What's it like?"

"Well, it's hard to put into words. Sleeping under the stars. The old chuck wagon comes along about once a week. It's the only life."

"Yeah? How'd you happen to leave it?"

"Well, two reasons. It's awful lonesome out there under the stars. Peaceful, but lonesome, and I used to miss my wife, and she used to miss me, so I got a job in town, and then I ran into a little luck. A gusher came in on the south forty." By now, Malloy was getting carried away with his fiction.

"Oil?"

"Yep. That meant I didn't have to work any more, and Sallie Lou and the kids could have all the advantages. We moved to the city."

"New York?"

"That's where we live now. No, I meant Abilene. Abilene, Texas. Population, 18,000. That was city to us in those days."

"But I'll bet you miss it, living on the ranch."

"It's in my blood. Oh, I still go out every year for roundup time. I got about four thousand head on the home ranch. Longhorns. I noticed you have the head of a Longhorn on that thing in your tie."

"That's not all I got. Take a look at this." The kid stood up and unbuttoned his coat to show his belt—hand-tooled leather with a silver buckle. "That cost me sixteen-fifty. I sent for it out to a place in Pendleton, Oregon."

"Oh, yes. I have some beauties like that. I have a Mexican named Pablo on the home ranch. I guess there isn't a better leather man in Deaf Smith County."

"Death Smith County?"

"Deaf. D-e-a-f. Maybe you pronounce it deef."

"That's a funny name for a county."

"You wouldn't say that out home. Deaf Smith was Vice-President of the old Texas Republic. Stone-deaf. Deaf as a hitching post, but to make up for it he could see in the dark, sharper than a coyote. They tell a lot of stories about him in that connection. I wish I had time. I'd tell you some'd curl your hair."

"You going right back to New York tonight, huh?"

"Yep. Stockholders' meeting in the morning. My oil company."

The kid smiled. "I just figured out something. See if I'm right. The Doozy, I'll bet you bought that when you struck it rich."

"Right on the nose! First, I bought the property in Abilene, then I said to myself I was going to have the biggest, longest, loudest, fastest automobile in West Texas, and out there she is. First automobile I ever owned. I guess I owned a hundred since then, but I held on to that son-of-a-gun out of sentiment. Sallie Lou keeps prodding me, why don't I get rid of that old thing. She won't ride in it. She got a couple Rolls-Royces, but I say to her, 'That's our lucky car. If the wells give out, maybe we'll be lucky to have the one we started with.'"

The kid nodded slowly, in complete approval of the sentiments. He jingled the nickels that he still held in his palm, and at the sound he looked down at them. "Funny you never heard of Spike Cooley. He's known as the King of Western Swing."

"Why, that nothing against him. Nothing against me either, son. The West is a mighty big place, mighty big. The only objection I have, I wish your friend didn't call himself the King. No man—no matter how big he is—no one man's big enough to call himself king of anything in the West, except we have the King Ranch, but that's a different proposition altogether. That's the name of the family who own it and they have a right to call it King Ranch. They would anyhow, even if their name wasn't King, cause that ranch is the king of 'em all. You could put my measly a hundred and forty thousand acres in the King Ranch and all they'd do'd be to use it for a corral, that's how big the King Ranch is." Malloy started to rise.

"Have another sandwich. There wasn't much to that," said the kid.

"Thanks very kindly, but I have to mosey along. I don't want to keep Sallie Lou waiting up for me." He looked around for the other waitress. "Say, miss," he said.

The kid shook his head no, and the waitress shook her head no, questioningly. "No check," said the kid.

"Oh, now, thanks very kindly, but I insist. I like to pay my own way."

"Maybe some time, maybe next year I'll be out in your country and I can stop at your ranch. How about that?"

"Fine, fine. But let me leave something for the girl," said Malloy.

"Sure, if you want to," said the kid. As Malloy laid a dollar bill on the table, he noticed that something was troubling the kid.

"Something bother you, son?"

"Well, if I did go out there next year—I know you're not supposed to ask a stranger's name . . ."

"Oh. My name. Humber Phillips," said Malloy.

"Humber Phillips. Abilene, Texas. Right." The kid smiled and walked to the door with Malloy. They shook hands, and Malloy, in the car, could see the kid standing in the open doorway, with his coat open and his thumbs in the cowboy belt. Malloy waved to him as the car began to move, and the kid tipped the brim of his hat. "So long, pardner," he heard the kid call out.

A Phase of Life

The radio was tuned in to an all-night recorded program, and the man at the good upright piano was playing the tunes that were being broadcast. He was not very original, but he knew all the tunes and the recordings, and he was having a pleasant time. He was wearing a striped pajama top which looked not only as though he had slept in it, but had lived in it for some days as well. His gray flannel slacks were wrinkled, spotted, and stained and were held up not with a belt but by being turned over all around at the waist, narrowing the circumference. On the rug in back of him, lined up, were a partly filled tall glass, a couple of bottles of beer, and a bottle of rye, far enough away from the vibration of the piano so they would not be spilled. He had the appearance of a man who had been affable and chunky and had lost considerable weight. His eyes were large and with the fixed brightness of a man who had had a permanent scare.

The woman on the davenport was reading a two-bit reprint of a detective story, and either she was rereading it or it had been read by others many times before. Twice a minute she would chew the corners of her mouth, every four or five minutes she would draw up one leg and straighten out the other, and at irregular intervals she would move her hand across her breasts, inside the man's pajamas she was wearing.

The one o'clock news was announced and the woman said, "Turn it off, will you, Tom?"

He got up and turned it off. He took a cigarette from his hip pocket. "You know what the first money I get I'm gonna do with?" he asked.

She did not speak.

"Buy a car," he said. He straddled the piano bench, freshened his drink. "We coulda been up in the Catskills for the week-end, or that place in Pennsylvania."

"And tonight in one of those traffic jams. Labor Day night. Coming back to the city. And you could walk it faster than those people."

"But, Honey, we could stay till tomorrow," he said.

"I'd be in favor of that, but not you. Three nights away from the city is all you can take. You always think they're gonna close everything up and turn out all the lights if you don't get back."

"I like *Saratoga*, Honey," he said.

"Show me the difference between Broadway, Saratoga, and Broadway, New York. Peggy, Jack, Phil, Mack, Shirl, McGovern, Rapport, Little Dutchy, Stanley Walden. Even the cops aren't different. Aren't you comfortable here, Honey? If we were driving back from Saratoga tonight you'd be having a spit hemorrhage in the traffic."

"Fresh air, though," said Tom.

He kept straddling the piano bench, hitting a few treble chords with his left hand, holding his drink and his cigarette in his right hand. "Do you remember that one?" he said.

"Hmm?" She had gone back to her mystery novel.

"That was one of the numbers I used when you sent over the note. That was 'Whenever they cry about somebody else, the somebody else is me.' I was getting three leaves a week. The High Hat Box. Three hundred bucks for sittin' and drinkin'."

"Mm-hmm. And some kind of a due bill," she said.

"Uh-huh."

"And nevertheless in hock," she said.

"On the junk, though, Honey," he said.

"If you wouldn't of been taking that stuff it'd been something else."

"You're right," he said.

"Well? Don't say you aren't better off now, even without any three hundred dollars a week. At least you don't go around looking like some creep."

"Oh, I'm satisfied, Honey. I was just remarking, I used to get that three every Thursday. Remember that blue Tux?"

"Mm-hmm."

"I had two of them, and in addition I had to have two white ones. You know with the white ones, those flowers I wore in the buttonhole, they were phonies. I forget what the hell they were made out of, but they fastened on with some kind of a button. They were made out of some kind of a wax preparation."

"I remember. You showed me," she said.

He put his drink on top of the upright and played a little. "Remember that one?"

"Hmm?"

He sang a little. " 'When will you apologize for being sorry?' I laid out two leaves for that. I liked it. Nobody else did."

"I did. It had a twist."

"The crazy one. Do you remember the cute crazy one? 'You mean to say you never saw a basketball game?' Where was it they liked that? Indianapolis."

"Yep," she said. She laid down the mystery novel, surrendering to the reminiscent mood. "I wore that blue sequin job. And of course the white beaded. Faust! Were they ever sore at me!"

"They loved you!" he said.

"I don't mean those characters from the cow barns. I mean the company manager and them."

He laughed. "Well, Honey, all you did was walk out on their show for some lousy society entertainer." He sneaked a glance at her. "I guess you been sorry ever since."

"Put that away for the night," she said, and picked up her mystery novel.

He played choruses of a half dozen tunes she liked, and was beginning to play another when the doorbell rang. They looked at each other.

"That wasn't downstairs. That was the *doorbell*," he whispered.

"Don't you think I know it?" she said. "Are you sure we're in the clear with the cops?"

"May my mother drop dead," he said.

"Well, go see who it is."

"Who the hell would it be tonight? Labor Day," he said.

"Go to the door and find out," she said. She got up and tip-toed down the short hall. He picked up the poker from the fireplace and held it behind his back, and went to the door.

"Who is it?" he called.

"Tom? It's Francesca."

"Who?" he said.

"Francesca. Is that Tom?"

He looked down the hall and Honey nodded. "Oh, O.K., Francesca," he said. He stashed the poker and undid the chain lock and held the door open. In came Francesca, and her half-brother, Cyril, and a girl and a man whom Tom never had seen before.

"Is there someone else here?" said Francesca.

"No," said Tom.

"Honey's here, I hope," said Francesca.

"Oh, yeah," said Tom. "Come in, sit down." He nodded in greeting to Cyril.

"This is Maggie, a friend of ours," said Francesca, "and Sid, also a friend of ours."

"Glad to know you," said Tom. There was no shaking of hands. "These are friends of yours," he said, studying Francesca.

"Definitely. You have nothing to worry about," said Francesca. She sat down, and her half-brother lit her cigarette. She was in evening clothes, with a polo coat outside. The girl Maggie was in evening clothes under a raincoat. Both men were wearing patent-leather pumps and black trousers with grosgrain stripes down the sides, and Shetland jackets. Sid's jacket was too small for him and most likely came out of Cyril's wardrobe. Francesca and Sid looked about the same age—late thirties—and Cyril was a few years younger, and Maggie could not have been more than twenty-one.

"I know we should have called up. We drove in from the country. But we decided to take a chance." Francesca liked being haughty with Tom.

"That's all right. It's quiet tonight," said Tom.

"I was going to *ask* you if it was quiet tonight," said Francesca.

"Yeah, we were just sitting here listening to the radio. I was playing the piano," said Tom.

"Really? Have you anything in the Scotch line?" said Francesca.

"Sure," said Tom. He named two good brands.

They ordered various Scotch drinks, doubles all, and Tom told Francesca that Honey'd be right out. He opened Honey's door on the way to the kitchen and saw that she was almost dressed. "Did you hear all that?" he said.

"Yes," she said.

"What do you want?"

"Brandy, prob'ly," she said.

He continued to the kitchen, and when he brought back the drinks Honey was sitting with the society group, very society herself with Francesca and Cyril, and breaking the ice for Maggie and Sid. Sid was holding Maggie's hand, but Tom broke it up by the way he handed those two their drinks.

"Oh, Von said to say hello," said Francesca.

"Really? What's with Von these days? We didn't see Von since early in the summer," said Honey.

"He was abroad for a while," said Francesca.

"He's thinking of getting married," said Cyril.

"God help her, whoever she is," said Honey.

Sid laughed heartily. "You're so right."

"Is that the Von we know?" said Maggie.

"Yes, but no last names here, Maggie," said Honey. "Except on checks." She laughed ladylike.

Maggie joined up with the spirit of the jest. "How do you know Von isn't marrying *me?*" she said.

"The gag still goes. If you're gonna marry Von, God help you. But my guess is you aren't," said Honey.

"I'm not, don't you worry," said Maggie.

"I'm not worried," said Honey.

"I oughta rise and defend my friend," said Sid. He was still laughing from his own comment.

"Have you *got* a friend?" said Honey.

"You're so right," said Sid, starting a new laugh.

"I understand you're moving," said Francesca.

"We were, but we had a little trouble. I'll speak to you about that, Frannie," said Honey.

"Anything I can do," said Francesca.

"Or me either," said Cyril.

"Well, it's the same thing, isn't it?" said Honey.

"Not entirely," said Cyril. "Frannie has the dough in this family."

"Ah, yes," said Francesca. "But you go to the office."

They all required more drinks and Tom renewed them. When he served the fresh ones the seatings had been changed. Honey and Francesca and Cyril were sitting on the davenport, and Maggie was sitting on the arm of Sid's chair. They sipped the new drinks and Francesca whispered to Honey and Honey nodded. "Will you excuse us?" she said, and she and Francesca and Cyril carried their drinks down the hallway. Tom went to the piano and played a chorus. He turned and asked Maggie and Sid if they wanted to hear anything.

"Not specially," said Maggie.

"No. Say, Old Boy, I understand you have some movies here," said Sid.

"Sure," said Tom. "Plenty. You ever been to Cuba?"

"*I* have. Have you, Maggie?"

"No. Why?"

"Well, then, let's go easy the first few, hah?" said Sid.

"Sit over here and I'll set everything up. I have to get the screen and the projection machine. By the way, if you ever want to buy any of these—"

"I'll let you know," said Sid.

Sid and Maggie moved to the davenport and crossed their legs while Tom set up the entertainment devices. "You want me to freshen your drinks before I start?" he said.

"That's a thought," said Sid.

Tom got the drinks and handed them over. "You know I have to turn out the lights, and some people prefer it if I keep the lights out between pictures. That's why I said did you want another drink now."

"Very damn considerate," said Sid. "When do we get to see the movies? Eh, Maggie?"

"I'm ready," she said.

The lights were turned off and the sound of the 16 mm. machine was something like the sound of locusts. The man and the girl on the davenport smoked their cigarettes and once in a while there was so much smoke that it made a shadow on the portable screen. Sid tried a few witty comments until Maggie told him, "Darling, don't speak."

In about fifteen minutes Tom spoke. "Do you want me to go ahead with the others?" he said.

"What about it, Kid? Can you take the others, or shall we look at those again, or what?" said Sid.

The girl whispered to him. He turned around. "Old Boy, have you got some place where we can go?"

"Sure," said Tom. "Room down the hall."

"Right," said Sid.

"I'll see if it's ready. I think it is, but I'll make sure."

He came back in a minute or so and stood in the lighted doorway of the hall and nodded. "Third door," he said.

"Thanks, Old Boy," said Sid. He put one of his ham-hands on Maggie's shoulder and they went to the third door.

Tom put the movie equipment away, and now that the lights were up he had nothing to do but wait.

The waiting never had been easy. As the years, then the months went on, it showed no sign of getting easier. The rye and beer did less and less for him, and the only time Honey got tough was if he played piano at moments exactly like this. He was not allowed to play piano, he *could* have a drink to pass the hour, but he could not leave the apartment because his clothes were in one room, and the little tin aspirin box that Honey did not know about was in another room. He was glad for that. He had fought that box for damn near a year, and lost not more than twice.

One of these days the thing to do was call up Francesca and get five palms out of her, just for the asking. Not spend it all on a Cadillac. A Buick, and wherever the horses were running at the time go there. What if Honey *did* get sore? What about giving up three leaves a week for her? And she'd always get along. What about tonight? Wasn't he ready to swing that poker for her? Where would Honey be if he let fly with that poker? Stepping over the body and on her way to Harrisburg, and leaving him to argue it out under the cold water with the Blues.

"What are you thinking about?"

It was Francesca.

"Me? I was just thinking," said Tom.

"Mm. A reverie," said Francesca. "What do I owe you?"

"Leave that up to you," said Tom.

"I don't mean Honey. I mean you," said Francesca.

"Oh," said Tom. "Including—"

"Including my friends," she said.

"Five thousand?" said Tom.

Francesca laughed. "Okay. Five thousand. Here's thirty, forty, forty-five on account. Forty-five from five thousand is five, four from nine leaves five. Forty-nine fifty-five. Tom, I never knew you had a sense of humor." She lowered her voice. "Tell Sid he owes you a hundred dollars. That'll make him scream."

"Sure."

"He has it, so make him pay," said Francesca. "He has something like two hundred dollars. Shall we wait for them, Cyril?"

"Oh, we have to," said Cyril.

"Here they are," said Francesca.

"Hundred dollars, Sid," said Tom.

"A what?" said Sid.

"Pay up or you'll never be asked again," said Francesca.

"A *hun*-dred *bucks*!" said Sid. "I haven't got that much."

"Pay up, Sid," said Francesca.

Maggie giggled. "I hope it was worth it," she said.

"Oh, by all means, but—am I giving the party?" said Sid.

"If you are you owe me plenty," said Francesca.

"I've some money," said Maggie.

"You know what that makes *you*, Sid," said Francesca. "Oh, Tom, I beg your pardon." She curtsied.

"Don't pay it then. Von never squawks," said Tom.

Sid took out his billfold and tossed Tom a hundred and twenty dollars and another ten. "Well, let's get the hell out of here," he said.

They all said good night to Tom and he to them. He counted the money and was recounting it when Honey came in.

"We got any more beer in the icebox?" she said.

"Three or four," said Tom.

"I see one fifty, two twenties, and a lot of tens. It's all yours, sweetie. For not going away to the country." She sank down in a chair. "You had a funny expression on your face when I came in. What were you thinking of?"

"Francesca."

She laughed a little. "Well, anyway I don't have to be jealous of that bum. The beer, Tommy, the beer."

He went to get the beer gladly. From now on the waiting would not be so bad.

WALTER T. CARRIMAN

Although he was only forty when he passed away last week, my friend, everybody's friend, Walter T. Carriman, may be said to have crowded into those comparatively few years a full life. Those who did not know Walter might be led to suspect that in those words I may be implying that they have missed being acquainted with a man of adventure, and I wish at the outset to make clear that such was not the case. I don't think any of us, his friends, would say that Walter Carriman was a swashbuckler in any sense of the word. At the same time, when I use the term a "full life" in speaking of my friend, it might be inferred that he had come to the end of a lifetime of service. Such was not the case either. It is rather difficult to tell all about Walter in the few lines that the *Herald Tribune* devoted to his obituary, and so I have decided to unlimber my own pen and without any attempt at eulogy (which I do not think Walter would have liked anyway, since he was a modest, almost retiring, man) to use this means to tell merely what I, one of his friends, knew about Walter. In the space available here it will be possible for me to present only certain "highlights" of my own arbitrary choosing, and if others of his friends and family wish to elaborate upon or extend these words, they are, of course, at liberty to do so. In that connection I apologize at the outset in the event that I fail to include in this article any anecdotes or items in his dossier that others of Walter's friends might consider characteristic and/or important. If I may repeat myself so early in the article, this is only my picture of Walter.

———

Walter Carriman was born on April 30, 1903 (and not April 20, as the *Herald Tribune* had it), on a farm in Mercer County, New Jersey. His full name was Walter Thomas Carriman, he being named after an Uncle Walter on his father's side and an Uncle Thomas on his mother's side. The first Carriman, Walter's grandfather, came to this country from England in 1841 and settled in New York City, where he was employed as bookkeeper in a tallow factory, and at the time of his death, in 1885, he was head bookkeeper. Walter's father, Albert Carriman, was born in New York City, a fact which was a source of great pride to Walter on his by no means infrequent trips to the city in his younger days, and again in later years, when he took up residence here. Although it may be assumed that Albert Carriman, by virtue of his father's years of employment at the factory, might have become one of the junior bookkeepers, he apparently did not consider the prospect a truly inviting one, and he became associated in a sales capacity with a firm of wholesale coffee-and-tea merchants with offices in downtown New York. The wisdom of Albert Carriman's choice becomes doubly apparent when one recalls first that the tallow factory long since has passed out of existence, and secondly there is the fact that the coffee-and-tea firm was absorbed by one of the larger corporations several years prior to Albert Carriman's death in 1928. Parenthetically it may be pointed out that the merger was a source of no little financial profit to the stockholders of the small (Carriman's) concern, and despite the fact that he himself did not participate in the monetary advantages of the amalgamation, Albert Carriman took an understandable pride in having known a good thing when he had seen it so early in his business career.

As a traveling man, Albert Carriman covered the territory consisting of the State of New Jersey north of Trenton, certain counties in eastern Pennsylvania, and New York State west of the Hudson River and south of Kingston. It was through these travels that he met the lady who was to become Mrs. Albert Carriman and, in time, the mother of my friend Walter Carriman. She was a Miss Anna Bond, of Easton, Pennsylvania, and through her Walter was able to trace his ancestry to one of the Hessian mercenaries who were defeated at the Battle of Trenton. At the time of Walter's birth his parents were living temporarily at the farm of an uncle and aunt of the former Miss Bond, Albert Carriman having severed his connection with the coffee-and-tea house. In the following year Carriman *père* accepted a position with Strawbridge & Clothier, the great Philadelphia department store, and it was to that city that Albert Carriman, his wife, Anna, and their infant son moved.

Not having been surrounded in his childhood by great riches, which have been known to disappear overnight, leaving their possessors with memories to dwell upon to the boredom of less comfortably placed friends of later years, Walter, on the other hand, was not raised in poverty and squalor, the details of which can, in their recital save in the hands of a Dickens or an equally great artist, prove equally boresome. Walter, an only child, could hold his end up when friends would exchange childhood recollections. I recall, for instance, his saying that he was given a carpentry set when he was nine years of age. I remember laughing with him when he recalled that his mother, for whom he entertained the greatest love and respect, had once made him a gift of a fielder's glove which she had purchased at Lit Brothers. The glove was made to fit the right hand, which of course was unsuitable for Walter, who was right-handed. This became a family joke, for, as Walter's father, a loyal employee of the competing firm of Strawbridge & Clothier, would say, "That is what you get for buying at Lit Brothers. It never would have happened at Strawbridge's." It is safe to say that Mrs. Carriman left the purchasing of sporting equipment to the male members of her household thereafter, and I have a sneaking suspicion that Lit Brothers lost a customer even though the glove was exchanged.

Walter attended the excellent public schools of the City of Brotherly Love and was graduated in the first third of his class from West Philadelphia High School, with the class of 1922, he having only just turned nineteen before graduation. As a boy he had been fond of baseball (*vide* the anecdote of the glove), roller-skating, and other sports. He kept up his interest in the Philadelphia Athletics until within a few years of his untimely death. However, his active participation in sports did not continue through high-school days, owing to defective vision, which necessitated his wearing spectacles. He was a candidate for track at W.P.H.S., but the training rules proved irksome to a lad of Walter's spirit and he dropped the sport in freshman year. (The truth is that Walter took his first cigarette at the age of fourteen and from then on was a rather heavy smoker.) He took a keen interest in cycling and made countless trips on his wheel to Camden, a distance of some miles from his home, where he would pass the day with friends. When he was no more than fifteen, he, in company with several fellow-members of a Fisk Bicycle Club, once rode on their bicycles as far as Norristown, Pennsylvania, which is quite a respectable distance from Philadelphia. This fondness for cycling was a cause for concern with his mother, who was alarmed lest the strenuous sport have its effect on her son's heart. Who shall say that the mother's alarm was not without its prophetic aspect? But of that more anon. Suffice it to say that Walter had a well-balanced attitude toward athletics, whether as baseball "fan" or as cyclist.

On the intellectual side Walter was somewhere between the studious and the casual. In pre-high-school studies his favorites were geography and arithmetic. Of the more advanced subjects his favorites were algebra and botany, with perhaps civics running a very close third. Indeed, Walter's "discovery" of the latter subject was responsible for his oft-avowed intention of becoming a lawyer. He could not, however, overcome his distaste for public speaking, and as he could not call himself a fully equipped attorney without being able to plead his cases at the bar, he gave up his legal ambitions. Walter also considered the advantages and opportunities for helping one's fellow-man that are inherent in the practice of mechanical dentistry, but this too he abandoned when he calculated the expense to his parents, who, truth to tell, were unable to undertake any such expense.

I think I may here interpose my own personal fund of information of Walter without offending the tenets of good taste. This I do because in the proper chronological order (or at least the conventional chronological order) it would be the moment to introduce the "romantic" element. I have no fear that Walter's relict will take offense at this passage in my writeup of her husband. Mrs. Walter Carriman is a woman of great character and she would be the very last to ask the exclusion of the fact (for fact it be) which I am about to disclose.

Some time after his honorable acceptance of his diploma from West Philadelphia High School, Walter attended a meeting of the Alumni Association, which was held at the Adelphia Hotel on Chestnut Street, in one of the ballrooms. Walter at the moment had just severed his connection with the vast Mastbaum enterprises, controllers of a great chain of theatres in Pennsylvania and elsewhere, and he was looking with a hopeful but at the same time disillusioned eye upon the "amusement capital," namely, New York. As an usher at the Stanley Theatre on Market Street he had had ample opportunity to study the likes and dislikes of the patronage. Stanley Theatres had in their grasp a lightninglike intelligence, a fellow-feeling for the common man, an usher who was superior to the bribes and blandishments which come the usher's way—but, sad to relate, Walter eluded their grasp in one of those turnovers of personnel which the larger corporations seem to have established as good business practice. Walter had turned in his uniform (and surely the uniform was made for the man and vice versa) and only the caprice of the moment led him to accept the invitation to attend the Alumni meeting.

Walter took the trolley down to the Adelphia, presented his credentials as a paid-up member of the W.P.H.S.A.A., and rather to his surprise was greeted effusively by a Miss X, who was acting sergeant-at-arms for the meeting. Miss X, the only daughter of a highly respected official of the P. R.T. (Philadelphia Rapid Transit—Mitten Management), was an authentic classmate of Walter's, but in the period intervening between graduation and the alumni(ae) meeting the young lady had "blossomed forth." Walter hardly knew her—and I have his own word for this. The exuberance of her welcome overwhelmed him and the two classmates exchanged more than one reminiscence of the good old days. Walter employed his subtle charm, with the result that Miss X (who since has been happily married and the mother of several charming children) not only sat with him during the meeting proper but accepted his proffer of escort to her home on Pennypacker Street. So pleasant was this chance encounter that Miss X and Walter could be found at Roseland at least once a month thereafter. Miss X was a more than average dancer and Walter's subsequent pleasure in an occasional fox trot may be traced to this association. Luckily for all concerned, Miss X developed an attachment for a chap who was more her type, an automobile salesman from one of the great agencies on North Broad. Walter wished her well (so typical of him) and the parting was without recriminations.

Although I do not seem to have heard any comment on this rather important part of Walter's makeup, his versatility was to me one of his outstanding characteristics. Consider, if you will, the many-sidedness of Walter: his interest in baseball, roller-skating, bicycling, the professions, the art of dancing, the sciences, and the truly Old World manner in which he handled *l'affaire* X. Then in addition there was his extensive knowledge of the city of Philadelphia, which in area is one of the largest cities in the world. Further consider the adaptability of the man, as evidenced in the years preceding and following his happy marriage to the charming and understanding Miss Edith Hoe, of whom it so often and so truly has been said, "Still waters run deep." I shall touch upon his felicitous union with Miss Hoe in a subsequent paragraph. At the moment it is Walter's versatility and adaptability that I am moved to stress.

After forsaking the entertainment world, Walter identified himself with no less than eight widely differing enterprises. He sought and found employment with the Philadelphia *Bulletin,* whose proud boast it is that "in Philadelphia nearly everybody reads the *Bulletin.*" Walter became one of the *Bulletin'*s crack ad-takers, mastering in a short time the technique of accepting classified advertisements over the telephone, a post requiring infinite patience, a good ear, a cheery speaking voice, and a legible hand, the last, by the way, an accomplishment of Walter's which I seem to have overlooked in my "roundup" of the man's numerous good points. As visitors to his home are well aware, Walter was the proud possessor of a beautifully framed certificate attesting his mastery of the Palmer Method. In the *Bulletin* job Walter also exercised another of his accomplishments: he also was the master of the Pitman-Howard shorthand system, and for a time he wore the lapel button proclaiming him one of the P-H students. It goes without saying that Walter was a fine typist, making up in sheer accuracy a slight, hardly discernible lack of speed. Following his newspaper association, Walter was a food-checker at the fashionable Arcadia Restaurant, where many of the Main Line élite were wont to lunch and dine. His next job was as freight clerk on the Reading Railway, this interesting occupation including the mailing of arrival notices to firms and individuals who were expecting freight, often from the far corners of the country. One of the attractive features of this job was the awarding of passes to employees of certain standing, which were good on the Reading and on the Central Railroad of New Jersey, thus enabling Walter to make periodic trips to Atlantic City and to New York. Had Walter chosen to remain with the Reading for five years, he would have been awarded an annual pass, good on any railroad in the entire United States! But like his father before him, Walter had the knack of knowing a good thing when he saw it, and from the Reading he went into the service of the American Tobacco Company. In this post he served as a sort of good-will ambassador for the American Tobacco Company, his job consisting chiefly of giving away Lucky Strike cigarettes. American provided Walter with an automobile and he visited such great institutions of learning as Princeton University, Penn State, Bucknell, Muhlenberg, and many other colleges and universities. Walter next returned to the transportation field, serving briefly as a conductor on the street railways of Asbury Park, New Jersey, during the busy summer season. When he returned to Philadelphia in the fall of that year (1927), Walter announced that he was, as he put it, "tired of knocking around," and he had come to the decision to settle down. Walter may have thought he was pulling the wool over our eyes, but we, his friends, could not help noticing that this decision happened to coincide with his now frequent references to a certain Miss Hoe, whom he had met in Asbury. This young lady, who was to play such an important part in the shaping of Walter T. Carriman's mature life, was engaged in caring for the two small children of a wealthy and socially prominent furniture manufacturer. Walter was not one to allow an inner turmoil to become public property, but one can imagine his sense of frustration, the turgid emotions of the emotional man who never loses control. He could not speak his mind or heart until he had the right so to do. Out of this grew the determination to find something and stick to it, and he became night clerk at the Benjamin Franklin Hotel. The moment he was transferred to the day shift he was at last free to speak. He proposed and was accepted and the marriage took place at the home of the bride in Germantown. It was not a splashy, splurgy wedding, but a simple one, the beautiful double-ring ceremony being used, and the event was attended only by relatives and very close friends of the happy couple, who departed for Ocean Grove on a late-afternoon train. Upon their return they set up housekeeping in a cozy apartment in congenial West Philadelphia and for a time their life together was idyllic. Unfortunately Walter's employers saw fit to retransfer him to the night shift and he stoutly refused to accept the change. He therefore cut himself off from the Benjamin Franklin just two weeks before the death of his father, who passed away quietly in his sleep, death being due to a coronary thrombosis. The young couple then moved into Walter's mother's apartment to relieve her loneliness. In due course Walter made an interesting connection as clerk at the ultra-exclusive Union League Club on South Broad Street. This opportunity to rub elbows with the powerful figures who, it may be said, really run Philadelphia was a source of inspiration to Walter, who, observing the great at such close quarters, became dissatisfied with his lot, for in their club these "tycoons" were relaxed, more or less like the rest of us, and this observation led Walter to conclude that what they could do, he could do. Accordingly he bided his time and at the right moment he resigned his position at the Union League and threw in his lot with the Prudential Insurance Company of America. Walter had found himself.

He remained with the Prudential until his last illness, an association of mutual advantage to Prudential and to our friend. Walter was a man who inspired trust and likewise he was of a quietly persuasive nature, a combination which had telling effect upon prospective investors in that safest of all investments (second only, of course, to War Bonds). He rose from collector to adjuster, through various other phases, until at his death he was said to be slated for assistant branch manager in one of Prudential's nearby agencies.

The years of progress with the well-loved company took Walter away from Philadelphia, scene of so many sad and happy moments in his life, back to the state of his birth, New Jersey, when he took a desk in the home office in Newark. Tragedy struck the Carriman home with the passing at a tender age of their only child, Irma, who went away when she was but two weeks old. But this, if anything, only brought the grief-stricken parents closer together. They lived quietly, Walter being engrossed in the work of providing protection for others bereaved. The Carrimans entertained on very rare occasions, preferring each other's company for the most part. Walter, who had a sly sense of humor, was a great admirer of Amos 'n' Andy until they went off the air, and his understanding of the "little fellow" made him a fascinated listener to the Major Bowes programs, and at his desk he often would give vent to a quiet chuckle as he recalled some wise and witty remark he had heard the night before while listening to Fibber McGee and Molly. He seldom missed a picture starring Gary Cooper, with whom, to be sure, he shared many attributes. He had no special preference among the ladies of the cinema unless it be the late Marie Dressler. He did also remark last year that he wondered what ever became of Polly Moran.

Walter cast his ballot for Franklin D. Roosevelt in 1932, proving that, lifelong Republican though he was, he recognized the need of a change. But Mr. Roosevelt failed to come up to Walter's rigid standards in subsequent years, and Walter became one of F.D.R.'s most outspoken critics. Walter was tolerant of all forms of religion, a fact to which his neighborly attitude toward Mr. and Mrs. Lewis Finkle and Mr. and Mrs. P. P. Lannigan bears testimony. The Finkles and the Lannigans were among the first to offer their sympathy when their neighbor passed away.

Walter had put on some weight in Newark, being tied to his desk and now and then complaining that he never got any exercise. For a man who had been so energetic in his youth, what with his interest in bicycling and other strenuous pastimes, the change to the sedentary life must have been too much for even that stout heart. If he had had any warning of an early demise, you may be sure that he kept it his own secret, for it was not his way to inflict his personal troubles on others. Save for an occasional cold and a painful attack of carbuncles when he was in his early thirties, Walter always seemed to enjoy good health. And yet perhaps the dark view his worried mother took of his bicycling may have been a kind of premonition. Perhaps in some way that most vital of all organs had sustained some hidden damage. Who is to say? At any rate, Walter came home that dreadful night last week. After dinner he complained of indigestion and announced to his wife that he would retire early. He prepared for bed. Mrs. Carriman, noticing that his distress continued, insisted upon telephoning the family physician, waving aside

Walter's protests. When she returned to the bedroom after telephoning, Walter was unconscious, and by the time the doctor arrived, Walter had yielded up his spirit.

Thanks to his foresight and the lessons he learned with Prudential, Walter left Mrs. Carriman comfortably fixed, although it seems probable that she will accept employment to fill the void that Walter's passing has left.

———

In preparing this article I have been giving more than passing thought to the composition of a suitable epitaph for my friend. I jotted down quite a few, but the one which I like best, which in its simplicity seems to suit Walter the best, is this: Walter T. Carriman, A Real American.

Now We Know

Where Mary Spellacy worked, in the office of a fairly big theatrical manager, the office rules were elastic. Nobody ever got there before Mary, and Mary never got there before ten-thirty. The boss, of course, had a key, and if he wanted to go to work before Mary opened up, there was nothing to stop him. The permanent staff was small: the boss, the press agent, the bookkeeper, the boss's secretary, and Mary, who called herself a receptionist, as indeed she was, along with her other duties of typing, running the tiny switchboard, and anything else she felt like doing. There were a lot of things she liked about her job: the pay was good and there were generous, unexpected bonuses when the boss had a hit or was drunk; Mary saw a lot of celebrities and knew precisely their relationships with the boss; she went to all of the boss's first nights and, through an understanding with other girls similarly placed in other offices, she got to quite a few first nights of other producers. The boss never bothered her and the press agent had not made a pass in three years. But the best, or certainly not the least attractive, feature of the job was the starting time in the morning. She had been hired to start at ten, but in three and a half years she had inched the starting time closer to eleven, with only a few ineffectual cracks from the bookkeeper, who gave up after she saw that Mary was in solid with the boss.

It wasn't that Mary was a lazy girl. But she liked a good time, and when you live a four-dollar taxi haul from Times Square you are likely to miss out on your sleep if you have dates in town. Mary liked her eight hours.

Because she lived in the far reaches of Queens, at the end of the bus line, Mary frequently was the first passenger on the bus which took her to the subway. Over a period of years she had known by sight, or to say hello to, dozens of bus-drivers, but Herbert was the only one with whom she got on more intimate terms.

One day Herbert was sitting in the bus waiting for time to start a new trip. Mary had been a passenger of his often enough so that they would nod and smile and say good morning, but this morning something seemed to have got into Herbert. Ordinarily he was a rather sad-eyed Jew with what Mary called a little muzzy that made him look somewhat like an ugly Ronald Colman. He had a beautiful smile, with that lingering sadness in it. But he was full of the devil this particular morning, and when Mary arrived at the bus he pretended not to have seen her. She tapped lightly on the glass door, and instead of touching the pneumatic door-opener, he looked down at his fingernails and pretended to polish them on his trousers and held up his hands as though he were seriously contemplating the effect of the polishing. Mary tapped again, but this time Herbert looked at his watch, frowned, then put the bus in gear and raced the engine, but he didn't release the clutch. Mary banged harder on the door, and now, pretending to notice her for the first time, Herbert slipped the bus out of gear and pulled the door-opener.

"You!" said Mary, studying him.

He smiled and said, "*Good* morning."

He spoke so affably, so politely, that Mary could not be sure of her suspicions. But Herbert did the same thing the next morning and Mary said, "Some people are blind in one eye and can't see out of the other. I wonder how they get jobs driving a bus."

"Do you mean me, for instance?"

"If the shoe fits, and also some people must be so hard of hearing they ought to wear a hearing device."

"I don't possibly see what you mean."

The third morning Mary simply walked to the door of the bus and did not tap on the door. This time Herbert made her wait a minute or so, then, looking to his left and up in the sky at an imaginary airplane, he distracted Mary's attention so that she too looked up to the sky, and at that moment Herbert touched the door-opener. He turned and burst out laughing.

"J-o-x—jokes," said Mary, dropping her money in the box.

The next morning Mary decided to fool *him*. Instead of going to the door of the bus, she walked straight to a spot just in front of the windshield and leaned against the bus, reading her paper. He let her read undisturbed for a full two minutes, then blasted away on the horn, and she jumped.

"Damn you!" she yelled. She wanted to get inside and crown him, but he sat there laughing and wouldn't open the door. When her anger subsided, she made up her mind not to ride with Herbert that day. She sat down on the wooden bench at the bus stop and resumed the appearance of reading her paper. Herbert opened the door, but Mary did not take her eyes off the paper. Herbert began to worry; not only was she really angry and obviously determined not to ride with him but he was a minute over his starting time. He got out.

"I apologize," he said.

"I refuse to accept your apology. I'll take the next bus, and I have a good notion to report you. The nerve."

"You wouldn't do that, would you? You know it was only kidding."

"Yes, and you take advantage of that. Just because you know I'm sap enough that I wouldn't report you."

"If I thought you were the kind that would turn me in, I never would of started the gag in the first place. I mean, it was a compliment."

"It wasn't any compliment blowing that horn. That terrorized me."

"I'm sincerely sorry and offer my humble apologies. Please get in."

She hesitated, then said, "Oh, all right, but cut the comedy. I have a job the same as you have."

They got in. She fished in her bag for the money.

"No, the ride's on me this morning. *Every* morning, I'd *like* it to be."

"A nickel won't break me," said Mary. "And anyway, I don't *know* you."

"I know. What's your name? I don't even know your name."

"Why do you want to know my name?"

"My name is Lewis. Herbert Lewis. If you wanted to turn me in any time, that's my name."

"Are you inferring that you're gonna pull the same kind of tricks again, because my patience is just about exhausted."

"A-a-a-h, it was just to relieve the monotony and I thought you looked like a good sport that could take it. Maybe I *was* fresh."

"*Maybe!*" She paid her fare and chose a seat toward the back of the bus to discourage any further conversation. She could tell by the fact he did not greet the other passengers that he was pretty darn miserable. At the subway station, instead of taking the center door, which would have been more convenient, she walked to the front of the bus, and just as she was leaving she turned to him and gave him her best smile and said, "Goo'bye." As she crossed the street and went into the station, she felt his eyes on her all the way, and she knew how he was looking.

For the next few days there were no more tricks, but warm smiles passed between them, and Mary guessed that he was beginning to look forward to their morning encounters just as much as she was, which was a lot. She got so now she sat near the front, near him. In that way they eventually found out the facts about each other: that he was married, two kids, 3-A, lived in Jackson Heights, had a Chevvie. He also told her that he had wanted to study medicine, took piano lessons for two years when he was a kid, gave up smoking for six months but put on so much weight his clothes would hardly fit him, had a brother in the Coast Guard, thought the movies were a waste of time, and had not seen a Broadway show since *Meet the People,* to which he had gone with his wife's sister and her husband. Mary supplied such information as the fact that she had been to Cuba on a cruise, put ammonia in a coke for a hangover, had more friends Jews than she did Irish, had taken piano lessons for two years when she was a kid, liked steak well done on the outside but rare on the inside, had wanted to become a nun when she was twelve, and lived with her mother and three sisters in the fourth house in that row of houses that you could see from the end of the bus line. In a few weeks they knew all they had to know about each other to fall in love, and after the period of unconscious caution it became a case of who would make the first move.

One morning Mary said to him, "I can get you two tickets for a show Tuesday night if you want to go."

"You mean passes?"

"Yes. My boss, we have a new show opening Friday and the way we do it, they like to show it to an audience before the critics see it, so Tuesday the employees of the Brooklyn Edison, I think it is, or maybe it's Bond Bread, anyway this kind of an employees' club gets tickets for nothing. It's the same seat and everything as the opening night but of course no critics are allowed in. We just want to get the audience reaction. Sort of a dress rehearsal with people out front so they can tell where the laughs are and what to cut, et cetera. Would you like to go and take your wife?"

"Listen, Mary, I hate my wife."

"Oh. Well, I just thought, you know."

"Don't think I don't appreciate your offer, because I do. Sincerely. But you go to a show, you're suppose to go to have a good time, take somebody you're fond of that you can have an enjoyable evening. My wife just don't fit in that category. I'm not saying anything behind her back. Everybody knows it, and it was her idea in the first place. I mean she took to disliking me before I took to disliking her. It's only the kids—A-a-a-a-h! You make a kind gesture and what do I do, I shoot off my mouth, but I might as well, Mary, because I love *you*, Mary. I'm gettin' changed over to another run. I might as well tell you that while I'm blabber-mouthing. You don't have to say anything. You don't have to take any responsibility or get the idea because I love you you have any—responsibility. But it's doing me no good torturing myself and now getting drunk, so I asked them to change me to another run."

"You did? When do you change?"

"Monday night I change with a fellow over at Forest Hills—he lives nearer, where it'll be more convenient for him. That's a week from Monday night. Christ, I think of you all day. She's all right, my wife, but a lot of people in this world—phooey. You're not saying anything. Well, I guess I know what you're thinking."

"Not by the way you say that you don't. I have to think."

"No you don't. I told you you didn't have any responsibility. I only told you for my own satisfaction."

"You're wrong there, Herbert. I have the responsibility that I let you be the first to say anything. If you hadn't said anything, I would have said something. Or showed it somehow, and prob'ly did. Well, at least we got it out in the open."

"Yes, I guess so. Anyway, now we know."

Too Young

It was the time of year when once again Bud was made to feel very young. It had happened last year, and it had happened the year before; it seemed as though it had been happening a great many more years than that. It *always* seemed that the Tuesday after Labor Day was around again; Father would be staying at the apartment in town, planning to come out for two or three weekends but not making it. The fathers of the other kids the same way. It just seemed that there were no older men at the beach club, giving you black looks or even coming right out and telling you if you did not get the heck off the tennis courts when they wanted to play their stiff and creaky mixed doubles. Through the summer, being with your own bunch, you did not think much about being young or old or anything. But when the fathers started to go back to town, and the young married people, only the mothers and the young boys and girls were left, and it made you remember that you were young.

Much too young to be in love with Kathy Mallet.

This had been the first summer Bud had come right out and called her Kathy. "Hyuh, Kathy," he often would say.

"Hello, Bud," she would say. "When are we going to have that match?"

"Any time you say," he would say.

She had started it. Watching him play one day in June, she had sat there and had seen him just *cream* Ned Work. He *creamed* him: 6–4, 6–2. It had been exciting knowing that Kathy was taking the trouble to wait and watch him before she went on to play. It was the best compliment he ever had from anybody. Then she had said, "Will you play me sometime, Bud?" And he had told her any time. They were always talking about it, but all summer they never got around to it, and now Bud was a little glad, because he could have beaten Kathy. He didn't want to do that, and yet he couldn't have played her and insulted her by easing up on her.

In ten years he would be twenty-five and Kathy would be twenty-nine. That wasn't so bad. Both in their late twenties. And by that time she no longer would be a little tall for him. He had heard a thousand times that on his mother's side they were all six-footers and all got their height in their teens, just sprouted up suddenly.

In no time he would be back at school, and naturally Kathy, back in college, would be going to New Haven and Princeton and New York all the time, because they had an awful lot of liberty where Kathy went to college and were in New York half the time. He would be very lucky to see her before next June. He wished he could do something or give her something that would make her just think of him once in a while during the school year. Well, there was one thing: he could beat her at tennis. That would make her remember him. He could make it up to her years from now. Some day in the future he would say to her, offhand, "Darling, I remember when I was just a kid—oh, back in thirty-nine—and I decided the only way to make you remember me that year was to beat you straight sets. Remember that time I practically forced you to play me?"

—

The hall clock said twenty after three, and he remembered that there was a touch-football game at three, so there wouldn't be many guys on the tennis courts and most of the girls of his own crowd would be watching the silly game. It seemed like an ideal day to challenge Kathy, if she happened to show up at the club, which she usually did every afternoon anyway. He put on white flannels and went out and took his mother's car and drove to the club. He noticed that Kathy's tan Ford convertible sedan was parked at the Mallets' porte cochere. That meant she was home. Good. On his way to the club he had a bad moment when he saw Martin standing beside his motorcycle. Martin was tough. Watkins, the other cop, wasn't so bad, but some of the guys said that Martin never gave anybody a break. If you didn't have a license, that was just too bad. Some of the guys said Martin actually carried a list of the kids that had licenses, and Bud had no license. But today Martin did not even notice Bud. Bud looked in the mirror to make sure, but Martin was already looking in the opposite direction.

At the club, Bud parked the car just inside the parking space, behind the high hedge, but on second thought he decided not to get out. He would stretch out and seem casual, and then when Kathy arrived he would sit up and say, "Oh, you wouldn't like a little tennis, would you, Kathy? We haven't much time left before college opens." No, it would be better to say when *school* opens; some people said school when they meant college, whereas if he said college, she would think he was being silly to talk about college when everybody knew he had three more years before he would get to college.

He stretched out, sure that he was looking casual enough. He stayed there quite a while and one or two cars came and went, and the casual attitude was becoming uncomfortable when he heard a car coming pretty fast, and then, faster, a motorcycle.

The motorcycle caught up to the car only a few yards away from the club entrance. Without looking, he knew who was on the motorcycle: Martin. He raised his head and sure enough, the car was Kathy's tan Ford.

Bud sank down in the seat, so that Martin would not see him, and he heard Martin start out the regular cop's line: "Well, baby, you *were* in a hurry."

He could not hear what Kathy said, but he hoped she said something that would put Martin in his place for calling her baby. The next thing Bud heard was unexpected. Martin said, "*You* can't duck *me* this way. Why weren't you there yesterday? I waited till seven o'clock."

"I told you I wouldn't be there," said Kathy.

"Oh, I *know* you *told* me. But *I* told *you* to *be* there, and you weren't. What is this, the brusheroo?"

"I told you I was never going there again. And I'm not," said Kathy.

"What's the matter with you? Why don't you stop this? All summer—you're the one, half the time you were the one that wanted to meet *me*."

"I know, I know. But it's over."

"No, get that out of your head. It isn't over."

"I'm not going to meet you again. I don't *want* to meet you again."

"Yes, but I want to meet you. You'll meet me. You be there at six o'clock."

"No, I won't, so don't wait for me," said Kathy.

"Listen, you little bitch, you *be* there," said Martin.

"No," said Kathy.

There was a moment's silence, then, "Are you gonna be there?"

"No," said Kathy. Then, "All right."

"O.K. I didn't hurt your arm. I'll be there at six o'clock," said Martin. The motorcycle spat a couple of times and went away.

Bud heard Kathy's Ford come into the parking space and heard her slam the door and the sound of her steps on the gravel. He waited until he heard the door of the bar slam to, then he got out of the car. No one must see him; he could tell his mother he had forgotten about her car. Right now he wanted to walk alone and to think thoughts that he hated and that would forever ruin his life. And the god-damn awful part was that there was nothing, nothing, nothing to do but what he was doing now. "Let me alone!" he said, to no one.

SUMMER'S DAY

There were not very many people at the beach when Mr. and Mrs. Attrell arrived. On this particular day, a Wednesday, possibly a little more than half the morning swimming crowd had come out of the water and gone home for lunch, some on their bicycles, some on the bus which stopped almost anywhere you asked to stop, and a still rather large number driving their cars and station wagons. The comparatively few persons who stayed at the club for lunch sat about in their bathing suits in groups of anywhere from two to seven.

Mrs. Attrell got out of the car—a shiny black 1932 Buick with fairly good rubber and only about thirty thousand miles on it—at the clubhouse steps and waited while Mr. Attrell parked it at the space marked "A. T. Attrell." Mr. Attrell then joined his wife, took her by the arm, and adapted his pace to her slightly shorter steps. Together they made their way to their bench. The bench, seating six, had a sign with "A. T. Attrell" on it nailed to the back, and it was placed a few feet from the boardwalk. On this day, however, it was occupied by four young persons, and so Mr. and Mrs. Attrell altered their course and went to a bench just a bit lower on the dune than their own. Mrs. Attrell placed her blue tweed bag and her book, which was in its lending-library jacket, in her lap. She folded her hands and looked out at the sea. Mr. Attrell seated himself on her left, with his right arm resting on the back of the bench. In this way he was not sitting too close to her, but he had only to raise his hand and he could touch her shoulder. From time to time he did this, as they both looked out at the sea.

It was a beautiful, beautiful day and some of the hungry young-sters of teen age forgot about lunch and continued to swim and splash. Among them was Bryce Cartwright, twelve, grandson of Mr. and Mrs. Attrell's friend T. K. Cartwright, whose bench they now occupied.

"Bryce," said Mr. Attrell.

"Mm-hmm," said Mrs. Attrell, nodding twice.

They filled their lungs with the wonderful air and did not speak for a little while. Then Mr. Attrell looked up the beach to his left. "Mr. O'Donnell," he said.

"Oh, yes. Mr. O'Donnell."

"Got some of his boys with him. Not all, though."

"I think the two oldest ones are at war," said Mrs. Attrell.

"Yes, I believe so. I think one's in the Army and the other's in, I *think,* the Navy."

Mr. O'Donnell was a powerfully built man who had played guard on an obscure Yale team before the last war. With him today, on parade, were his sons Gerald, Norton, Dwight, and Arthur Twi-ning Hadley O'Donnell, who were sixteen, fourteen, twelve, and nine. Mrs. O'Donnell was at home with the baby which no one be-lieved she was going to have until she actually had it. Mr. O'Don-nell and the boys had been for a walk along the beach and now the proud father and his skinny brown sons were coming up the board-walk on their way to lunch. A few yards away from the Cartwright bench Mr. O'Donnell began his big grin for the Attrells, looking at Mrs. Attrell, then at Mr. Attrell, then by compulsion at Mr. Attrell's hatband, that of a Yale society, which Mr. O'Donnell had nothing against, although he had not made it or any other.

"Mr. and Mrs. Attrell," he said, bowing.

"How do you do, Mr. O'Donnell?" said Mr. Attrell.

"How do you do, Mr. O'Donnell?" said Mrs. Attrell.

"You don't want to miss that ocean today, Mr. Attrell," said Mr. O'Donnell. "Magnificent." He passed on, and Mr. Attrell laughed politely. Mr. O'Donnell's greetings had, of course, done for the boys as well. They did not speak, nor did they even, like their father, slow down on their way to the bathhouse.

"He's an agreeable fellow, Henry O'Donnell," said Mr. Attrell.

"Yes, they're a nice big family," said his wife. Then she removed the rubber band which marked her page in her book and took out her spectacles. Mr. Attrell filled his pipe but made no move to light it. At that moment a vastly pregnant and pretty young woman—no one he knew—went down the boardwalk in her bathing suit. He turned to his wife, but she was already reading. He put his elbow on the back of the bench and he was about to touch his wife's shoulder again when a shadow fell across his leg.

"Hello, Mrs. Attrell, Mr. Attrell. I just came over to say hello." It was a tall young man in a white uniform with the shoulder-board stripe-and-a-half of a lieutenant junior grade.

"Why, it's Frank," said Mrs. Attrell. "How are you?"

"Why, hello," said Mr. Attrell, rising.

"Just fine," said Frank. "Please don't get up. I was on my way home and I saw your car in the parking space so I thought I'd come and say hello."

"Well, I should think so," said Mr. Attrell. "Sit down? Sit down and tell us all about yourself."

"Yes, we're using your bench. I suppose you noticed," said Mrs. Attrell.

"Father'll send you a bill for it, as you well know," said Frank. "You know Father."

They all had a good laugh on that.

"Where are you now?" said Mr. Attrell.

"I'm at a place called Quonset."

"Oh, yes," said Mrs. Attrell.

"Rhode Island," said Frank.

"Oh, I see," said Mrs. Attrell.

"Yes, I think I know where it is," said Mr. Attrell. "Then do you go on a ship?"

"I hope to. You both look extremely well," said Frank.

"Well, you know," said Mr. Attrell.

"When you get our age you have nothing much else to do," said Mrs. Attrell.

"Well, you do it beautifully. I'm sorry I've got to hurry away like this but I have some people waiting in the car, but I had to say hello. I'm going back this afternoon."

"Well, thank you for coming over. It was very nice of you. Is your wife down?" said Mrs. Attrell.

"No, she's with her family in Hyannis Port."

"Well, remember us to her when you see her," said Mrs. Attrell.

"Yes," said Mr. Attrell. They shook hands with Frank and he departed.

Mr. Attrell sat down. "Frank's a fine boy. That just shows how considerate, seeing our car. How old is Frank, about?"

"He'll be thirty-four in September," said Mrs. Attrell.

Mr. Attrell nodded slowly. "Yes, that's right," he said. He began tamping down the tobacco in his pipe. "You know, I think that water—would you mind if I had a dip?"

"No, dear, but I think you ought to do it soon, before it begins to get chilly."

"Remember we're on daylight saving, so it's an hour earlier by the sun." He stood up. "I think I'll just put on my suit and get wet, and if it's too cold I'll come right out."

"That's a good idea," she said.

In the bathhouse Mr. Attrell accepted two towels from the Negro attendant and went to his booth, which was open and marked "A. T. Attrell," to undress. From the voices there could not have been more than half a dozen persons in the men's side. At first he paid no attention to the voices, but after he had untied the double knot in his shoelaces he let the words come to him.

"And who is T. K. Cartwright?" a young voice was saying.

"He's dead," said the second young voice.

"No, he isn't," said the first young voice. "That's the old buzzard that's sitting in front of us."

"And what makes you think *he* isn't dead, he and the old biddy?"

"You're both wrong," said a third young voice. "That isn't Mr. Cartwright sitting there. That's Mr. Attrell."

"So what?" said the first young voice.

"All right, so what, if you don't want to hear about them, old Attrell and his wife. They're the local tragedy. Ask your mother; she used to come here. They had a daughter or, I don't know, maybe it was a son. Anyway, whichever it was, he or she hung himself."

"Or herself," said the first young voice.

"I think it was a girl. They came home and found her hanging in the stable. It was an unfortunate love affair. I don't see why—"

"Just a minute, there." Mr. Attrell recognized the voice of Henry O'Donnell.

"Yes, sir?" asked one young voice.

"You sound to me like a pack of goddam pansies. You oughta be over on the girls' side," said Mr. O'Donnell.

"I'd like to know what business of—" a young voice said, then there was a loud smack.

"Because I made it my business. Get dressed and get outa here," said O'Donnell. "I don't give a damn whose kids you are."

Mr. Attrell heard the deep breathing of Henry O'Donnell, who waited a moment for his command to be obeyed, then walked past Mr. Attrell's booth with his head in the other direction. Mr. Attrell sat there, many minutes probably, wondering how he could ever again face Henry O'Donnell, worrying about how he could face his wife. But then of course he realized that there was really nothing to face, really nothing.

THE KING OF THE DESERT

Dave, by far the biggest of the three men, gently tapped the edge of the table off the beat of the old record of "You Go to My Head" that was on the nickel-a-record phonograph. He was smiling, but not at anything, not even at himself. It was his regular smile that his face relaxed into when he was not revealing one of his emotions. Artie looked at the smile and turned and grinned at Ben.

"It must be nice to be like that," said Artie. "How is it to be like that, Dave old boy?"

"Like what, Artie?" said Dave.

"Like you. Nothing to worry about. Go-as-you-please and happy-go-lucky. Let a smile be your umbrella."

"That's where you're wrong," said Dave. "I got plenty to worry about. If I could tell you the stuff I worry about."

"You can," said Artie. "Go ahead, tell us. We're here till the station wagon comes. Make it a good story and we'll miss the bus, eh, Ben? Anything to keep from going back to that ranch. Only fooling. No, come on, Dave. What kind of thing would worry a big, rangy, easygoing feller like you?"

"Lots of things. I worry, but I'm sitting here enjoying a drink with a couple good fellers, why should I talk about my worries?" Dave smiled and then stopped smiling. "I got the ranch to worry about."

"Aah, don't give me that. The ranch? It runs itself. I could run it and I don't know a maverick from a congressman. Maverick the congressman. Skip it. No, now Dave, you can't give us that about the ranch." Artie patted his hands together several times. "Look, you got a piece of California desert. You put a house on it, dig yourself a well, put a couple horses on it, get credit. A feller like you can get credit anywhere, with that honest face."

"That's what *you* think," said Dave, grinning.

"All right, say you have a dishonest face and you can't get credit. Then you strike oil and you don't *need* credit. Not a gusher. Just enough oil to get you started running a dude ranch and a few quarts left over for the car, the windmill, the sewing machine. Will we let him have a few quarts left over, Bennie?"

"Sure. About a gallon and a half."

"Fine," said Artie. "So you have the whole setup *plus—plus*, mind you—this gallon of oil—"

"I said a gallon and a half! I let him have a gallon and a half!" screamed Bennie.

"A gallon's plenty. He wouldn't know what to do with a gallon and a half, a big boy like Dave. I decided to let him have four quarts, one gallon, and that's enough to start with. If he needs more, let him come to me and maybe I'll let him have my credit card at the filling station, good at any station in the U.S.A. It is, too. Here it is. You want to see it, Dave?" He pulled out his wallet and started to hand it to Dave, who reached for it. As he reached, Artie slapped his hand, playfully but sharply. "Take your hands off, you with your dishonest face. If you can't get credit. Anyway, you have the ranch. You advertise. Bennie and I see the ad and we get into our Super-Nooper Twin Sixteen Diesel and drive all the way from the film capital. Hollywood. One hundred fifteen miles. Between the two of us we pay you one hundred and twenty dollars a week for a room about the size of one of those shelfs they put stiffs on at the morgue. Not that I ever went there, please God, but *I* read the *Life* magazine. Anyway, for a room and seven threes, twenty-one, times two, forty-two meals that we don't eat we pay you a one, a two, a zero. That's your overhead. The profit on us takes care of your overhead. For a month, if I'm any guesser."

"Two months," said Bennie.

"A gallon and a *half*!" said Artie. "Then multiply that by forta forta forta forta times sibba sibba sibba sabba, and what have you got?"

"He's got worries," said Bennie.

"Precisely," said Artie. "Precisely. Dave, you haven't a thing to worry about. Unless it's a woman. . . . *Ahh-hhh*."

Artie rolled his eyes. He stood up and shook his hips and sat down. "Ahhhh."

"Ah-ah-ah-ah-ah," said Bennie.

"Is it a woman, Dave? I'm glad you came to me instead of one of those quacks on the next floor," said Artie. "Is it a woman, Artie? I mean Dave. My name's Artie."

"Aw, you guys're too fast for me," said Dave. He shifted in his chair and turned his head around to look at the other people in the bar. Artie kept looking at him. They sipped their drinks.

"That bus takes *long* enough," said Bennie. "How about another drink?" The waiter took their order.

Artie kept looking at Dave. "Now you've hurt Dave's feelings with your talk. Bus. *Station wagon,* you vulgarian. Dave spends frannis hundred dollars for a station wagon and you vulgarians from the film capital come down here and call it a bus. I know, though, don't I, Dave?"

"That's right, Artie," said Dave. "I think I'll put a nickel in the machine." He started to get up. Artie put his hands on his shoulders.

"I wouldn't think of it. Let me. Waiter!" said Artie. The waiter was coming with the drinks, and when he got to the table Artie gave him a quarter and told him to put five nickels in the phonograph. "You're the king of the desert but your money's no good here, Dave."

"O.K.," said Dave. "Only don't call me king of the desert. I'm not that."

"Well, prince then. What the hell," said Artie. "You know, Dave, they tell me you use to play a lot of football for Southern Cal. Is there any truth in that rumor?"

"I got my letter."

"When was that, Dave? About ten years ago?"

"Just about," said Dave.

"You were a tackle, probably?"

"No, I was an end. I only weighed about one-ninety then," said Dave.

"Is that so? Now you're around two-thirty," said Artie.

"Hell, no. Two-eighteen's bad enough." He patted the heavy engraved-silver buckle of his belt.

"I see. Are you what they call a native son, Dave?"

"Well, I am, but my folks aren't Californians."

"Oh? Back East?" said Artie.

"Both sides of the family. From New England. Father's family came from Gloucester, Mass.—"

"Oh, sure. A whaling family?"

"Well, fishing. I guess some whaling," said Dave.

"And your mother's family, they from Gloucester too?" said Artie.

"Nope. All from Boston. Both my mother *and* my father's family came to this country right around the time of the *Mayflower*."

"I see. That makes you real old American stock, then."

"I guess just about as old as they come," said Dave.

"That's wonderful. I guess you can look down on these Whitneys and Vanderbilts and all these jerks that come out here during the racing season."

"Oh, I don't know. I imagine they go pretty far back. Anyway, what difference does it make?"

"What difference does it make? Why, you ought to take pride in a thing like that, oughtn't he, Ben? These days with all these un-Americanisms. Like rheumatism."

"What?"

"Now, come on, Dave, admit it. Down underneath, you having all these family ancestors and old New England stock, you feel that they're a little better than the rest of the common herd, don't you now, honest?"

"Sure I do, if it comes right down to it," said Dave.

Artie turned to Bennie. "What'd I tell you? A bit of a jerk."

He did not finish the long smile that he had begun. His face was not there. He was lying on the floor, and Dave, who had hit him sitting down, now stood up and started around the table after Bennie. Bennie was on his feet, but Dave grabbed him, raised his fist, and was about to hammer down on him, but changed his mind.

"What the hell's the idea?" said Bennie.

Dave started to laugh. "Sit down," he said, and threw Bennie back in his chair. The other people in the saloon were standing watching, but they stayed where they were.

"If you want your stuff, you can send out for it, but don't come yourself," said Dave.

"We'll fix you in Hollywood, mister," said Bennie.

A young cop appeared. "What's the matter, Dave?"

"It's all right, Marv," said Dave. "A couple of wise guys."

"What about him?" said the cop, looking at Artie, who was out on the floor.

"His boy friend can worry about him," said Dave. "I got enough to worry about." Now he suddenly laughed.

BREAD ALONE

It was the eighth inning, and the Yankees had what the sports-writers call a comfortable lead. It was comfortable for them, all right. Unless a miracle happened, they had the ball game locked up and put away. They would not be coming to bat again, and Mr. Hart didn't like that any more than he was liking his thoughts, the thoughts he had been thinking ever since the fifth inning, when the Yanks had made their five runs. From the fifth inning on, Mr. Hart had been troubled with his conscience.

Mr. Hart was a car-washer, and what colored help at the Elbee Garage got paid was not much. It had to house, feed, and clothe all the Harts, which meant Mr. Hart himself; his wife, Lolly Hart; his son, Booker Hart; and his three daughters, Carrie, Linda, and the infant, Brenda Hart. The day before, Mr. Ginsburg, the bookkeeper who ran the shop pool, had come to him and said, "Well, Willie, you win the sawbuck."

"Yes sir, Mr. Ginsburg, I sure do. I was watchin' them newspapers all week," said Mr. Hart. He dried his hands with the chamois and extended the right.

"One, two, three, four, five, six, seven, eight, nine, anduh tenner.

Ten bucks, Willie," said Mr. Ginsburg. "Well, what are you gonna do with all that dough? I'll bet you don't tell your wife about it."

"Well, I don't know, Mr. Ginsburg. She don't follow the scores, so she don't know I win. I don't know what to do," said Mr. Hart. "But say, ain't I suppose to give you your cut? I understand it right, I oughta buy you a drink or a cigar or something."

"That's the custom, Willie, but thinking it over, you weren't winners all year."

"No sir, that's right," said Mr. Hart.

"So I tell you, if you win another pool, you buy me *two* drinks or *two* cigars. Are you going in this week's pool?"

"Sure am. It don't seem fair, though. Ain't much of the season left and maybe I won't win again. Sure you don't want a drink or a cigar or something?"

"That's all right, Willie," said Mr. Ginsburg.

On the way home, Mr. Hart was a troubled man. That money belonged in the sugar bowl. A lot could come out of that money: a steak, stockings, a lot of stuff. But a man was entitled to a little pleasure in this life, the only life he ever had. Mr. Hart had not been to a ball game since about fifteen or twenty years ago, and the dime with which he bought his ticket in the pool every week was his own money, carfare money. He made it up by getting rides home, or pretty near home, when a truck-driver or private chauffeur friend was going Harlem-ward; and if he got a free ride, or two free rides, to somewhere near home every week, then he certainly was entitled to use the dime for the pool. And this was the first time he had won. Then there was the other matter of who won it for him: the Yankees. He had had the Yankees and the Browns in the pool, the first time all season he had picked the Yanks, and it was they who made the runs that had made him the winner of the ten dollars. If it wasn't for those Yankees, he wouldn't have won. He owed it to them to go and buy tickets and show his gratitude. By the time he got home his mind was made up. He had the next afternoon off, and, by God, he was going to see the Yankees play.

There was, of course, only one person to take; that was Booker, the strange boy of thirteen who was Mr. Hart's only son. Booker was a quiet boy, good in school, and took after his mother, who was quite a little lighter complected than Mr. Hart. And so that night after supper he simply announced, "Tomorrow me and Booker's going over to see the New York Yankees play. A friend of mine happened to give me a choice pair of seats, so me and Booker's taking in the game." There had been a lot of talk, and naturally Booker was the most surprised of all—so surprised that Mr. Hart was not sure his son was even pleased. Booker was a very hard one to understand. Fortunately, Lolly believed right away that someone had really given Mr. Hart the tickets to the game; he had handed over his pay as usual, nothing missing, and that made her believe his story.

But that did not keep Mr. Hart from having an increasingly bad time from the fifth inning on. And Booker didn't help him to forget. Booker leaned forward and he followed the game all right but never said anything much. He seemed to know the game and to recognize the players, but never *talked*. He got up and yelled in the fifth inning when the Yanks were making their runs, but so did everybody else. Mr. Hart wished the game was over.

DiMaggio came to bat. Ball one. Strike one, called. Ball two. Mr. Hart wasn't watching with his heart in it. He had his eyes on DiMaggio, but it was the crack of the bat that made Mr. Hart realize that DiMaggio had taken a poke at one, and the ball was in the air, high in the air. Everybody around Mr. Hart stood up and tried to watch the ball. Mr. Hart stood up too. Booker sort of got up off the seat, watching the ball but not standing up. The ball hung in the air and then began to drop. Mr. Hart was judging it and could tell it was going to hit about four rows behind him. Then it did hit, falling the last few yards as though it had been thrown down from the sky, and smacko! it hit the seats four rows behind the Harts, bounced high but sort of crooked, and dropped again to the row directly behind Mr. Hart and Booker.

There was a scramble of men and kids, men hitting kids and kids darting and shoving men out of the way, trying to get the ball. Mr. Hart drew away, not wanting any trouble, and then he remembered

Booker. He turned to look at Booker, and Booker was sitting hunched up, holding his arms so's to protect his head and face.

"Where the hell's the ball? Where's the ball?" Men and kids were yelling and cursing, pushing and kicking each other, but nobody could find the ball. Two boys began to fight because one accused the other of pushing him when he almost had his hand on the ball. The fuss lasted until the end of the inning. Mr. Hart was nervous. He didn't want any trouble, so he concentrated on the game again. Booker had the right idea. He was concentrating on the game. They both concentrated like hell. All they could hear was a mystified murmur among the men and kids. "Well, somebody must of got the goddam thing." In two minutes the Yanks retired the side and the ball game was over.

"Let's wait till the crowd gets started going, Pop," said Booker.

"O.K.," said Mr. Hart. He was in no hurry to get home, with the things he had on his mind and how sore Lolly would be. He'd give her what was left of the ten bucks, but she'd be sore anyhow. He lit a cigarette and let it hang on his lip. He didn't feel so good sitting there with his elbow on his knee, his chin on his fist.

"Hey, Pop," said Booker.

"Huh?"

"Here," said Booker.

"What?" said Mr. Hart. He looked at his son. His son reached inside his shirt, looked back of him, and then from the inside of the shirt he brought out the ball. "Present for you," said Booker.

Mr. Hart looked down at it. "Lemme see that!" he said. He did not reach for it. Booker handed it to him.

"Go ahead, take it. It's a present for you," said Booker.

Suddenly Mr. Hart threw back his head and laughed. "I'll be a goddam holy son of a bitch. You got it? The ball?"

"Sure. It's for you," said Booker.

Mr. Hart threw back his head again and slapped his knees. "I'll be damn—boy, some Booker!" He put his arm around his son's shoulders and hugged him. "Boy, some Booker, huh? You givin' it to me? Some Booker!"

GRAVEN IMAGE

Greate O'Hara — archetypal !

The car turned in at the brief, crescent-shaped drive and waited until the two cabs ahead had pulled away. The car pulled up, the doorman opened the rear door, a little man got out. The little man nodded pleasantly enough to the doorman and said "Wait" to the chauffeur. "Will the Under Secretary be here long?" asked the doorman.

"Why?" said the little man.

"Because if you were going to be here, sir, only a short while, I'd let your man leave the car here, at the head of the rank."

"Leave it there *anyway*," said the Under Secretary.

"Very good, sir," said the doorman. He saluted and frowned only a little as he watched the Under Secretary enter the hotel. "Well," the doorman said to himself, "it was a long time coming. It took him longer than most, but sooner or later all of them—" He opened the door of the next car, addressed a colonel and a major by their titles, and never did anything about the Under Secretary's car, which pulled ahead and parked in the drive.

The Under Secretary was spoken to many times in his progress to the main dining room. One man said, "What's your hurry, Joe?"

to which the Under Secretary smiled and nodded. He was called Mr. Secretary most often, in some cases easily, by the old Washington hands, but more frequently with that embarrassment which Americans feel in using titles. As he passed through the lobby, the Under Secretary himself addressed by their White House nicknames two gentlemen whom he had to acknowledge to be closer to The Boss. And, bustling all the while, he made his way to the dining room, which was already packed. At the entrance he stopped short and frowned. The man he was to meet, Charles Browning, was chatting, in French, very amiably with the maître d'hôtel. Browning and the Under Secretary had been at Harvard at the same time.

The Under Secretary went up to him. "Sorry if I'm a little late," he said, and held out his hand, at the same time looking at his pocket watch. "Not so very, though. How are you, Charles? Fred, you got my message?"

"Yes, sir," said the maître d'hôtel. "I put you at a nice table all the way back to the right." He meanwhile had wigwagged a captain, who stood by to lead the Under Secretary and his guest to Table 12. "Nice to have seen you again, Mr. Browning. Hope you come see us again while you are in Washington. Always a pleasure, sir."

"Always a pleasure, Fred," said Browning. He turned to the Under Secretary. "Well, shall we?"

"Yeah, let's sit down," said the Under Secretary.

The captain led the way, followed by the Under Secretary, walking slightly sideways. Browning, making one step to two of the Under Secretary's, brought up the rear. When they were seated, the Under Secretary took the menu out of the captain's hands. "Let's order right away so I don't have to look up and talk to those two son-of-a-bitches. I guess you know which two I mean." Browning looked from right to left, as anyone does on just sitting down in a restaurant. He nodded and said, "Yes, I think I know. You mean the senators."

"That's right," said the Under Secretary. "I'm not gonna have a cocktail, but you can. . . . I'll have the lobster. Peas. Shoestring potatoes. . . . You want a cocktail?"

"I don't think so. I'll take whatever you're having."

"O.K., waiter?" said the Under Secretary.

"Yes, sir," said the captain, and went away.

"Well, Charles, I was pretty surprised to hear from you."

"Yes," Browning said, "I should imagine so, and by the way, I want to thank you for answering my letter so promptly. I know how rushed you fellows must be, and I thought, as I said in my letter, at your convenience."

"Mm. Well, frankly, there wasn't any use in putting you off. I mean till next week or two weeks from now or anything like that. I could just as easily see you today as a month from now. Maybe easier. I don't know where I'll be likely to be a month from now. In more ways than one. I may be taking the Clipper to London, and then of course I may be out on my can! Coming to New York and asking *you* for a job. I take it that's what you wanted to see me about."

"Yes, and with hat in hand."

"Oh, no. I can't see you waiting with hat in hand, not for anybody. Not even for The Boss."

Browning laughed.

"What are you laughing at?" asked the Under Secretary.

"Well, you know how I feel about him, so I'd say least of all The Boss."

"Well, you've got plenty of company in this goddam town. But why'd you come to me, then? Why didn't you go to one of your Union League or Junior League or whatever-the-hell-it-is pals? There, that big jerk over there with the blue suit and the striped tie, for instance?"

Browning looked over at the big jerk with the blue suit and striped tie, and at that moment their eyes met and the two men nodded.

"You *know* him?" said the Under Secretary.

"Sure, I know him, but that doesn't say I *approve* of him."

"Well, at least that's something. And I notice he knows you."

"I've been to his house. I think he's been to our house when my father was alive, and naturally I've seen him around New York all my life."

"Naturally. Naturally. Then why didn't you go to *him?*"

"That's easy. I wouldn't like to ask him for anything. I don't approve of the man, at least as a politician, so I couldn't go to him and ask him a favor."

"But, on the other hand, you're not one of our team, but yet you'd ask me a favor. I don't get it."

"Oh, yes you do, Joe. You didn't get where you are by not being able to understand a simple thing like that."

Reluctantly—and quite obviously it was reluctantly—the Under Secretary grinned. "All right. I was baiting you."

"I know you were, but I expected it. I have it coming to me. I've always been against you fellows. I wasn't even for you in 1932, and that's a hell of an admission, but it's the truth. But that's water under the bridge—or isn't it?" The waiter interrupted with the food, and they did not speak until he had gone away.

"You were asking me if it isn't water under the bridge. Why should it be?"

"The obvious reason," said Browning.

" 'My country, 'tis of thee'?"

"Exactly. Isn't that enough?"

"It isn't for your Racquet Club pal over there."

"You keep track of things like that?"

"Certainly," said the Under Secretary. "I know every goddam club in this country, beginning back about twenty-three years ago. I had ample time to study them all then, you recall, objectively, from the outside. By the way, I notice you wear a wristwatch. What happens to the little animal?"

Browning put his hand in his pocket and brought out a small bunch of keys. He held the chain so that the Under Secretary could see, suspended from it, a small golden pig. "I still carry it," he said.

"They tell me a lot of you fellows put them back in your pockets about five years ago, when one of the illustrious brethren closed his downtown office and moved up to Ossining."

"Oh, probably," Browning said, "but quite a few fellows, I believe, that hadn't been wearing them took to wearing them again out of simple loyalty. Listen, Joe, are we talking like grown men? Are you sore at the Pork? Do you think you'd have enjoyed being a member of it? If being sore at it was even partly responsible for getting you where you are, then I think you ought to be a little grateful to it. You'd show the bastards. O.K. You showed them. Us. If you hadn't been so sore at the Porcellian so-and-so's, you might have turned into just another lawyer."

"My wife gives me that sometimes."

"There, do you see?" Browning said. "Now then, how about the job?"

The Under Secretary smiled. "There's no getting away from it, you guys have got something. O.K., what are you interested in? Of course, I make no promises, and I don't even know if what you're interested in is something I can help you with."

"That's a chance I'll take. That's why I came to Washington, on just that chance, but it's my guess you can help me." Browning went on to tell the Under Secretary about the job he wanted. He told him why he thought he was qualified for it, and the Under Secretary nodded. Browning told him everything he knew about the job, and the Under Secretary continued to nod silently. By the end of Browning's recital the Under Secretary had become thoughtful. He told Browning that he thought there might be some little trouble with a certain character but that that character could be handled, because the real say-so, the green light, was controlled by a man who was a friend of the Under Secretary's, and the Under Secretary could almost say at this moment that the matter could be arranged.

At this, Browning grinned. "By God, Joe, we've got to have a drink on this. This is the best news since—" He summoned the waiter. The Under Secretary yielded and ordered a cordial. Browning ordered a Scotch. The drinks were brought. Browning said, "About the job. I'm not going to say another word but just keep my fingers crossed. But as to you, Joe, you're the best. I drink to you." The two men drank, the Under Secretary sipping at his, Browning taking half of his. Browning looked at the drink in his hand. "You know, I was a little afraid. That other stuff, the club stuff."

"Yes," said the Under Secretary.

"I don't know why fellows like you—you never would have made it in a thousand years, but"—then, without looking up, he knew everything had collapsed—"but I've said exactly the wrong thing, haven't I?"

"That's right, Browning," said the Under Secretary. "You've said exactly the wrong thing. I've got to be going." He stood up and turned and went out, all dignity.

March 13, 1943

THE NEXT-TO-LAST DANCE OF THE SEASON

It was not the last dance of the summer. There would be one more, which was to be as much of a gala as there could be under the present circumstances. The women were marshaling and pooling their points for the dinner parties that would take place before the final dance. They were saving their nicest dresses and watching their gasoline coupons so they could wait until the next Friday, the very last minute, to drive the fifteen miles—thirty for the round trip—to the nearest good hairdresser. This harassed individual was having the devil's own time trying to satisfy all her customers with appointments for that one day, and almost every request for a half-hour of her time carried with it some pleading, a bribe, or both. But of course no threats of discontinued patronage. Not this year.

A good many of the husbands were not coming down to the country for this dance. They too were saving up for the final one. Some of them were going to do some extra work, and a few had no great amount of work in mind, but in either case the men who stayed in town this weekend were doing so because the final dance was a must. Sons in the armed forces knew without being reminded that they were wanted and expected next week. The younger girls were urging them to be on their good behavior and remain eligible for leaves. Servants were given extra time off against the extra work they would inevitably be asked to do the next week. The tradespeople were being handled with extraordinary care, and especially the proprietors of the three filling stations, who were rather spoiled already.

The flags and the bunting were stored in the club office. Sonny Wine had promised he would appear with an augmented orchestra. The House Committee had O.K.'d the bar order back early in August, to assure delivery in plenty of time. All things considered, the final dance of the season was being well planned, and you didn't really have to add "under the present circumstances."

And yet sometime late in the afternoon of the semi-final dance there began to be something in the air. There was the obvious fact that it threatened rain. Around three o'clock the lovely breeze from the southwest shifted to the west and northwest, but suddenly shifted back again a few minutes past five. By that time the good, browning sun had gone for the day and the swimmers were on their way home or on the tennis courts. But it was something other than the weather that affected people this particular afternoon. It may have been the simple fact that tonight's dance was going to be a relaxed sort of affair, with none of the elaborate preparations that were being made for the final shindig. Only five or six women planned to dress for tonight's dance and not a few of the men were wearing the same white ducks they had worn to the beach in the morning. At the most there were three small dinner parties planned at the club for the evening; everybody else was eating at home. Not a single sizable cocktail party had been arranged. And yet around five-thirty things began to happen.

It is manifestly impossible to determine which was the first occurrence that started the rather remarkable series of events on the evening of the next-to-last dance of the season. But, sticking to the actual facts, it is absolutely true that at exactly five twenty-eight Mary Choate said "Hello, Doris" to Doris Cantwell. Both girls were on their bicycles on their way to their respective homes. As everyone in the community knew, Mary Choate never in her life had spoken to Doris Cantwell. Mary spoke to no one who had not been summering in the community for thirteen years, or, roughly, since the Crash. The girls were of an age—thirty. They never had quarreled, nor was there any trouble between the Cantwells and the Choates. It was just that Mary never had said a word to Doris Cantwell until this particular afternoon. Doris nearly fell off her bicycle, and Mary had pedaled away before Doris was able to return the greeting. The confusion engendered in Doris's mind may well be imagined.

A minute later, in another part of the village, Sam Ainsley, who was down to his shorts, said to his wife, Vera, who still had on the white sharkskin dress she'd been playing tennis in, "Go ahead. You take your bath first."

"What!" exclaimed Vera. This reversal of the Ainsleys' bathing order shattered a tradition of nineteen years' standing, or, in other words, took them back to the second summer of their marriage. Unfortunately, Vera did not take advantage of Sam's offer. Being a practical woman, she argued that Sam was ready for his bath and she was still dressed. Sam pointed out that what she had on could be taken off in less than sixty seconds, but Vera was stern. Sam warned her she might catch cold, and Vera replied that she never had before so why didn't he stop arguing. Sam yielded, went in, and was singing of D.K.E., the mother of jollity, whose children are gay and free, and thus did not hear Vera's sneeze. This served her right, as at that precise moment she was wondering if perhaps Sam wasn't getting some of his mail at the University Club.

Things were quiet in the village for the next ten minutes. Then Rouge, a three-gaited bay mare owned by some people called Scott, reared up while being rubbed down, jumped a six-foot fence, and was shot by Coast Guardsmen at one-thirty the next morning. Rouge would have been nine years old the first of the year.

At six, or thereabouts, Elton Ponsonby, who is a man in his late forties, telephoned Mrs. Hagedorn, a lady old enough to be his mother, and said, "Mizz Hagedorn, thiz Elton Ponsonby. I just heard you said I never draw a sober breath."

"Now, Elton," said Mrs. Hagedorn, who had known Elton's mother very well.

"Well, come on overt our place tomorrow afternoon about three o'clock. I'm gonna draw one." He then hung up.

Sonny Wine and his regular, unaugmented band arrived on the six-five, but Artie Burns' drums had been put off the train at some earlier station. Musically, this may have been all to the good, since Artie was not exactly a Sonny Greer in percussion circles and he was more than likely, after the long intermission, to permit Elton Ponsonby or the youngest Boone kid to sit in in his place. Elton Ponsonby no more belonged at the drums in a dance band than the late E. T. Stotesbury and young Boone hadn't even entered Mercersburg yet. Still, the accident of the jettisoned drums somehow fitted in the general picture, it not having happened ever before.

The coming fact bears only the remotest relation to the preceding and those to follow, and it is germane only for obvious reasons: at twenty past six Norman Chew, one of the village policemen, missed a cross-corner shot which, if he had made it, would have equaled the high run of forty-eight balls which is the record at the Elks'. Norman had not intended to be present at the dance, as he hated the summer people, but he usually helped the late stayers with his flashlight. He was so disappointed at failing to equal the Elks' high run that he spent the rest of the evening playing pinochle. That was sad, because some people rather counted on Norman.

Not that this is important either, but Dr. Gordon Macgregor, who possessed a collection of eighty-four pipes, could not find a match in the whole goddam house. That was going on twenty of seven.

At six forty-five more than two hundred of the sporting enthusiasts (natives and summer people) tried to tune in on Stan Lomax. They all either turned off their radios or changed to some other station, so bad was the static. This proves that there may have been something in the air after all. Dressed, ready for dinner, hungry, and thwarted by the static and with at least fifteen minutes on his hands, a certain lad of fifteen made a serious pass at his mother's maid, and this time she slapped him right across the face. This was noteworthy principally because she had been threatening to for over a year, but never had.

There was no hot water at the Barbours'. This was infuriating and embarrassing to Mr. Barbour, because the hot-water system was practically brand-new (1941) and Mr. Barbour, who was a Tau Beta Pi from M.I.T., went over the whole system and couldn't find a single thing wrong with it.

A girl named Sallie Lynes, who was staying with the Stevenses, came across a dozen pairs of nylons while looking around her room for a safety pin. So delighted was Augusta Stevens that she shared this wonderful find with her honorable guest. Augusta couldn't remember ever having bought them and absolutely insisted that Sallie take half a dozen pairs.

The preceding two items are placed at roughly seven o'clock. At three minutes past seven—1903, as time is indicated in the services— the burglar alarm at the bank went off by accident. This was quite a coincidence, as Wayne Buffington, assistant cashier at the bank, was born in 1903 and has a son in the Navy who will be nineteen next March (third month of the year). Wayne, as is the local custom, was married very young. He fits into the picture because he is one of the few natives who are members of the club and as a matter of fact was planning to attend the dance. Wayne has always gotten along very well with the summer people and has won several cups with his knockabout in competition with the club members. He decided not to go to the dance at the last minute, as he only lives down the street from the bank and he thought, after the alarm went off, that he ought to stick around in case there was anything to it. The Buffingtons are an interesting old family and sometime it might be worth someone's while to go into their history.

Practically everyone sat down to dinner shortly after seven and apparently no one had any adventures worth repeating, or if they did, perhaps they were not *fit* to repeat. A few of the young kids turned up at the dance a little before nine o'clock, at which time the music began. By ten-thirty the floor was about half full. At ten past eleven three couples came and stood on the porch for a while but decided the party didn't look too tempting, so they went home and four of them played bridge and the other two played gin rummy.

The club lost money on the dance, not even making enough to pay the orchestra, but that was more or less anticipated, with all the big plans for the final dance. Nevertheless, as almost everybody re-marked the next day, many remarkable things occurred on what most people thought was going to be the dullest Saturday of the season.

WHERE'S THE GAME?

The moment his wife began to remove the dishes from the table Mr. Garfin got up and went to their bedroom and counted his money. Eighty dollars. Actually a little more than eighty dollars, but not enough more to put his bankroll in the ninety-dollar class. There would be enough left over, if he lost the eighty, to bring him home in a taxi and maybe have a rarebit or something.

He put on his hat and coat in the narrow hall and called out to his wife: "I don't know what time I'll be home."

She came out of the kitchen, rubbing her hands on her apron. "Wud you say?"

"I said I don't know what time I'll be home danight."

"You called me out to tell me that? Who *cares, when* you'll be home?" She returned to the kitchen and the dirty dishes.

"Nuts," he said, and went out.

He walked down the short steep street, his cigar sticking up out his mouth. A man spoke to him and he nodded and said, "Moe." Moe, henpecked Moe. For a moment his contempt for Moe gave way to pity. He almost asked Moe to accompany him, but that was out of the question. Tonight might be the night when he would get into a decent game, the game he had been looking for for three, four months. Why run the risk of spoiling it with penny-ante Moe? No, tonight he had a feeling that he would at last get into a decent game, a game where they played for folding money instead of stamp money. The hell with Moe.

A driver in a parked taxi at the corner said, "Taxi?" and Mr. Garfin almost succumbed but he resisted. He would take a taxi home. Now he would take the subway. He bought an early edition of the *News* and read the sports pages until he came to his station. A very shapely blonde girl got off the train when he did; she must have been in another car or surely he would have noticed her on the way down. She was too tall for him but he followed her up the steps anyway. She was a delight to follow up the steps, that figure. And the way her coat fit her over the hips. They got outside and he followed her along 149th Street, taking a kind of proprietary pleasure in the way men looked at her. She looked more like the kind of a broad you might see at the Paradise downtown. She probably was a hostess at one of the dime-a-dance places in this neighborhood, and he was so sure of this guess that he thought of following her into one and having a little fun. Buy a couple bucks' worth of tickets and get something started. Maybe not tonight. Tonight just show her he was a spender. But no, not tonight. Tonight he had other uses for his money.

And then, in front of a cigar store, a young man, dressed flashy, detached himself from a group, and went off with the blonde.

Mr. Garfin continued until he came to a Bar & Grill. He spoke to the cashier, a tired dame with too much lipstick on her. "Hello, dear. The boys here?"

"What boys?"

"The *boys*. Wilkey. Bloom. Harry Smith," said Mr. Garfin.

"Oh, sure. They're sitting in the last booth."

The girl was a dope. Why did she pretend she didn't know him? For three, four months now he had been coming in this joint, two or three nights a week sometimes; and she knew damn well he always sat with Wilkey and Bloom and Harry Smith whenever they were there. A dope girl like that could keep steady customers away.

He went back to the last booth, and when he reached it he stood still. Smith was telling the other two a story and they did not see Garfin coming because their heads were together and they were looking at the salt cellars and Smith was watching the effect of his story on the others. Smith saw Garfin first and nodded, but went on with his story. As the other two saw him they also nodded but continued to listen. At the end of the story the three men burst out laughing, and having laughed, the three looked at Garfin. Wilkey and Bloom said nothing. Smith said: "Hello, Big Shot. What's new?"

"Harry. Willie. Abe," said Garfin. "Oh, I don't know. I guess you boys were on that goat yesterday. That Fanciful."

"At Fair Grounds? You mean that one?" said Smith.

"That's the one," said Garfin. "Fanciful."

"No, I wasn't," said Smith. "Were you? You sound like it."

"For a little," said Garfin. "I made a little."

"Like what?" said Bloom.

"Like eighty bucks," said Garfin.

"You don't call that a little," said Bloom. "Don't tell me you can't use eighty dollars. *Any* time."

"He better not tell you," said Willie Wilkey. "Who'd believe him? What I doubt is if he was on her at all." Wilkey was sitting on the aisle. The others were sitting across the table from him. Wilkey made no sign of making room for Garfin, but Garfin took off his coat and hat and pushed in beside Wilkey.

"You got that prosperous look, Big Shot," said Smith. "I bet you were on that Fanciful for plenty. Come on, level with us. How much are you in?"

"Eighty bucks. A little over," said Garfin. "You boys just eat?"

"No, we're just here keeping the seats warm for some fellows from out of town," said Wilkey.

"I ate, but I think I'll have a piece of lemon pie," said Garfin. He called Gus, a waiter, and gave his order. Then he said to Smith: "Where's the game tonight?"

"What game? I didn't hear there was any game. Do you know where one is?"

"Aw, now, Harry," said Garfin.

"No. On the level," said Smith. "What kind of a game? You mean the *hockey* game, down at the Garden? Or, uh, the basketball game. New York U.?"

"Quid it, quid it," said Garfin, smiling. Gus brought the pie and Garfin began to eat, shaking his head and smiling. "You guys."

Wilkey watched him eat and after a bit said: "Garfin, lemme ask you a personal question if you don't mind."

"Not too personal I don't mind."

"Garfin—that's your name, isn't it?" said Wilkey.

"You know it's my name."

"Sure. Well, I often wanted to ask you, what do you do for a living?" said Wilkey.

"I could ask you the same question," said Garfin.

"Everybody knows what I do for a living, Garfin," said Wilkey. "I'm a part-time stool pigeon trying to find out who killed Rothstein. Do you know? I could use that information."

"Everybody knows I killed Rothstein," said Garfin. Smith and Bloom laughed with him.

"Well, then, I guess my work is ended," said Wilkey. "But seriously, when you're not killing Rothstein what do you do? That was a long time ago. You must do something besides that. Come on, level with me."

"You really want to know?"

"Really."

"I'm a salesman."

"Selling what? Papers?" said Wilkey.

"Furniture," said Garfin.

"Furniture. Well, Garfin, I don't want any," said Wilkey.

"That's your privilege," said Garfin.

"That's right. It's my privilege. And you know what else is my privilege? My privilege is I don't like your kisser. You're always coming around here always asking the same question: 'Where's the game tonight?' You always get the same answer, but you keep on asking, 'Where's the game tonight?' I wonder why that is, Garfin. Nobody knows anything about you—"

"Bloom knows me. Bloom went to school with me," said Garfin.

"Bloom told me. He went to school with you for like six months. That was a long time ago, Garfin. Sixth grade, or around there. Twenty years ago at least."

"I used to see him since then, off and on."

"Off and on," said Bloom.

"Right. And Abe was away a few years, remember that," said Wilkey. "Well, this is the way it adds up, Garfin. Bloom is away a few years and then a few months ago you happen to run into him on the street. Happen to. So he can't get rid of you and you come here with him and he introduced you to us and right away you start coming here all the time. A couple times a week. And every night the same question: 'Where's the game tonight?' till I begin to wonder about you, Garfin."

"Why?"

"This is why. I remember about six months ago at an apartment, some fellows I happen to know slightly, they had a game. A poker game. They were playing cards this night in this apartment, and about four o'clock in the morning there was a stick-up. These guys were just friends having a poker game and not letting the whole world know about it, but somebody must have found out because there was a stick-up and the gorills took away about twelve hundred dollars and shot one of the fellows that was playing poker. Do you remember?"

"I read the papers," said Garfin.

"He reads the papers," said Wilkey. "All right. Well, I like to play poker, Garfin. I like all forms of gambling but the best one I like is poker. Now supposing I was sitting here some night and some friends of mine invited me to join them in a game, and you came in and asked your usual question and suppose I said, 'Why, Garfin, old pal. The game is at some address on Tremont Avenya.' Then would you say you hadda make a phone call and when you came back would you say you hadda go home to the little woman, and then I would say too bad and then we would go and play poker without you, and along about four o'clock in the morning some gorills come in and take our money and shoot one of us? Would that ever happen?"

"Certainly not. What do you think I am?"

"I don't know, Garfin. I don't know. But do me a favor, Garfin. Do me a favor and stay out of here. I and the boys talked this over and we decided we don't want you butting in on a private conversation. Do me a favor and get out now. I'll pay for the piece of pie and coffee."

Garfin stared at Wilkey and then quickly looked at Smith and Bloom. They were looking at him coldly, dead-pan. "O.K.," he said. He got up and put on his hat and coat. "O.K."

At the desk he told the cashier, "Mr. Wilkey is taking care of my check." He went out into 149th Street and walked a couple of blocks. He caught himself looking at a pretty girl, who stared back at him and sniffed. The hell with her, he thought; he wasn't even thinking about her. Every now and then he would be sick with fear, knowing now what they thought of him. But almost as bad was knowing that he never could go back there again, the only place where he wanted to be. And so he went down into the subway and home.

MRS. WHITMAN

The following, apparently the rough draft of a letter, was picked up on South Broad Street near Walnut in Philadelphia. It is printed here for its value as an American document.

—

Dear (blurred): This is not the story of Ella Miller Whitman. The story of Ella Miller Whitman and her lifelong devotion to the Gibbsville (Pa.) *Standard* could only have been written by one man: Bob Hooker, editor and publisher of the *Standard,* and he not only has written the story, but published it in a beautifully bound presentation volume which was one of the nicest surprises at the dinner given Mrs. Whitman recently upon the occasion of her retirement from the *Standard.* Mrs. Whitman had been with the *Standard* for forty-five years. Indeed, as Bob Hooker said in his speech: "Not only has Mrs. Whitman been with the *Standard* for five and forty years. There have been times when you might even say that Ella has *been* the *Standard*!" At this there was a suspicious moisture in Mrs. Whitman's usually twinkling eyes, but the smile never left her unlined face. It had been hoped that Mrs. Whitman might round out the full fifty years of devotion to the *Standard,* but Herbert Hooker, Bob's nephew and business manager of the *Standard*, wisely realized that although Mrs. Whitman's health seemed as good as can be reasonably expected at her age, there was always the chance that she might not be around five years longer. Herbert was above all things a business man, a realist, and reluctantly or not he also faced the possibility that his Uncle Bob might not be in the land of living on the day that Mrs. Whitman achieved the half-century mark of her career. He therefore wrote his uncle, then vacationing in one of the less ostentatious Florida resorts, and suggested tactfully that Mrs. Whitman be retired and a commemorative dinner be given in her honor. With the full approval of Bob Hooker the nephew went about lining up many of the important folk of Gibbsville to be present at the event or at least to send messages to the honored guest. It is true that the mayor, the fire chief, the honorable county judges, and several other locally famed figures did not know Mrs. Whitman personally, or at any rate had been unaware that she had been serving the *Standard* these many years, but that was an inevitable consequence of Mrs. Whitman's lifelong avoidance of the limelight. So long as she is spared, Mrs. Whitman may derive daily satisfaction from the beautifully bound volume containing the pretty tributes from her grateful employers and from virtually all persons of importance in Gibbsville. These included the briefer messages as well as the speeches by the mayor, the presiding judge, the secretary of the chamber of commerce, Mrs. Whitman's own pastor, and, of course, Bob Hooker himself. In addition the leading merchants were afforded the opportunity to participate in the celebration, just as they had been a few years earlier when "Fighting Bob" was discovered to have passed a full fifty years as a newspaper man. At that time only full-page congratulatory advertisements were accepted. For Mrs. Whitman this regulation was relaxed as was the rate, in order to enable a more representative group, including Mrs. Whitman's neighborhood shops, to be represented in the volume. So co-operative, however, were the department stores, specialty shops, nationally famous newsprint manufacturers, the Mergenthaler and Hoe people, insurance firms and private individuals (several of whom were content to remain, simply, "A Friend") that not only was the expense of the dinner itself defrayed, but a neat purse was turned over to Mrs. Whitman. Although not officially announced at the dinner or in the *Standard*'s account on the following day, the amount of the purse was said to be in the neighborhood of four figures. This sum, of course, was over and above Mrs. Whitman's pension, under the terms of which she is to receive half pay so long as she is spared. Moreover, mention at this junction should be made of the beautiful silver coffee set—coffee pot with ebonized handles, cream pitcher, sugar bowl, and tray—which was the gift of Mrs. Whitman's fellow workers. This beautiful, useful, and long-lasting gift was made possible through popular subscription, but 'tis said the lion's share was borne by the editor and publisher. At any rate the tray bears the legend: "To Ella M. Whitman, In Appreciation of Forty-five Years of Service—From Bob Hooker and The Gang at The Gibbsville Standard."

The presentation volume mentioned above was, as may be inferred, the dinner program in a special leather-and-gold binding, hand-tooled. On the front cover is a golden replica of the *Standard*'s masthead, a superb example of the bookbinder's art. Directly beneath the masthead is the dedication: "To Ella M. Whitman, In Appreciation of Forty-five Years of Service—From Bob Hooker and The Gang at The Gibbsville Standard." On the spine are Mrs. Whitman's initials, the year, and the word *Standard,* also in gold. But beautiful as is the bookbinder's contribution to the presentation volume, it is the contents of the program itself which one may assume will bring forth a tiny tear when in her richly earned years of retirement Mrs. Whitman pauses to peruse the happy memento.

As one opens the book first to greet the eye is a full-page reproduction of the most recent available photograph of Mrs. Whitman. There is a sentimental touch to the inclusion of this photograph which could be recognized only by those in the know. This same picture was made in the *Standard*'s own "shop" by Murray Weiss, staff photographer and assistant sports editor of the *Standard.* Originally it was taken for inclusion along with the other members of the *Standard*'s "Twenty-five Year Club," an informal organization which was founded by Herbert Hooker while he was preparing the celebration of Fighting Bob's fiftieth anniversary in the newspaper business. Mrs. Whitman, of course, more than qualified for "membership" in the "club" for at that time she had been with the *Standard* approximately forty years, but it is believed that Herbert in making Mrs. Whitman a member of the "Twenty-five Year" group was exercising tact in two ways: it was, after all, his uncle's day, and too it may have passed through his mind that a lady's age is her own secret. At any rate the photograph remained in the *Standard*'s files until the program for her own celebration was being prepared. With characteristic fairness Herbert Hooker gave Mrs. Whitman her day: her photograph is the first in the book; Bob Hooker's does not appear until the second following page, and Herbert's two pages after that.

What might be called the title page reads as follows: "Programme—Testimonial Banquet to Ella M. Whitman, In Appreciation of Forty-five Years of Service—Tendered by Bob Hooker and The Gang at the Gibbsville Standard." The date appears at the bottom of the page, along with the name of the hotel, which was, of course, the Gibbs Hotel. A word here may for all time clear up the single minute criticism which was directed against the *Standard*'s sincere and touching tribute to Mrs. Whitman. It is customary in Gibbsville to hold affairs of the kind in the King Coal Room of the Gibbs House, as it formerly was known. The King Coal Room was the name given the main dining room when the hotel was completely redecorated and refurnished in 1929, and the room is regarded as one of the most attractive rooms of its kind in that section of Pennsylvania, if not in the entire State. The murals are regional in theme, depicting as they do coal-mining scenes which were painted by a professional artist from Philadelphia. To residents of Gibbsville and the surrounding territory the words King Coal Room are so well known that the room need not be otherwise identified. It has been the scene of countless fashionable banquets, wedding receptions, and balls, and throughout the Thirties it was the scene of the regular Saturday-night dances, which were attended by leading members of Gibbsville society, although open to the public. In the course of the pleasant but by no means small task of arranging for Mrs. Whitman's celebration Herbert Hooker inevitably and automatically decided upon the King Coal Room, but, as he later confided to friends, when this decision was casually mentioned to Bob Hooker the latter voiced his doubt that the King Coal Room was suitable. He pointed out that a lady of Mrs. Whitman's retiring habits might find herself so ill at ease in such worldly surroundings that she would be completely ill at ease, with the result that what had been intended as an occasion for her own personal enjoyment might turn out to be little short of a trying ordeal. Herbert therefore changed the plan and the banquet was held in the more informal, more friendly Coffee Shoppe, where Mrs. Whitman was wont to lunch each working day. Also, if pressed Herbert will admit that he had Mrs. Whitman's best interests in mind in another direction: the *Standard,* of course, assumed the entire expense of the celebration and a certain sum was budgeted to cover that expense. Since the per-plate cost of dinner in the King Coal Room is nearly double that of the Coffee Shoppe, it stood to reason that within the limitations of the budgeted sum the Coffee Shoppe was the more desirable, since it left a tidy amount which could be and was devoted to the purse which was tendered Mrs. Whitman as the climax of the banquet. And later in the evening Mrs. Whitman had her King Coal Room after all, for at the conclusion of the festivities she was hostess to a small party of friends among whom were City Editor Jack O'Brien, Sports Editor Walt Southard, Composing Room Foreman Jake Spitz, and their wives. Also present as one of Mrs. Whitman's guests was J. Russell Meredith, for thirty years political and county editor of the *Standard.* (Mr. Meredith had resigned from the *Standard* shortly after the banquet plans were announced, giving ill health as his reason. He was not present at the banquet. Mr. Meredith's many friends will be delighted to hear that he is well on the way to recovery and has accepted a position in the County Recorder's office under County Recorder Will M. Templeton.)

For obvious mechanical reasons it was possible to include in the printed program only those laudatory messages which had been prepared in advance. Mrs. Whitman herself had, as was to be expected, declined the opportunity to present her own response to these tributes in the program. In fact she had consented to the celebration on condition that she not be called upon for any speech. But in that she reckoned without the persuasiveness of Editor Bob Hooker, who departed from the announced program and led the assemblage in applause which had the desired effect of bringing Mrs. Whitman to her feet to say a few words. It was a never-to-be-forgotten sight as the well-loved jovial editor-in-chief placed his arm about the shoulders of the faithful employee, now on her way to a well-earned rest. "And now," said Editor Bob, "I yield, as, truth to tell, I have more than once yielded in the past, to my favorite coworker, and permit me to state, permit me to admit right here in open court, as it were, that many times in the five decades past I have had good reason to be happy in deferring to the wise judgment of Ella Whitman on such occasions as I have consulted her. Boys and girls of the *Standard* gang, I give you Ella M. Whitman." At this there was renewed applause which must have drowned out the sound of the orchestra playing in the King Coal Room on the floor above. Mrs. Whitman waited until the applause had died down and then she spoke with all the assurance of a veteran speaker. As reported in the *Standard* the next day, her remarks were simple but eloquent: "Mr. Hooker, ladies and gentlemen: I am very grateful to you all, not only for what has been said here this evening, but even more so for the friendships and the kindnesses I have been shown during my forty-five years with the *Standard*. Forty-five years is a long time, and I suppose I am an old lady and that my usefulness is at an end, and so I shall not be with you after this evening. Some of you know what is in my heart tonight and to you I say thank you, and thirty." This last, the word thirty, is the traditional signing-off signal of the newspaper business, which Mrs. Whitman had learned as typesetter and proofreader on the *Standard,* before taking charge of the classified advertising of the paper, a position which she occupied for twenty-three of her forty-five years' service. When she finished her graceful speech the assemblage rose as one man, and with Herbert Hooker at the piano and Editor Bob Hooker leading, all present sang *Auld Lang Syne* and Ella Whitman had entered upon the *emerita* phase of her career.

No, this is not the story of Ella Miller Whitman. It is a bigger story than that. It is the story of Free Enterprise in a Free Country. It is the story of employer and employee working hand-in-hand, one for the other in a manner all too rare in these times. If it be the story of Ella Miller Whitman, then it is also the story of Bob Hooker. Truly, it is the story of neither, and of both.

With (blurred)

PRICE'S ALWAYS OPEN

The place where everybody would end up before going home was Price's. This was the second summer for Price's. Before that it had been a diner and an eyesore. The last man to run the diner had blown town owing everybody, and somehow or other that had put a curse on the place. No one, not even the creditors, wanted to open up again, and time and the weather got at the diner and for two years it had stood there, the windows all smashed by passing school-boys, the paint gone, and the diner itself sagging in the middle like an old work horse. Then last summer Mr. Price got his bonus and he went into the all-night-restaurant business.

The first thing he did was to get permission to tear down the diner and put up his own place. It was a corner plot, and he built his place twice as wide as the diner had been. The Village Fathers were only too glad to have Mr. Price build. In other times they never would have let the place go the way the diner had. The neatness of the village was always commented upon by new summer people and bragged about by those who had been coming there for gen-erations. But things being the way they were . . . So Mr. Price built a sort of rustic place, which, while not in keeping with the rest of the village architecture, was clean and attractive in its way. All the signboards were simulated shingles, and the lettering has been described as quaint. Mr. Price frankly admitted he got his idea from a chain of places in New York. There was one neon sign that stayed on all night, and it said, simply, "PRICE'S." Nothing about what Price's was; everyone knew.

Mr. Price had one leg, having left the other somewhere in a dressing station back of Château-Thierry. He was not a cook but a house painter, and he had had to employ a couple of short-order cooks from New York and Boston. But Mr. Price was always there. Not that anyone ever wondered about it, but it might have been interesting to find out just when he slept. He was at his position near the cash register all night, and he certainly was there at noon when the chauffeurs and a few summer-hotel clerks and people like that would come in for lunch. As a matter of fact, he did not need much sleep. No day passed without his leg bothering him, and seeing people took his mind off his leg. Best of all, he liked late at night.

Saturday night there was always a dance at the yacht club. That was a very late crowd. The dances were supposed to stop at one, but if the stricter older members had gone home, the young people would keep the orchestra for another hour or two, and even after that they would hang around while one of the boys played the piano. The boy who played the piano was Jackie Girard.

They were a nice bunch of kids, practically all of them, and Mr. Price had known their fathers and mothers for years, or many of them. Sometimes the wife's family had been coming to this island for years and years; then she married the husband, a stranger, and the husband and wife would start coming here and keep coming. Sometimes it was the husband who was old summer people. Most of the present younger crowd had been coming here every summer for fifteen, twenty years. One or two of them had been born here. But Jackie Girard was Mr. Price's favorite. He was born here, and unlike the others, he lived here all year round.

Jackie had a strange life with the summer people, and it probably was that that made Mr. Price feel closer to him than to the others. The others were nice and respectful, and they always said *Mister* Price, just as Jackie did. But they were summer people, and the winters were long. Not that Jackie was here in the winter any more, but at least he came home several times in the winter. Jackie was at college at Holy Cross, and naturally his holidays were spent here.

The strange life that Jackie had apparently did not seem strange to him. He was not a member of the yacht club, naturally. Jackie's father was a carpenter, the best in the village; the best out of three, it's true, but head and shoulders above the other two. Henry Girard was a French Canuck and had been in the Twenty-sixth Division with Mr. Price, but never an intimate of Mr. Price's. Jackie had three sisters; one older, two younger. Jackie's mother played the organ in the Catholic church. The older sister was married and lived in Worcester, and the younger ones were in high school. Anyway, Jackie was not a member of the yacht club, but he was almost always sure of being invited to one of the dinners before the regular Saturday-night dance. He was one of the clerks at the hotel, and that, plus an occasional five or ten from his sister in Worcester, gave him just enough money to pay for gas and his incidental expenses. He could hold his end up. The only trouble was, except for Saturday and Sunday, he did not have much end to hold up.

There were gatherings, if not parties, practically every night of the week. Every Thursday, for instance, the large group of young people would split up into smaller groups, sometimes three, four, five, and after dinner they would go to the boxing matches. Jackie was not invited to these small dinner parties. He had been invited two or three times, but his mother had told him he had better not go. For herself, she wished he could have gone, but his father would not have approved. After Jackie had regretted the few invitations he got, the summer people figured it out that all he cared about was the yacht-club dances. He was the only town boy who was invited to yacht-club dances, and they figured that that was all he wanted. It did not take them long to decide that this was as it should be all around. They decided that Jackie would feel embarrassed at the smaller parties, but that he did not need to feel embarrassed at the club dances, because in a sense he was earning his way by playing such perfectly marvelous piano. But this was not the way Mr. Price saw it.

Almost every night but Saturday Jackie would drop in. Two nights a week he had been to the movies, which changed twice a week, but Mr. Price at first wondered what Jackie would do to kill time the other nights. Jackie would show up around eleven-thirty and sit at the counter until some of the summer crowd began to arrive. They would yell at him, "Hi, Jackie! Hi, keed! How's it, Jackie?" And Jackie would swing around on his stool, and they would yell at him to come on over and sit at a table with them. And he would sit at the table with whichever group arrived first. In the early part of the summer that did not mean any special group, because when the other groups would arrive, they would put all the tables together and form one party. Then there would be some bickering about the bill, and more than once Mr. Price saw Jackie grab the check for the whole party. It was not exactly a big check; you could not eat much more than forty cents' worth at Mr. Price's without making a pig of yourself, and the usual order was a cereal, half-milk-half-cream, and a cup of coffee; total, twenty cents. But you take fourteen of those orders and you have a day's pay for Jackie.

As the summer passed, however, the large group did break into well-defined smaller groups; one of six, several of four. By August there would be the same foursomes every night, and of these one included the Leech girl.

The Leeches were not old people in the sense that some of them were. The Leeches belonged to the newcomers who first summered in this place in 1930 and 1931. They had come from one of the more famous resorts. Louise Leech was about twelve when her family first began to come to this place. But now she was eighteen or nineteen. She had a Buick convertible coupé. She was a New York girl, whereas most of the other boys and girls were not New Yorkers; they all went to the same schools and colleges, but they did not come from the same home towns. Some came from as far west as Denver, as Mr. Price knew from cashing their checks. And even what few New York girls did come to this place were not New York friends of the Leeches. Mr. Leech was here only on week-ends and his wife was away most of the time, visiting friends who had not had to give up Narragansett. Louise herself was away a good deal of the time.

It was easy to see, the first summer Louise was grown up, that she was discontented. She did not quite fit in with the rest of the crowd, and she not only knew it but she was content not to make the best of it. Mr. Price could hear the others, the first summer he was in business, making remarks about Louise and her thinking she was too good for this place. And they had been saying something like it the early part of this summer, too. But after the Fourth of July, somewhere around there, they began to say better things about her. Mostly they said she really wasn't so bad when you got to know her. To which a few of the girls said, "Who wants to?" And others said, "She doesn't like us any better. We're still not good enough for her. But Sandy is." Which did explain a lot.

Sandy—Sandy Hall—was from Chicago, but what with prep school and college and this place and vacation trips, he probably had not spent a hundred days in Chicago in the last seven years. In a bathing suit he was almost skinny, except for his shoulders; he looked cold, he was so thin. But Mr. Price had seen him in action one night when one of the Portuguese fishermen came in drunk and got profane in a different way from the way the summer people did. Sandy had got up and let the Portuguese have two fast hard punches in the face, and the fisherman went down and stayed down. Sandy looked at the man on the floor—it was hard to tell how long he looked at him—and suddenly he kicked him. The man was already out, and so there was no need to kick him, but the kick had several results. One was that Mr. Price brought a blackjack to work the next night. The other result was something Mr. Price noticed on Louise's face.

He had not had much time to take it all in, as he had had to leave the cash register to help the night counterman drag the fisherman out of the place. But he remembered the expression on the girl's face. It began to appear when the fisherman went down from the punches, and when Sandy kicked the man, it was all there. Mr. Price, standing where he did, was the only one who caught it. He thought of it later as the way a girl would look the first time she saw Babe Ruth hit a home run, provided she cared about home runs. Or the way she would look if someone gave her a bucketful of diamonds. And other ways, that would come with experiences that Mr. Price was sure Louise never had had.

Sandy had not come with Louise that night, but Mr. Price noticed she went home with him. And after that night they were always together. They were part of a foursome of whom the other two were the dullest young people in the crowd. It took Mr. Price some time to determine why this was, but eventually he did figure it. The foursome would come into Price's, and Louise and Sandy would watch the others while they ordered; then Sandy would say he and Louise wanted the same, and from then on neither Sandy nor Louise would pay any attention to the other two. Stooges.

Another thing that Mr. Price noticed was that Jackie could not keep his eyes off Louise.

Along about the latter part of August, it was so obvious that one night Mr. Price kidded Jackie about it. It was one of the nights Jackie dropped in by himself, and Mr. Price said, "Well, she isn't here yet."

"Who isn't here?"

"The Leech girl."

"Oh," said Jackie. "Why, did anybody say anything to you? Is that how you knew I liked her?"

"No. Figured it out for myself. I have eyes."

"You're a regular Walter Winchell. But don't say anything, Mr. Price."

"What the hell would I say, and who to?"

"I'll be back," said Jackie. He was gone for more than an hour, and when he returned, the crowd was there. They all yelled as usual, but this time one of the girls added, "Jackie's tight." He was, rather. He had a somewhat silly grin on his face, and his nice teeth made a line from ear to ear. Several tables wanted him to join them and they were friendly about it. But he went to the table where sat Louise and Sandy and the others.

"Do you mind if I sit down?" he said.

"Do you mind?" said Sandy.

"No," said Louise.

"Thank you. Thank you," said Jackie. "Go fights?"

"Mm-hmm," said Sandy.

"Any good? Who won?"

"The nigger from New Bedford beat the townie," said Sandy. "Kicked the Jesus out of him."

"Oh, uh townie. You mean Bobbie Lawless. He's nice guy. Za friend of mine. I used to go to high school—"

"He's yellow," said Sandy.

"Certainly was," said Louise.

"Nope. Not yellow. Not Bobbie. I used to go to high school with Bobbie. Plain same football team."

"Where do you go to school now?" said Sandy.

"Holy Cross. We're gonna beat you this year."

"What is Holy Cross?" said Louise.

Sandy laughed. Jackie looked at her with tired eyes.

"No, really, what is it?"

" 'Tsa college. It's where I go to college. Dint you ever hear of Holy Cross? Give another hoya and a choo-choo rah rah—"

"O.K.," said Sandy.

"I'll sing if I wanta. I'll sing one of your songs. Oh, hit the line for Harvard, for Harvard wins today—"

"Oh, go away," said Sandy.

"Yes, for God's *sake*," said Louise.

"Oh, very well, Miss Leech. Very well." Jackie put his hands on the table to steady himself as he got to his feet, but he stared down into her eyes and for two seconds he was sober.

"Come on, Jackie, you're stewed." Mr. Price had come around from the cash register and had taken Jackie by the right arm. At that moment Sandy lashed out with a right-hand punch, and Jackie fell down. But he had hardly reached the floor before Mr. Price snapped his blackjack from his pocket and slapped it down on the front of Sandy's head. Sandy went down and there was blood.

"Anybody else?" said Mr. Price. By this time the night counterman had swung himself over the counter, and in his hand was a baseball bat, all nicked where it had been used for tamping down ice around milk cans. None of the summer crowd made a move; then Mr. Price spoke to two of the young men. "Get your friend outa here, and get out, the whole goddam bunch of you." He stood where he was, he and the counterman, and watched the girls picking up their wraps.

"Aren't you going to do anything?" Louise screamed. "Chuck! Ted! All of you!"

"You get out or I'll throw you out," said Mr. Price. She left.

There were murmurs as well as the sounds of the cars starting. Thinking it over, Mr. Price agreed with himself that those would be the last sounds he ever expected to hear from the summer crowd.

THE COLD HOUSE

The house in the country was cold, and Mrs. Carnavon sat with her hat on, her sealskin coat open, her bag in her lap, her left hand lying flat on the bag. The slight exertion—but not slight to her—of getting out of the car, stepping down, walking up the three steps of the porte cochere, had left her breathing heavily, and the thumb of her right hand was beating against the forefinger. She had had a long nap in the car, coming up from New York. Driscoll drove so you could sleep. He had to; that was his job. She knew Driscoll, and how he would look in the mirror to see if she was asleep before he would increase his speed. Driscoll was so thoroughly trained in moderate speed that she often had had to feign sleep in order to get some place in a hurry. But today she had not had to feign sleep. Up at six-thirty, away at seven-thirty, and now it was almost time for lunch. But first a rest, a little rest. The house was very cold. Mrs. Carnavon rang for the maid.

"I didn't expect you till late afternoon," said the maid. "I'll build you a fire."

"Never mind, Anna."

"But it'll only *take* a *minute*, ma'am. I kin—"

"No, never *mind*."

"Well, but of course if you—"

"I won't change my mind. Is the phone connected? I mean here in the house."

"No, only over the garage, where we are."

"Then will you go out and telephone the Inn and tell Mr. McCall—ask him if I could have a chop and a baked potato. Or anything. Nothing much. Cup of tea."

"I could fix you something."

"Too much trouble to start a fire. No, just tell Mr. McCall, and find out how soon he can have it."

"Of course he'll more than likely have to go out and buy it, and—"

"All right. He can go out and buy it." Mrs. Carnavon hated to be short with Anna, but Anna had the hide of an elephant. She knew that Anna would not be hurt; she watched Anna leave the room and knew that Anna was thinking: "The poor woman is all upset."

She looked out of the window and saw Anna, with a very ugly shawl over her head and shoulders, looking rather pathetic, hurrying to the garage to telephone Mr. McCall. Mrs. Carnavon lit a cigarette. It steadied her a little. It steadied her body, her hands; there was no unsteadiness to the lump in her heart, the thing in her mind. She held the cigarette as high as her face, taking regular, deep inhales. She idly opened a china cigarette box on the table beside her, just tilting the lid. There were four cigarettes in the box. She took one out and it was as crisp as a twig. She broke it with her fingers. It was from last summer. A cigarette that her son could have smoked. She looked at it and saw that it was a cigarette that Harry would *not* have smoked; it was a brand he never had liked. But still, when he had had a few drinks she had seen him smoking just that brand without noticing any difference. "Mom, why do you have those things in the house? Everybody passes them up. They're really vile. They are. They're vile. I hate to tell you what they remind me of." One time he had emptied all the available boxes of that brand. But she noticed that when some friends of his were at the house, they would ask Anna if there didn't happen to be some of that brand—"on the premises," one boy had said. She didn't remember much about the boy, but she remembered that strange expression.

Now that she was here—"I came up here for something," she said aloud. Well, what? The cracked windowpane that she had noticed the first time one morning after Harry and his friends had been to a dance. Two decks of cards on the desk. The copy of *Life* magazine on the rack. The summer *Social Register*, with its warped cover curling up. She heard a screen door slam, an odd sound in this kind of weather, when the flies had died. It was Anna, of course. Anna's hands were cold; Mrs. Carnavon noticed them when Anna reached up to take off her shawl.

"He said he'd be glad to serve you in about three-quarters of an hour," said Anna. "I was right. He does have to go out and buy the chops. About three-quarters of an hour, he said. I think what he's doing, I think he wants to warm up the dining room a little, too. You know, it was awful this winter for Mr. McCall. I don't believe he had more than two or three people there a week. A couple regulars, like salesmen, passing through, but overnight I don't believe he had more than two or three people. Just for lunch, the regulars. I don't think it paid him to keep open."

"Anna, will you go upstairs in Mr. Harry's room, there's a picture in a silver frame—"

"Of Dr. Carnavon. I have it out in our room."

"How dare you!"

"I'm sorry, ma'am, I only meant to do the right thing. I didn't want anybody to steal—"

"You had no right to touch anything in that room. Go bring it to me!"

The tears came and Anna fled, and Mrs. Carnavon was weary of herself, flaring up at this miserable soul, who had no way of knowing that that room was not to be disturbed. No order had been given. Indeed, Mrs. Carnavon admitted that until now she had not thought of leaving that room the way it was, the way it had been all winter. It was part of her confusion, trying to find some reason for making this trip. Trying to find some excuse, she admitted, that would explain the trip to the servants, to Anna. And then, finally, finding the worst excuse of all: Anna would know she had not driven all this distance merely to take home a picture of a husband long dead. Weary, wearily, Mrs. Carnavon climbed the stairs to her son's room.

On the wall the same diamond-shaped plaque, with the clasped hands and the Greek letters; another wooden diamond, with the head of a wolf; a photograph of a baseball team, with names badly printed in white ink under the picture; a large bare spot where there had been a reproduction which he had liked well enough to take back to town. A magazine that he may have read. She opened it: ". . . and it will become increasingly apparent that the forces of Fascism are laboring night and day . . . choice may have to be made sooner than you expect; but no matter when it comes, when it does come it will be sooner than you like. . . ." A young friend, an *old* friend, of Harry's had written that. An intense young man had come to see her a month or so ago; he had been abroad, he had just learned, he couldn't *believe* it. Why, he and Harry, for eight years . . . Eight years? What about twenty-four years? What was *eight* years? Well, for one thing, it was eight years during which he had seen Harry a great deal more than she had, like it or not.

Everything in this room would have to go. Those things, those shields, those pictures, all that would have to go. She would send them to the right people. Everything would have to go. She now saw that in the back of her mind, as she was climbing the stairs, had been some vague plan to lock this room and leave everything as she found it; but now when she saw this she felt chilled and disgusted. Let him be dead, but let him be dead! Let him be what he was, and let it have ended with no awful sanctuary or crypt of useless things. Oh, how useless were these things! "I do not even know what Upsilon means," she whispered. "Those baseball players. Do I want to see *them*?" She recoiled from the nearness of a danger, the danger of keeping this room the way it was, and the lone, secret visits she would have paid it, looking at things that had no meaning to her.

She could see clearly, like watching a motion picture of herself, what she would have done, what she had been in terrible danger of doing: next August, next September, a year from next August and a year from next July, she would have come up here, unlocked the door, come in this room and stood. She saw herself, a woman in white, trying to squeeze out a tear at the sight of these things of wood and brass and paper and glass—and all the while distracted by the sounds of passing cars, the children next door, the telephone downstairs, the whirring vacuum cleaner. And she even knew the end of this motion picture: she would end by hating a memory that she only knew how to love.

She walked out, leaving the door open, and went downstairs. Anna was standing in the hall, with fear in her eyes. Mrs. Carnavon looked at her watch. "Tell Driscoll to bring the car around."

"He's having a bite with us," said Anna.

"Tell him to bring that *car* around!" said Mrs. Carnavon. "I'm going back by train."

The train was quicker.

ARE WE LEAVING TOMORROW?

It was cool, quite cool, the way the weather is likely to be at an in-between resort when the Florida season is over but the Northern summer season has not yet begun. Every morning the tall young man and his young wife would come down the steps of the porch and go for their walk. They would go to the mounting block where the riders would start for the trails. The tall young man and his wife would stand not too close to the block, not speaking to anyone; just watching. But there might have been a little in his attitude, in his manner, of a man who felt that he was starting the riders, as though his presence there made their start official. He would stand there, hatless and tan, chin down almost to his chest, his hands dug deep in the pockets of his handsome tweed topcoat. His wife would stand beside him with her arm in his, and when she would speak to him she would put her face in front of him and look up. Almost always his answer would be a smile and a nod, or perhaps a single word that expressed all he wanted to put into words. They would watch the riders for a while, and then they would stroll over to the first tee of the men's golf course to watch the golfers start off. There it would be the same: not much talk, and the slightly superior manner or attitude. After they had watched their quota of golfers they would go back to the porch and she would go up to their rooms and a Negro bellboy would bring him his papers, the *Montreal Star* and the *New York Times*. He would sit there lazily looking at the papers, never so interested in a news item that he would not look up at every person who came in or went out of the hotel, or passed his chair on the porch. He watched every car come up the short, winding drive, watched the people get in and out, watched the car drive away; then when there was no human activity he would return to his paper, holding it rather far away, and on his face and in his eyes behind the gold-rimmed spectacles there was always the same suspicion of a smile.

He would go to his room before lunch, and they would come down together. After lunch, like most everyone else, they would re-tire, apparently for a nap, not to appear until the cocktail hour. They would be the first, usually, in the small, cheery bar, and until it was time to change for dinner he would have a high-ball glass, constantly refilled, in his hand. He drank slowly, sipping teaspoon-fuls at a time. In that time she might drink two light highballs while he was drinking eight. She always seemed to have one of the maga-zines of large format in her lap, but at these times it was she who would look up, while he hardly turned his head.

Not long after they came she began to speak to people; to bow and pass the time of day. She was a pleasant, friendly little woman, not yet thirty. Her eyes were too pretty for the rest of her face; in sleep she must have been very plain indeed, and her skin was sen-sitive to the sun. She had good bones—lovely hands and feet—and when she was in sweater and skirt her figure always got a second look from the golfers and riders.

Their name was Campbell—Douglas Campbell, and Sheila. They were the youngest people over fifteen in the hotel. There were a few children, but most of the guests were forty or thereabouts. One afternoon the Campbells were in the bar and a woman came in and after hesitating at the entrance she said, "Good afternoon, Mrs. Campbell. You didn't happen to see my husband?"

"No, I didn't," said Mrs. Campbell.

The woman came closer slowly and put her hand on the back of a chair near them. "I was afraid I'd missed him," she said to no one; then suddenly she said, "Do you mind if I sit with you while he comes?"

"No, not at all," said Mrs. Campbell.

"Please do," said Campbell. He got to his feet and stood very erect. He set his glass on the little table and put his hands behind his back.

"I'm sorry I don't remember your name," said Mrs. Campbell.

"Mrs. Loomis."

Mrs. Campbell introduced her husband, who said, "Wouldn't you like a cocktail meanwhile?"

Mrs. Loomis thought a moment and said she would—a dry Daiquiri. Then Campbell sat down, picking up his drink and beginning to sip.

"I think we were the first here, as usual," said Mrs. Campbell, "so we couldn't have missed Mr. Loomis."

"Oh, it's all right. One of us is always late, but it isn't important. That's why I like it here. The general air of informality." She smiled. "I've never seen you here before. Is this your first year?"

"Our first year," said Mrs. Campbell.

"From New York?"

"Montreal," said Mrs. Campbell.

"Oh, Canadians. I met some awfully nice Canadians in Palm Beach this winter," said Mrs. Loomis. She named them off, and Mrs. Campbell said they knew them, and he smiled and nodded. Then Mrs. Loomis tried to remember the names of some other people she knew in Montreal (they turned out to have been Toronto people), and Mr. Loomis arrived.

A white-haired man, a trifle heavy and about fifty, Mr. Loomis wore young men's clothes. He was brown and heavy-lidded. He had good manners. It was he who corrected his wife about the people from Montreal who actually were from Toronto. That was the first time the Loomises and the Campbells had done more than speak in passing, and Mrs. Campbell was almost gay that afternoon.

The Campbells did not come down to dinner that evening, but they were out for their stroll the next morning. Mr. Loomis waved to them at the first tee, and they waved—*she* waved, Campbell nodded. They did not appear for cocktails that afternoon. For the next few days they took their stroll, but they had their meals in their room. The next time they came to the cocktail lounge they took a small table at the side of the bar, where there was room only for the table and two chairs. No one spoke to them, but that night was one of the nights when the hotel showed movies in the ballroom, and after the movie the Loomises fell in with them and insisted on buying them a drink, just a nightcap. That was the way it was.

Mr. Loomis brought out his cigar case and offered Mr. Campbell a cigar, which was declined, and gave the orders for drinks, "Scotch, Scotch, Scotch, and a Cuba Libre." Mrs. Loomis was having the Cuba Libre. As the waiter took the order Mr. Campbell said, "And bring the bottle."

There was a fraction of a second's incredulity in Mr. Loomis's face; incredulity, or more likely doubt that he had heard his own ears. But he said, "Yes, bring the bottle." Then they talked about the picture. It had been a terrible picture, they all agreed. The Loomises said it was too bad, too, because they had crossed with the star two years ago and she had seemed awfully nice, not at all what you'd expect a movie star to be like. They all agreed that the Mickey Mouse was good, although Mr. Loomis said he was getting a little tired of Mickey Mouse. Their drinks came, and Mrs. Loomis was somewhat apologetic about her drink, but ever since she had been in Cuba she'd developed a taste for rum, always rum. "And before that gin," said Mr. Loomis. Mr. Campbell's glass was empty and he called the waiter to bring some more ice and another Cuba Libre, and he replenished the high-ball glasses from the bottle of Scotch on the table.

"Now this was my idea," said Mr. Loomis.

"Only the first one," said Mr. Campbell. They let it go at that, and the ladies returned to the subject of the star of the picture, and soon Mr. Loomis joined in. They got all mixed up in the star's matrimonial record, which inevitably brought up the names of other movie stars and *their* matrimonial records. Mr. and Mrs. Loomis provided the statistics, and Mrs. Campbell would say yes or no as the statement or opinion required. Mr. Campbell sipped his drink wordlessly until the Loomises, who had been married a long time, became simultaneously aware of Mr. Campbell's silence, and they began directing their remarks at him. The Loomises were not satisfied with Mrs. Campbell's ready assents. They would address the first few words of a remark to the young wife, because she had been such a polite listener, but then they would turn to Mr. Campbell and most of what they had to say was said to him.

For a while he would smile and murmur "Mm-hmm," more or less into his glass. Then it seemed after a few minutes that he could hardly wait for them to end an item or an anecdote. He began to nod before it was time to nod, and he would keep nodding, and he would say, "Yes, yes, yes," very rapidly. Presently, in the middle of an anecdote, his eyes, which had been growing brighter, became very bright. He put down his drink and leaned forward, one hand clasping and unclasping the other. "And—yes—and—yes," he kept saying, until Mrs. Loomis had finished her story. Then he leaned farther forward and stared at Mrs. Loomis, with that bright smile and with his breathing become short and fast.

"Can I tell you a story?" he said.

Mrs. Loomis beamed. "Why, of course."

Then Campbell told a story. It had in it a priest, female anatomy, improbable situations, a cuckold, unprintable words, and no point.

Long before Campbell finished his story Loomis was frowning, glancing at his wife and at Campbell's wife, seeming to listen to Campbell but always glancing at the two women. Mrs. Loomis could not look away; Campbell was telling her the story, and he looked at no one else. While Mrs. Campbell, the moment the story was begun, picked up her drink, took a sip, and put the glass on the table and kept her eyes on it until Campbell signaled by his chuck-ling that the story was at an end.

He kept chuckling and looking at Mrs. Loomis after he had fin-ished, and then he smiled at Loomis. "Huh," came from Loomis, and on his face a muscular smile. "Well, dear," he said. "Think it's about time—"

"Yes," said Mrs. Loomis. "Thank you so much. Good night, Mrs. Campbell, and good night." Campbell stood up, erect, bowing.

When they were entirely out of the room he sat down and crossed his legs. He lit a cigarette and resumed his drinking and stared at the opposite wall. She watched him. His eyes did not even move when he raised his glass to his mouth.

"Oh," she said suddenly. "I wonder if the man is still there at the travel desk. I forgot all about the tickets for tomorrow."

"Tomorrow? Are we leaving tomorrow?"

"Yes."

He stood up and pulled the table out of her way, and when she had left he sat down to wait for her.

No Mistakes

The church was crowded, and they were late, and McDonald could blame no one but himself. To begin with, he had overslept, and he no longer could blame Jean for that. For three months now he had taken the responsibility of their getting up in time, and he had been very good about it until today, of all days. Finally it was she who was awake first and had had to rouse him. "Come on, come *on*," she had said. "This is your party, remember." Then there were no clean starched collars. Oh, there were plenty of winged collars, clean as could be, lying useless in a collar box. But no turned-down ones, and this was an occasion for the dark-blue suit and a turned-down collar. So he had had to go through the laundry and pick out the cleanest of the dirty collars—one he had worn three nights ago with a dinner jacket. It wasn't too clean, either, but it was the best there was. Then the taxi-driver never had heard of Shakespeare Avenue. He was a Brooklyn taxi-driver, and McDonald was not too sure himself how to get to Shakespeare Avenue. They got there, and the church was crowded, Mass had begun, and they had to kneel in the aisle.

McDonald got up and went to the usher. "Listen, I have an invitation—"

"I can't help that," the usher said. "You see what it says: 'Kindly be in your pew fifteen minutes before Holy Mass begins.'"

"I know, but we came all the way from Nineteenth Street, and my wife can't kneel on that hard floor."

"Sh-h-h. Other people are kneeling."

"But she's pregnant. She shouldn't kneel at all. Anyway, she's a Protestant."

That was what made the difference. "Well, I'll see if I can get somebody to move over. You won't get two together, though."

"That's all right. Just so she won't have to kneel. Thanks," said McDonald.

"I'll see what I can do." The usher walked down the aisle slowly, counting the people in the pews on the Epistle side, and then returning, counting the people in the pews on the Gospel side. Halfway down he stopped at a pew and leaned over to the man at the first seat. Apparently he knew the man, because he smiled and the man smiled and nodded vigorously, and the usher came back and told McDonald he had a seat for Jean.

"You go ahead," McDonald said.

"But—I don't know when to stand up and everything."

"Just watch the others. Anyway, just sit," he said. "I'll be right here. Go on."

She went to the pew, accompanied by the usher. The usher's friend, holding his hat in one hand and a string of rosary beads in the other, got up and stood in the aisle, and Jean entered and the man followed her in. It was a tight fit, and McDonald saw Jean being glared at by the hard-faced Irishwoman on her left. The usher came back and McDonald thanked him again, and at last was able to watch O'Connor.

Naturally he expected Gerald O'Connor to do everything according to the rubrics, even though it was O'Connor's first High Mass. Still, even though McDonald expected it, he was glad to see that Okie made no mistakes. McDonald told himself that even he, after all these years, probably could fake a Mass. As an altar boy he had served probably hundreds of them. Even now he remembered practically all of the Latin responses—even the Suscipiat and the Confiteor. The Suscipiat, although shorter, was harder, for some reason. The Confiteor—all you had to do was memorize the first half, up to "... *mea culpa, mea culpa, mea maxima culpa,*" and then you went into *"Ideo precor,"* and changed the case endings of the first half. Something like that. It was like swimming or riding a bicycle, or more like shorthand. Once you learned it, you never completely forgot it. Still, even though Okie had been studying it every day for ten years, it was nice to see he didn't get rattled and go to the wrong place or get in the way of the deacon or the subdeacon. The old priest, who wore the dalmatic of the deacon—he probably was the pastor of this church. The young guy, the subdeacon—he probably was some classmate of Okie's from the seminary.

All the new friends Okie must have, and yet Okie had remembered to send him an invitation. McDonald wondered just how much or how little Okie knew about him. He had not written to Okie for five years or more; much more. More like eight years. And he had not seen him since the year Okie had entered the seminary. Yet Okie surely must have found out by this time that he had married out of the Church and was living in New York. The invitation had been sent to the McDonald home in Waterbury, and, like all such mail, it had been forwarded to the office.

He listened to Okie, who had a deep voice, softly, weakly singing "Glo-o-oria in excelsis De-e-o." He watched him coming down from the altar. His vestments didn't seem to fit him. The—what was it?—the amice almost looked like a scarf, and was no whiter than Okie's face. The chasuble *was* too big for him, and at the bottom step the alb got in his way and he half tripped. It seemed strange to see that old priest, the deacon, formally assisting Okie, a big young man who had been called a tower of strength against Colgate, Harvard, and Boston College. McDonald wondered what Jean was thinking of it all. He was afraid he knew what she was thinking. In her church a man who wore a tie and a business suit would get up and read, and then preach, and hymns would be sung in English.... Yes, he was afraid he knew what Jean was thinking.

The Mass went on, and presently it was very quiet and the quiet was not really broken by the bells, and McDonald bowed his head but did not lower his eyes. He wanted to watch Jean, he wanted to be with her, to touch her hand. She turned around and smiled, and he smiled at her.

Then after a long while the Mass was over and people began to go, and Jean got up and joined him. She took his arm, and they did not say anything until they were out of the church.

He couldn't help feeling the way he did; the whole thing was exhilarating. But he didn't have to say so. "We can get a taxi at the corner and go to Okie's house. We won't have to stay long, but I want you to meet him."

"All right. What was it when everybody got very quiet and O'Connor leaned over and sort of kissed the altar? Only he didn't kiss it."

"When the bells rang?"

"Yes."

"The bells rang three times, and then a minute later three times again?"

"Yes."

"That was the Consecration."

"Oh, *that* was the Consecration. I liked that part. I liked some of the singing, but I guess I'd have liked it better if I knew Latin."

He laughed. "How many people there do you think know Latin?"

"Well," she said, "I was wondering. There were quite a few that didn't look as though they knew English, let alone Latin. There was a terrible woman sitting next to me. She kept pushing me all through the service, except for that one part."

In the taxi he held her hand. It was not far to Okie's house. A butler, probably hired for the occasion, opened the door, and a huge gray-haired man in a cutaway greeted them. He said he was Dr. O'Connor, Gerald's father, and this was Gerald's mother—Mr. and

Mrs. McDonald. Oh, yes. Mac. Gerald's roommate in college. Well, well—and McDonald was fairly sure that the Doctor took a professional look at Jean. Well, well. Gerald would be down right away. Meanwhile, a little champagne never hurt anybody, and they had champagne, and a well-dressed girl, thirty or so, introduced herself. Okie's sister. And introduced other people to the McDonalds, Gerald's roommate at college and his wife. Well, well. I'll bet you're proud of Gerald today. His roommate. He'll make a fine priest. And another man in a cutaway, a lawyer, a man about thirty-five, whom people called Counselor. Okie's brother. "I thought I recognized you from the Stork Club," said this O'Connor. And a lot of old ladies, who Never Touched It. "Neither touch, taste, nor handle," he heard two of them say.

"He'll be here in a minute. I hope," said McDonald. "Let's sit down over here."

He took Jean to a chair, which everyone was politely leaving vacant for everyone else. Then after a few minutes Okie appeared, beaming over his Roman collar.

"He looks like Spencer Tracy," said Jean.

"You're crazy," said her husband.

"Well, reminds me of him. In that earthquake picture."

"*San Francisco*. But you're crazy. He looks about as much like Spencer Tracy as I do."

There was no use getting up. Okie had a lot of blessings to give. One or two of the old ladies, apparently anticipating the time when Okie would have the ring of a bishop, kissed his hand. The old ladies, and the young ladies, and the men and the children, they all would ask Father O'Connor for his blessing, and McDonald could read Okie's lips saying, "Be glad to," and they would kneel and Okie would mumble, very fast, the blessing, and so on he moved until he saw McDonald. At that moment someone was asking for his blessing, but he hurried to McDonald.

"Mac! You old rat. How are you? Were you at the Mass?"

"I sure was. Okie, I want you to meet my wife. Jean, this is Father O'Connor."

"How are you, Jean?"

"How do you do, Father?"

"When did all this happen, Mac? And why didn't I get an invitation?"

"Well," said McDonald. "There weren't any. We, uh—"

"Waterbury girl?" said Okie.

"No. New York."

"You should have waited—when'd you say you were married?"

"About six months ago," said McDonald.

"Ah, you should have waited. Then I could have married you," said Father O'Connor, looking at Jean. "Or *could* I?"

"No, I guess you couldn't, Okie," said McDonald.

"I see," said the priest. Then, "Well, it was nice of you to come. Help yourself to some champagne."

A woman tugged at his cuff. "Father, can I have your blessing? I remember when you used to—"

"Glad to," said O'Connor. "Excuse me," he said to the McDonalds.

McDonald sat beside his wife and they watched Okie moving around to the other side of the room, and when he had reached the farthest corner Jean spoke. "Go?" she said.

"Yes, I guess so," said McDonald.

THE IDEAL MAN

Breakfast in the Jenssen home was not much different from breakfast in a couple of hundred thousand homes in the Greater City.
Walter Jenssen had his paper propped up against the vinegar cruet
and the sugar bowl. He read expertly, not even taking his eyes off
the printed page when he raised his coffee cup to his mouth. Paul
Jenssen, seven going on eight, was eating his hot cereal, which had
to be sweetened heavily to get him to touch it. Myrna L. Jenssen,
Walter's five-year-old daughter, was scratching her towhead with
her left hand while she fed herself with her right. Myrna, too, was
expert in her fashion: she would put the spoon in her mouth, slide
the cereal off, and bring out the spoon upside down. Elsie Jenssen
(Mrs. Walter) had stopped eating momentarily the better to ex-
plore with her tongue a bicuspid that seriously needed attention.
That was the only thing she held against the kids—what having
them had done to her teeth. Everybody'd warned her, but she
wanted—

"Holy hell!" exclaimed Walter Jenssen. He slammed down his
coffee cup, splashing the contents on the tablecloth.

"What kind of talk is that in front of the children?" said Elsie.

"In front of the children! A hell of a fine one you are to be worrying about the children," said Walter. "Just take a look at this. Take a *look* at it!" He handed her the paper as though he were stabbing her with it.

She took the paper. Her eyes roved about the page and stopped. "Oh, *that*? Well, I'd like to know what's wrong with that. Hereafter I'll thank you to keep your cursing and swearing—"

"You! You!" said Walter.

"Myrna, Paul, off to school. Get your coats and hats and bring them in here. Hurry now," said Elsie. The children got up and went to the hall. "Just hold your temper till the children are where they won't hear you, with your raving like somebody *in*sane." She buttoned Myrna's coat and made Paul button his and warned him to keep it buttoned and warned Myrna not to let go of Paul's hand; then she shooed them off with a smile that would have been approved by the Good Housekeeping Institute. But as soon as they were out of the apartment, the smile was gone. "All right, you big baboon, go ahead and curse your head off. I'm used to it."

Walter said, "Gimme back that paper."

"You can have it," said Elsie. She handed him the paper. "Go ahead, read it till you get a stroke. You oughta see yourself."

Walter began to read aloud. " 'Is your husband as attentive to you now that you are married as when he was courting you? Answer: Mrs. Elsie Jenssen, West 174th Street, housewife: Yes, in fact more so. Before we were married my husband was not exactly what would be called the romantic type. He was definitely shy. However, since our marriage he has become the ideal man from the romantic point of view. None of your Tyrone Powers or Clark Gables for me.' For God's sake!"

"Well, so what?" said Elsie.

"So *what*? Do you think that's funny or something? What the hell kind of a thing is that you're putting in the paper? Go around blabbing private matters. I guess all the neighbors know how much we owe on the car. I suppose you tell everybody how much I get. How do you think a person's going to have any self-respect if you go running around and shooting off your face to newspaper reporters?"

"I didn't go around anywhere. He stopped me."

"Who stopped you?"

"The reporter. On Columbus Circle. I was just coming around the corner and he came up and tipped his hat like a gentleman and asked me. It says so there."

Walter wasn't listening. "The office," he said. "Oh, God. What they're going to do to me at that office. McGonigle. Jeffries. Hall. Wait'll they see it. They prob'ly read it already. I can just see them waiting till I get in. I go to my desk and then they all start calling me Tyrone Power and Clark Gable." He stared at her. "You know what's gonna happen, don't you? They'll start kidding till they get too loud, and the boss'll want to know what it's all about, and he'll find out. Maybe they won't come right out and snitch, but he'll find out. And he'll call me in his office and say I'm fired, and he'll be right. I oughta be fired. Listen, when you work for a finance corporation you don't want your employees going around getting a lot of silly publicity. What happens to the public confidence if—"

"It doesn't say a word about you. It says Elsie Jenssen. It doesn't say where you work or anything else. You look in the phone book and there's any number of Walter Jenssens."

"Three, including Queens, too."

"Well, it could be another one."

"Not living on 174th Street. Even if the public doesn't know, they'll know at the office. What if they don't care about the publicity part? All the boss'll want to know is I have a wife that—that goes blabbing around, and believe you me, they don't want employees with wives that go blabbing around. The public—"

"Oh, you and the public."

"Yes, me and the public. This paper has a circulation of two million."

"Oh, hooey," said Elsie, and began to stack the breakfast dishes.

"Hooey. All right, hooey, but I'm not going to that office today. You call up and tell them I have a cold."

"You big baby. If you want to stay home, call them up yourself," said Elsie.

"I said you call them up. I'm not going to that office."

"You go to the office or I'll—who do you think you are, anyway? The time you had off this year. Your uncle's funeral and your brother's wedding. Go ahead, take the day off, take the week off. Let's take a trip around the world. Just quit your job and I'll go back and ask Mr. Fenton to give me back my old job. I'll support you. I'll support you while you sit here, you big baboon." She put down the dishes and put her apron to her eyes and ran out of the room.

Walter took out a cigarette and put it in his mouth but did not light it. He took it out of his mouth and tapped it on the table and lit it. He got up and looked out the window. He stood there a rather long time, with one foot on the radiator and his chin in his hand, looking at the wall across the court. Then he went back to his chair and picked the paper off the floor and began to read.

First he reread his wife's interview, and then for the first time he read the other interviews. There were five others. The first, a laughing Mrs. Bloomberg, Columbus Avenue, housewife, said her husband was so tired when he came home nights that as far as she was concerned romance was only a word in the dictionary.

A Mrs. Petrucelli, East 123rd Street, housewife, said she hadn't noticed any difference between her husband's premarital and present attentiveness. But she had only been married five weeks.

There were three more. The husband of one woman was more attentive, but she did not compare him with Tyrone Power and Clark Gable. The husband of another woman was less attentive, but she did not get sarcastic like Mrs. Bloomberg. The last woman said her husband was radio operator on a ship and she didn't really have much way of telling because she only saw him about every five weeks.

Jenssen studied their photographs, and one thing you had to say for Elsie: she was the prettiest. He read the interviews once more, and he reluctantly admitted that—well, if you had to give an interview, Elsie's was the best. Mrs. Bloomberg's was the worst. He certainly would hate to be Bloomberg when his friends saw that one.

He put down the paper and lit another cigarette and stared at his shoes. He began by feeling sorry for Mr. Bloomberg, who was probably a hard-working guy who really did come home tired. He ended— he ended by beginning to plan what retorts he would have when the gang at the office began to kid him. He began to feel pretty good about it.

He put on his coat and hat and overcoat and then he went to the bedroom. Elsie was lying there, her face deep in the pillow, sobbing.

"Well, I guess I'll go to the office now," he said. She stopped sobbing.

"What?" she said, but did not let him see her face.

"Going downtown now," he said.

"What if they start kidding you?"

"Well, what if they do?" he said.

She sat up. "Are you cross at me any more?" she said.

"Nah, what the hell?" he said.

She smiled and got up and put her arm around his waist and walked down the hall with him to the door. It wasn't a very wide hall, but she kept her arm around him. He opened the door and set his hat on his head. She kissed his cheek and his mouth. He rearranged his hat again. "Well," he said. "See you tonight." It was the first thing that came into his head. He hadn't said *that* in years.

DO YOU LIKE IT HERE?

The door was open. The door had to be kept open during study period, so there was no knock, and Roberts was startled when a voice he knew and hated said, "Hey, Roberts. Wanted in Van Ness's office." The voice was Hughes'.

"What for?" said Roberts.

"Why don't you go and find out what for, Dopey?" said Hughes.

"Phooey on you," said Roberts.

"Phooey on *you*," said Hughes, and left.

Roberts got up from the desk. He took off his eyeshade and put on a tie and coat. He left the light burning.

Van Ness's office, which was *en suite* with his bedroom, was on the ground floor of the dormitory, and on the way down Roberts wondered what he had done. It got so after a while, after going to so many schools, that you recognized the difference between being "wanted in Somebody's office" and "Somebody wants to see you." If a master wanted to see you on some minor matter, it didn't always mean that you had to go to his office, but if it was serious, they always said, "You're wanted in Somebody's office." That meant Somebody would be in his office, waiting for you, waiting specially for you. Roberts didn't know why this difference existed, but it did, all right. Well, all he could think of was that he had been smoking in the shower room, but Van Ness never paid much attention to that. Everybody smoked in the shower room, and Van Ness never did anything about it unless he just happened to catch you.

For minor offenses Van Ness would speak to you when he made his rounds of the rooms during study period. He would walk slowly down the corridor, looking in at each room to see that the proper occupant, and no one else, was there; and when he had something to bawl you out about, something unimportant, he would consult a list he carried, and he would stop in and bawl you out about it and tell you what punishment went with it. That was another detail that made the summons to the office a little scary.

Roberts knocked on Van Ness's half-open door and a voice said, "Come in."

Van Ness was sitting at his typewriter, which was on a small desk beside the large desk. He was in a swivel chair and when he saw Roberts he swung around, putting himself behind the large desk, like a damn judge.

He had his pipe in his mouth and he seemed to look over the steel rims of his spectacles. The light caught his Phi Beta Kappa key, which momentarily gleamed as though it had diamonds in it.

"Hughes said you wanted me to report here," said Roberts.

"I did," said Van Ness. He took his pipe out of his mouth and began slowly to knock the bowl empty as he repeated, "I did." He finished emptying his pipe before he again spoke. He took a long time about it, and Roberts, from his years of experience, recognized that as torture tactics. They always made you wait to scare you. It was sort of like the third degree. The horrible damn thing was that it always did scare you a little, even when you were used to it.

Van Ness leaned back in his chair and stared through his glasses at Roberts. He cleared his throat. "You can sit down," he said.

"Yes, sir," said Roberts. He sat down and again Van Ness made him wait.

"Roberts, you've been here now how long—five weeks?"

"A little over. About six."

"About six weeks," said Van Ness. "Since the seventh of January. Six weeks. Strange. Strange. Six weeks, and I really don't know a thing about you. Not much, at any rate. Roberts, tell me a little about yourself."

"How do you mean, Mister?"

"How do I mean? Well—about your life, before you decided to honor us with your presence. Where you came from, what you did, why you went to so many schools, so on."

"Well, I don't know."

"Oh, now. Now, Roberts. Don't let your natural modesty overcome the autobiographical urge. Shut the door."

Roberts got up and closed the door.

"Good," said Van Ness. "Now, proceed with this—uh—dossier. Give me the—huh—huh—*lowdown* on Roberts, Humphrey, Second Form, McAllister Memorial Hall, et cetera."

Roberts, Humphrey, sat down and felt the knot of his tie. "Well, I don't know. I was born at West Point, New York. My father was a first lieutenant then and he's a major now. My father and mother and I lived in a lot of places because he was in the Army and they transferred him. Is that the kind of stuff you want, Mister?"

"Proceed, proceed. I'll tell you when I want you to—uh—halt." Van Ness seemed to think that was funny, that "halt."

"Well, I didn't go to a regular school till I was ten. My mother got a divorce from my father and I went to school in San Francisco. I only stayed there a year because my mother got married again and we moved to Chicago, Illinois."

"Chicago, Illinois! Well, a little geography thrown in, eh, Roberts? Gratuitously. Thank you. Proceed."

"Well, so then we stayed there about two years and then we moved back East, and my stepfather is a certified public accountant and we moved around a lot."

"Peripatetic, eh, Roberts?"

"I guess so. I don't exactly know what that means." Roberts paused.

"Go on, go on."

"Well, so I just went to a lot of schools, some day and some boarding. All that's written down on my application blank here. I had to put it all down on account of my credits."

"Correct. A very imposing list it is, too, Roberts, a very imposing list. Ah, to travel as you have. Switzerland. How I've regretted not having gone to school in Switzerland. Did you like it there?"

"I was only there about three months. I liked it all right, I guess."

"And do you like it here, Roberts?"

"Sure."

"You do? You're sure of that? You wouldn't want to change anything?"

"Oh, I wouldn't say that, not about any school."

"Indeed," said Van Ness. "With your vast experience, naturally you would be quite an authority on matters educational. I suppose you have many theories as to the strength and weaknesses inherent in the modern educational systems."

"I don't know. I just—I don't know. Some schools are better than others. At least I like some better than others."

"Of course. Of course." Van Ness seemed to be thinking about something. He leaned back in his swivel chair and gazed at the ceiling. He put his hands in his pants pockets and then suddenly he leaned forward. The chair came down and Van Ness's belly was hard against the desk and his arm was stretched out on the desk, full length, fist closed.

"Roberts! Did you ever see this before? Answer me!" Van Ness's voice was hard. He opened his fist, and in it was a wristwatch.

Roberts looked down at the watch. "No, I don't think so," he said. He was glad to be able to say it truthfully.

Van Ness continued to hold out his hand, with the wristwatch lying in the palm. He held out his hand a long time, fifteen seconds at least, without saying anything. Then he turned his hand over and allowed the watch to slip onto the desk. He resumed his normal position in the chair. He picked up his pipe, slowly filled it, and lit it.

He shook the match back and forth long after the flame had gone. He swung around a little in his chair and looked at the wall, away from Roberts. "As a boy I spent six years at this school. My brothers, my two brothers, went to this school. My *father* went to this school. I have a deep and abiding and lasting affection for this school. I have been a member of the faculty of this school for more than a decade. I like to think that I am part of this school, that in some small measure I have assisted in its progress. I like to think of it as more than a mere steppingstone to higher education. At this very moment there are in this school the sons of men who were my classmates. I have not been without my opportunities to take a post at this and that college or university, but I choose to remain here. Why? Why? Because I love this place. I love this place, Roberts. I cherish its traditions. I cherish its good name." He paused, and turned to Roberts. "Roberts, there is no room here for a thief!"

Roberts did not speak.

"There is no room here for a thief, I said!"

"Yes, sir."

Van Ness picked up the watch without looking at it. He held it a few inches above the desk. "This miserable watch was stolen last Friday afternoon, more than likely during the basketball game. As soon as the theft was reported to me I immediately instituted a search for it. My search was unsuccessful. Sometime Monday afternoon the watch was put here, here in my rooms. When I returned here after classes Monday afternoon, this watch was lying on my desk. Why? Because the contemptible rat who stole it knew that I had instituted the search, and like the rat he is, he turned yellow and returned the watch to me. Whoever it is, he kept an entire dormitory under a loathsome suspicion. I say to you, I do not know who stole this watch or who returned it to my rooms. But by God, Roberts, I'm going to find out, if it's the last thing I do. If it's the last thing I do. That's all, Roberts. You may go." Van Ness sat back, almost breathless.

Roberts stood up. "I give you my word of honor, I—"

"I said you may go!" said Van Ness.

Roberts was not sure whether to leave the door open or to close it, but he did not ask. He left it open.

He went up the stairs to his room. He went in and took off his coat and tie, and sat on the bed. Over and over again, first violently, then weakly, he said it, "The bastard, the dirty bastard."

THE DOCTOR'S SON

My father came home at four o'clock one morning in the fall of 1918, and plumped down on a couch in the living room. He did not get awake until he heard the noise of us getting breakfast and getting ready to go to school, which had not yet closed down. When he got awake he went out front and shut off the engine of the car, which had been running while he slept, and then he went to bed and stayed, sleeping for nearly two days. Up to that morning he had been going for nearly three days with no more than two hours' sleep at a stretch.

There were two ways to get sleep. At first he would get it by going to his office, locking the rear office door, and stretching out on the floor or on the operating table. He would put a revolver on the floor beside him or in the tray that was bracketed to the operating table. He had to have the revolver, because here and there among the people who would come to his office, there would be a wild man or woman, threatening him, shouting that they would not leave until he left with them, and that if their baby died they would come back and kill him. The revolver, lying on the desk, kept the more violent patients from becoming too violent, but it really did no good so far as my father's sleep was concerned; not even a doctor who had kept going for days on coffee and quinine would use a revolver on an Italian who had just come from a bedroom where the last of five children was being strangled by influenza. So my father, with a great deal of profanity, would make it plain to the Italian that he was not being intimidated, but would go, and go without sleep.

There was one other way of getting sleep. We owned the building in which he had his office, so my father made an arrangement with one of the tenants, a painter and paperhanger, so he could sleep in the room where the man stored rolls of wallpaper. This was a good arrangement, but by the time he had thought of it, my father's strength temporarily gave out and he had to come home and go to bed.

Meanwhile there was his practice, which normally was about forty patients a day, including office calls and operations, but which he had lost count of since the epidemic had become really bad. Ordinarily if he had been ill his practice would have been taken over by one of the young physicians; but now every young doctor was as busy as the older men. Italians who knew me would even ask me to prescribe for their children, simply because I was the son of Mister Doctor Malloy. Young general practitioners, who would have had to depend upon friends of their families and fraternal orders and accidents and gonorrhea for their start, were seeing—hardly more than seeing—more patients in a day than in normal times they could have hoped to see in a month.

The mines closed down almost with the first whiff of influenza. Men who for years had been drilling rock and had chronic miner's asthma never had a chance against the mysterious new disease; and even younger men were keeling over, so the coal companies had to shut down the mines, leaving only maintenance men, such as pump men, in charge. Then the Commonwealth of Pennsylvania closed down the schools and churches, and forbade all congregating. If you wanted an ice cream soda you had to have it put in a cardboard container; you couldn't have it at the fountain in a glass. We were glad when school closed, because it meant a holiday, and the epidemic had touched very few of us. We lived in Gibbsville; it was in the tiny mining villages—"patches"—that the epidemic was felt immediately.

The State stepped in, and when a doctor got sick or exhausted so he literally couldn't hold his head up any longer, they would send a young man from the graduating class of one of the Philadelphia medical schools to take over the older man's practice. This was how Doctor Myers came to our town. I was looking at the pictures of the war in the *Review of Reviews,* my father's favorite magazine, when the doorbell rang and I answered it. The young man looked like the young men who came to our door during the summer selling magazines. He was wearing a short coat with a sheepskin collar, which I recognized as an S. A. T. C. issue coat.

"Is this Doctor Malloy's residence?" he said.

"Yes."

"Well, I'm Mr. Myers from the University."

"Oh," I said. "My father's expecting you." I told my father, and he said: "Well, why didn't you bring him right up?"

Doctor Myers went to my father's bedroom and they talked, and then the maid told me my father wanted to speak to me. When I went to the bedroom I could see my father and Doctor Myers were getting along nicely. That was natural: my father and Doctor Myers were University men, which meant the University of Pennsylvania; and University men shared a contempt for men who had studied at Hahnemann or Jefferson or Medico-Chi. Myers was not an M.D., but my father called him Doctor, and as I had been brought up to tip my hat to a doctor as I did to a priest, I called him Doctor too, although Doctor Myers made me feel like a lumberjack; I was so much bigger and obviously stronger than he. I was fifteen years old.

"Doctor Myers, this is my boy James," my father said, and without waiting for either of us to acknowledge the introduction, he went on: "Doctor Myers will be taking over my practice for the time being and you're to help him. Take him down to Hendricks' drugstore and introduce him to Mr. Hendricks. Go over the names of our patients and help him arrange some kind of a schedule. Doctor Myers doesn't drive a car, you'll drive for him. Now your mother and I think the rest of the children ought to be on the farm, so you take them there in the big Buick and then bring it back and have it overhauled. Leave the little Buick where it is, and you use the Ford. You'll understand, Doctor, when you see our roads. If you want any money your mother'll give it to you. And no cigarettes, d'you understand?" Then he handed Doctor Myers a batch of prescription blanks, upon which were lists of patients to be seen, and said good-bye and lay back on his pillow for more sleep.

Doctor Myers was almost tiny, and that was the reason I could forgive him for not being in the Army. His hair was so light that you could hardly see his little mustache. In conversation between sentences his nostrils would twitch and like all doctors he had acquired a posed gesture which was becoming habitual. His was to stroke the skin in front of his right ear with his forefinger. He did that now downstairs in the hall. "Well . . . I'll just take a walk back to the hotel and wait till you get back from the farm. That suit you, James?" It did, and he left and I performed the various chores my father had ordered, and then I went to the hotel in the Ford and picked up Doctor Myers.

He was catlike and dignified when he jumped in the car. "Well, here's a list of names. Where do you think we ought to go first? Here's a couple of prescription blanks with only four names apiece. Let's clean them up first."

"Well, I don't know about that, Doctor. Each one of those names means at least twenty patients. For instance, Kelly's. That's a saloon, and there'll be a lot of people waiting. They all meet there and wait for my father. Maybe we'd better go to some single calls first."

"O.K., James. Here's a list." He handed it to me. "Oh, your father said something about going to Collieryville to see a family named Evans."

I laughed. "Which Evans? There's seventy-five thousand Evanses in Collieryville. Evan Evans. William W. Evans. Davis W. Evans, Junior. David Evans?"

"David Evans sounds like it. The way your father spoke they were particular friends of his."

"David Evans," I said. "Well—he didn't say who's sick there, did he?"

"No. I don't think anybody. He just suggested we drop in to see if they're all well."

I was relieved, because I was in love with Edith Evans. She was nearly two years older than I, but I liked girls a little older. I looked at his list and said: "I think the best idea is to go there first and then go around and see some of the single cases in Collieryville." He was ready to do anything I suggested. He was affable and trying to make me feel that we were pals, but I could tell he was nervous, and I had sense enough to know that he had better look at some flu before tackling one of those groups at the saloons.

We drove to Collieryville to the David Evans home. Mr. Evans was district superintendent of one of the largest mining corporations, and therefore Collieryville's third citizen. He would not be there all the time, because he was a good man and due for promotion to a bigger district, but so long as he was there he was ranked with the leading doctor and the leading lawyer. After him came the Irish priest, the cashier of the larger bank (of which the doctor or the lawyer or the superintendent of the mines is president), the brewer, and the leading merchant. David Evans had been born in Collieryville, the son of a superintendent, and was popular, a thirty-second-degree Mason, a graduate of Lehigh, and a friend of my father's. They would see each other less than ten times a year, but they would go hunting rabbit and quail and pheasant together every autumn and always exchanged expensive Christmas gifts. When my mother had large parties she would invite Mrs. Evans, but the two women were not close friends. Mrs. Evans was a Collieryville girl, half Polish, and my mother had gone to an expensive school and spoke French, and played bridge long before Mrs. Evans had learned to play "500." The Evanses had two children: Edith, my girl, and Rebecca, who was about five.

The Evans Cadillac, which was owned by the coal company, was standing in front of the Evans house, which also was owned by the coal company. I called to the driver, who was sitting behind the steering wheel, hunched up in a sheepskin coat and with a checkered cap pulled down over his eyes. "What's the matter, Pete?" I called. "Can't the company get rid of that old Caddy?"

"Go on wid you," said Pete. "What's the wrong wid the doctorin' business? I notice Mike Malloy ain't got nothin' better than Buicks."

"I'll have you fired, you round-headed son of a so and so," I said. "Where's the big lad?"

"Up Mike's. Where'd you t'ink he is?"

I parked the Ford and Doctor Myers and I went to the door and were let in by the pretty Polish maid. Mr. Evans came out of his den, wearing a raccoon coat and carrying his hat. I introduced Doctor Myers. "How do you do, sir," he said. "Doctor Malloy just asked me to stop in and see if everything was all right with your family."

"Oh, fine," said Mr. Evans. "Tell the dad that was very thoughtful, James, and thank you too, Doctor. We're all O.K. here, thank the Lord, but while you're here I'd like to have you meet Mrs. Evans. Adele!"

Mrs. Evans called from upstairs that she would be right down. While we waited in the den Mr. Evans offered Doctor Myers a cigar, which was declined. Doctor Myers, I could see, preferred to sit, because Mr. Evans was so large that he had to look up to him. While Mr. Evans questioned him about his knowledge of the anthracite region, Doctor Myers spoke with a barely discernible pleasant hostility which was lost on Mr. Evans, the simplest of men. Mrs. Evans appeared in a housedress. She looked at me shyly, as she always did. She always embarrassed me, because when I went in a room where she was sitting she would rise to shake hands, and I would feel like telling her to sit down. She was in her middle thirties and still pretty, with rosy cheeks and pale blue eyes and nothing "foreign"-looking about her except her high cheekbones and the lines of her eyebrows, which looked as though they had been drawn with crayon. She shook hands with Doctor Myers and then clasped her hands in front of her and looked at Mr. Evans when he spoke, and then at Doctor Myers and then at me, smiling and hanging on Mr. Evans' words. He was used to that. He gave her a half-smile without looking at her and suggested we come back for dinner, which in Collieryville was at noon. Doctor Myers asked me if we would be in Collieryville at that time, and I said we would, so we accepted his invitation. Mr. Evans said: "That's fine. Sorry I won't be here, but I have to go to Wilkes-Barre right away." He looked at his watch. "By George! By now I ought to be halfway there." He grabbed his hat and kissed his wife and left.

When he had gone Mrs. Evans glanced at me and smiled and then said: "Edith will be glad to see you, James."

"Oh, I'll bet she will," I said. "Where's she been keeping herself anyway?"

"Oh, around the house. She's my eldest," she said to Doctor Myers. "Seventeen."

"Seventeen?" he repeated. "You have a daughter seventeen? I can hardly believe it, Mrs. Evans. Nobody would ever think you had a daughter seventeen." His voice was a polite protest, but there was nothing protesting in what he saw in Mrs. Evans. I looked at her myself now, thinking of her for the first time as something besides Edith's mother. . . . No, I couldn't see her. We left to make some calls, promising to be back at twelve-thirty.

Our first call was on a family named Loughran, who lived in a neat two-story house near the Collieryville railroad station. Doctor Myers went in. He came out in less than two minutes, followed by Mr. Loughran. Loughran walked over to me. "You," he said. "Ain't we good enough for your dad no more? What for kind of a thing is this he does be sending us?"

"My father is sick in bed, just like everybody else, Mr. Loughran. This is the doctor that is taking all his calls till he gets better."

"It is, is it? So that's what we get, and doctorin' with Mike Malloy sincet he come from college, and always paid the day after payday. Well, young man, take this back to Mike Malloy. You tell him for me if my woman pulls through it'll be no thanks to him. And if she don't pull through, and dies, I'll come right down to your old man's office and kill him wid a rock. Now you and this one get the hell outa here before I lose me patience."

We drove away. The other calls we made were less difficult, although I noticed that when he was leaving one or two houses the people, who were accustomed to my father's quick, brusque calls, would stare at Doctor Myers' back. He stayed too long, and probably was too sympathetic. We returned to the Evans home.

Mrs. Evans had changed her dress to one that I thought was a little too dressy for the occasion. She asked us if we wanted "a little wine," which we didn't, and Doctor Myers was walking around with his hands in his trousers pockets, telling Mrs. Evans what a comfortable place this was, when Edith appeared. I loved Edith, but the only times I ever saw her were at dancing school, to which she would come every Saturday afternoon. She was quite small, but long since her legs had begun to take shape and she had breasts. It was her father, I guess, who would not let her put her hair up; she often told me he was very strict and I knew that he was making her stay in Collieryville High School a year longer than was necessary because he thought her too young to go away. Edith called me Jimmy—one of the few who did. When we danced together at dancing school she scarcely spoke at all. I suspected her of regarding me as very young. All the little kids at dancing school called me James, and the oldest girls called me sarcastic. "James Malloy," they would say, "you think you're sarcastic. You think you're clever, but you're not. I consider the source of that remark." The remark might be that I had heard that Wallace Reid was waiting for that girl to grow up—and so was I. But I never said things like that to Edith. I would say: "How's everything out in the metropolis of Collieryville?" and she would say they were all right. It was no use trying to be sarcastic or clever with Edith, and no use trying to be romantic. One time I offered her the carnation that we had to wear at dancing school, and she refused it because the pin might tear her dress. It was useless to try to be dirty with her; there was no novelty in it for a girl who had gone to Collieryville High. I told her one story, and she said her grandmother fell out of the cradle laughing at that one.

When Edith came in she took a quick look at Doctor Myers, which made me slightly jealous. He turned and smiled at her, and his nostrils began to twitch. Mrs. Evans rubbed her hands together nervously, and it was plain to see that she was not sure how to introduce Doctor Myers. Before she had a chance to make any mistakes I shook hands with Edith and she said, "Oh, hello, Jimmy," in a very offhand way, and I said; "Edith, this is Doctor Myers."

"How do you do?" said Edith.

"How are you?" said the doctor.

"Oh, very well, thank you," Edith said, and realized that it wasn't quite the thing to say.

"Well," said Mrs. Evans. "I don't know if you gentlemen want to wash up. Jimmy, you know where the bathroom is." It was the first time she had called me Jimmy. I glanced at her curiously and then the doctor and I went to wash our hands. Upstairs he said: "That your girl, James?"

"Oh, no," I said. "We're good friends. She isn't that kind."

"What kind? I didn't mean anything." He was amused.

"Well, I didn't know what you meant."

"Edith certainly looks like her mother," he said.

"Oh, I don't think so," I said, not really giving it a thought, but I was annoyed by the idea of talking about Edith in the bathroom. We came downstairs.

Dinner was a typical meal of that part of the country: sauerkraut and pork and some stuff called nep, which was nothing but dough, and mashed potatoes and lima beans, coffee, tea, and two kinds of pie, and you were expected to take both kinds. It was a meal I liked, and I ate a lot. Mrs. Evans got some courage from somewhere and was now talkative, now quiet, addressing most of her remarks to Doctor Myers and then turning to me. Edith kept looking at her and then turning to the doctor. She paid no attention to me except when I had something to say. Rebecca, whose table manners were being neglected, had nothing to contribute except to stick out her plate and say: "More mash potatoes with butter on."

"Say please," said Edith, but Rebecca only looked at her with the scornful blankness of five.

After dinner we went to the den and Doctor Myers and I smoked. I noticed he did not sit down; he was actually a little taller than Edith, and just about the same height as her mother. He walked around the room, standing in front of enlarged snapshots of long-deceased setter dogs, one of which my father had given Mr. Evans. Edith watched him and her mother and said nothing, but just before we were getting ready to leave, Mrs. Evans caught Edith staring at her and they exchanged mysterious glances. Edith looked defiant and Mrs. Evans seemed puzzled and somehow alarmed. I could not figure it out.

———

In the afternoon Doctor Myers decided he would like to go to one of the patches where the practice of medicine was wholesale, so I suggested Kelly's. Kelly's was the only saloon in a patch of about one hundred families, mostly Irish, and all except one family were Catholics. In the spring they have processions in honor of the Blessed Virgin at Kelly's patch, and a priest carries the Blessed Sacrament the length of the patch, in the open air, to the public school grounds, where they hold Benediction. The houses are older and stauncher than in most patches, and they look like pictures of Ireland, except that there are no thatched roofs. Most patches were simply unbroken rows of company houses, made of slatty wood, but Kelly's had more ground between the houses and grass for the goats and cows to feed on, and the houses had plastered walls. Kelly's saloon was frequented by the whole patch because it was the postoffice substation, and it had a good reputation. For many years it had the only telephone in the patch.

Mr. Kelly was standing on the stoop in front of the saloon when I swung the Ford around. He took his pipe out of his mouth when he recognized the Ford, and then frowned slightly when he saw that my father was not with me. He came to my side of the car. "Where's the dad? Does he be down wid it now himself?"

"No," I said. "He's just all tired out and is getting some sleep. This is Doctor Myers that's taking his place till he gets better."

Mr. Kelly spat some tobacco juice on the ground and took a wad of tobacco out of his mouth. He was a white-haired, sickly man of middle age. "I'm glad to make your acquaintance," he said.

"How do you do, sir?" said Doctor Myers.

"I guess James here told you what to be expecting?"

"Well, more or less," said Doctor Myers. "Nice country out here. This is the nicest I've seen."

"Yes, all right I guess, but there does be a lot of sickness now. I guess you better wait a minute here till I have a few words with them inside there. I have to keep them orderly, y'understand."

He went in and we could hear his loud voice: "... young Malloy said his dad is seriously ill ... great expense out of his own pocket secured a famous young specialist from Philadelphee so as to not have the people of the patch without a medical man ... And any lug of a lunkhead that don't stay in line will have me to answer to ..." Mr. Kelly then made the people line up and he came to the door and asked Doctor Myers to step in.

There were about thirty women in the saloon as Mr. Kelly guided Doctor Myers to an oilcloth-covered table. One Irishman took a contemptuous look at Doctor Myers and said, "Jesus, Mary and Joseph," and walked out, sneering at me before he closed the door. The others probably doubted that the doctor was a famous specialist, but they had not had a doctor in two or three days. Two others left quietly but the rest remained. "I guess we're ready, Mr. Kelly," said Doctor Myers.

Most of the people were Irish, but there were a few Hunkies in the patch, although not enough to warrant Mr. Kelly's learning any of their languages as the Irish had had to do in certain other patches. It was easy enough to deal with the Irish: a woman would come to the table and describe for Doctor Myers the symptoms of her sick man and kids in language that was painfully polite. My father had trained them to use terms like "bowel movement" instead of those that came more quickly to mind. After a few such encounters and wasting a lot of time, Doctor Myers more or less got the swing of prescribing for absent patients. I stood leaning against the bar, taking down the names of patients I didn't know by sight, and wishing I could have a cigarette, but that was out of the question because Mr. Kelly did not approve of cigarettes and might have told my father. I was standing there when the first of the Hunkie women had her turn. She was a worried-looking woman who even I could see was pregnant and had been many times before, judging by her body. She had on a white knitted cap and a black silk shirtwaist—nothing underneath—and a nondescript skirt. She was wearing a man's overcoat and a pair of Pacs, which are short rubber boots that men wear in the mines. When Doctor Myers spoke to her she became voluble in her own tongue. Mr. Kelly interrupted: "Wait a minute, wait a minute," he said. "You sick?"

"No, no. No me sick. Man sick." She lapsed again into her own language.

"She has a kid can speak English," said Mr. Kelly. "Hey, you. Leetle girl Mary, you daughter, her sick?" He made so-high with his hand. The woman caught on.

"Mary. Sick. Yah, Mary sick." She beamed.

Mr. Kelly looked at the line of patients and spoke to a woman. "Mame," he said. "You live near this lady. How many has she got sick?"

Mame said: "Well, there's the man for one. Dyin' from the way they was carryin' on yesterday and the day before. I ain't seen none of the kids. There's four little girls and they ain't been out of the house for a couple of days. And no wonder they're sick, runnin' around wild widout no—"

"Never mind about that, now," said Mr. Kelly. "I guess, Doctor, the only thing for you to do is go to this woman's house and take a look at them."

The woman Mame said: "To be sure, and ain't that nice? Dya

hear that, everybody! Payin' a personal visit to the likes of that but the decent people take what they get. A fine how-do-ya-do."

"You'll take what you get in the shape of a puck in the nose," said Mr. Kelly. "A fine way you do be talkin' wid the poor dumb Hunkie not knowing how to talk good enough to say what's the matter wid her gang. So keep your two cents out of this, Mamie Brannigan, and get back into line."

Mamie made a noise with her mouth, but she got back into line. Doctor Myers got through the rest pretty well, except for another Hunkie who spoke some English but knew no euphemisms. Mr. Kelly finally told her to use monosyllables, which embarrassed Doctor Myers because there were some Irishwomen still in line. But "We can't be wasting no time on politeness," said Mr. Kelly. "This here's a doctor's office now." Finally all the patients except the Hunkie woman were seen to.

Mr. Kelly said: "Well, Doctor, bein's this is your first visit here you gotta take a little something on the house. Would you care for a brandy?"

"Why, yes, that'd be fine," said the doctor.

"James, what about you? A sass?"

"Yes, thank you," I said. A sass was a sarsaparilla.

Mr. Kelly opened a closet at the back of the bar and brought out a bottle. He set it on the bar and told the doctor to help himself. The doctor poured himself a drink and Mr. Kelly poured one and handed it to the Hunkie woman. "There y'are, Mary," he said. "Put hair on your chest." He winked at the doctor.

"Not joining us, Mr. Kelly?" said the doctor.

Mr. Kelly smiled. "Ask James there. No, I never drink a drop. Handle too much of it. Why, if I took a short beer every time I was asked to, I'd be drunk three-quarters of the time. And another advantage is when this here Pro'bition goes into effect I won't miss it. Except financially. Well, I'll take a bottle of temperance just to be sociable." He opened a bottle of ginger ale and took half a glassful. The Hunkie woman raised her glass and said something that sounded more like a prayer than a toast, and put her mouth around the mouth of the glass and drank. She was happy and grateful. Doctor Myers wanted to buy another round, but Mr. Kelly said his money was no good there that day; if he wanted another drink he was to help himself. The doctor did not want another, but he said he would like to buy one for the Hunkie woman, and Mr. Kelly permitted him to pay for it, then we said good-bye to Mr. Kelly and departed, the Hunkie woman getting in the car timidly, but once in the car her bottom was so large that the doctor had to stand on the running board until we reached the house.

A herd of goats in various stages of parturition gave us the razz when we stopped at the house. The ground around the house had a goaty odor because the wire which was supposed to keep them out was torn in several places. The yard was full of old wash boilers and rubber boots, tin cans and the framework of an abandoned baby carriage. The house was a one-and-a-half-story building. We walked around to the back door, as the front door is reserved for the use of the priest when he comes on sick calls. The Hunkie woman seemed happier and encouraged, and prattled away as we followed her into the house, the doctor carefully picking his way through stuff in the yard.

The woman hung up her coat and hat on a couple of pegs on the kitchen wall, from which also hung a lunch can and a tin coffee bottle, the can suspended on a thick black strap, and the bottle on a braided black cord. A miner's cap with a safety lamp and a dozen buttons of the United Mine Workers of America was on another peg, and in a pile on the floor were dirty overalls and jumper and shirt. The woman sat down on a backless kitchen chair and hurriedly removed her boots, which left her barefoot. There was an awful stink of cabbage and dirty feet in the house, and I began to feel nauseated as I watched the woman flopping around, putting a kettle on the stove and starting the fire, which she indicated she wanted to do before going to look at the sick. Her bosom swung to and fro and her large hips jounced up and down, and the doctor smirked at these things, knowing that I was watching, but not knowing that I was trying to think of the skinniest girl I knew, and in the presence of so much woman I was sorry for all past thoughts or desires. Finally the woman led the way to the front of the house. In one of the two front rooms was an old-fashioned bed. The windows were curtained, but when our eyes became accustomed to the darkness we could see four children lying on the bed. The youngest and the oldest were lying together. The oldest, a girl about five years old, was only half covered by the torn quilt that covered the others. The baby coughed as we came in. The other two were sound asleep. The half-covered little girl got awake, or opened her eyes and looked at the ceiling. She had a half-sneering look about her nose and mouth, and her eyes were expressionless. Doctor Myers leaned over her and so did her mother, speaking to the girl, but the girl apparently made no sense even in the Hunkie language. She sounded as though she were trying to clear her throat of phlegm. The doctor turned to me and said dramatically: "James, take this woman out and get her to boil more water, and go out to the car and get your father's instrument case." I grabbed the woman's arm and pulled her to the kitchen and made signs for her to boil the water, then I went out to the Ford and wrestled with the lid of the rear compartment, wondering what the hell Myers wanted with the instrument case, wondering whether he himself knew what he wanted with it. At last I yanked the lid open and was walking back with the leather case in my hand when I heard a loud scream. It sounded more deliberate than wild, it started so low and suddenly went so high. I hurried back to the bedroom and saw Doctor Myers trying to pull the heavy woman away from her daughter. He was not strong enough for her, but he kept pulling and there were tears in his eyes: "Come away, God damn it! Come away from her, you God-damn fool!" He turned to me for help and said: "Oh, Jesus, James, this is awful. The little girl just died. Keep away from her. She has diphtheria!"

"I couldn't open the back of the car," I said.

"Oh, it wasn't your fault. Even a tracheotomy wouldn't have saved her, the poor little thing. But we've got to do something for these others. The baby has plenty of spots, and I haven't even looked at the other two." The other two had been awakened by their mother's screams and were sitting up and crying, not very loud. The woman had the dead girl in her arms. She did not need the English language to know that the child was dead. She was rocking her back and forth and kissing her and looking up at us with fat streams of tears running from her eyes. She would stop crying for a second, but would start again, crying with her mouth open and the tears, unheeded, sliding in over her upper lip.

Doctor Myers took some coins from his pocket and tried to make friends with the in-between kids, but they did not know what money was, so I left him to go in to see how the man was. I walked across the hall to the other bedroom and pulled up the curtains. The man was lying in his underwear; gaunt, bearded, and dead.

I knew he was dead, but I said: "Hyuh, John, hyuh." The sound of my voice made me feel silly, then sacrilegious, and then I had to vomit. I had seen men brought in from railroad wrecks and mine explosions and other violent-accident cases, but I had been prepared for them if only by the sound of an ambulance bell. This was different. Doctor Myers heard me being sick and came in. I was crying. He took a few seconds to see that the man was dead and then he took me by the arm and said: "That's all right, kid. Come out in the air." He led me outside into the cold afternoon and I felt better and hungry.

He let go of my arm. "Listen," he said. "As soon as you feel well enough, take the car and go to the hospital. The first thing you do there is to get them to give you twenty thousand units of antitoxin, and while you're doing that tell them to send an ambulance out here right away. Don't go near anybody if you can help it except a doctor." He paused. "You'd better find out about an undertaker."

"You'll need more than twenty thousand units of antitoxin," I said. I had had that much in my own back when I was eight years old.

"Oh, no. You didn't understand me. The antitoxin's for you. You tell whoever's in charge at the hospital how many are sick out here, and they'll know what to send."

"What about you?"

"Oh, I'll stay here and go back in the ambulance. Don't worry about me. I want to stay here and do what I can for these kids." I suddenly had a lot of respect for him. I got into the Ford and drove away. Doctors' cars carried cardboard signs which said By Order State Department of Health, which gave them the right to break speed laws, and I broke them on my way to the hospital. I pulled in at the porte cochere and met Doctor Kleiber, a friend of my father's, and told him everything. He gave me antitoxin. He smiled when I mentioned getting an undertaker. "Lucky if they get a wooden rough box, even, James. These people aren't patients of Daddy's, are they, James?"

"No."

"Well then, I guess maybe we have to send an Army doctor. I'm full up so I haven't a minute except for Daddy's patients. Now go home and I'll take care of everything. You'll be stiff in the back and you want to rest. Good-bye now." So I drove home and went to bed.

I was stiff the next morning from the antitoxin, but it had not been so bad as the other time I had taken it, and I was able to pick up Doctor Myers at the hotel. "I feel pretty damn useless, not being able to drive a car," he said. "But I never had much chance to learn. My mother never had enough money to get one. You know that joke: we can't afford a Ford."

"Oh, well," I said, "in Philadelphia you don't need one. They're a nuisance in the city."

"All the same I'd like to have one. I guess I'll have to when I start practicing. Well, where to first?" We outlined a schedule, and for the next couple of days we were on the go almost continually. We hardly noticed how the character of the region was changed. There was little traffic in the streets, but the few cars tore madly. Most of them were Cadillacs: black, company-owned Cadillacs which were at the disposal of young men like Doctor Myers and the two drunken Gibbsville doctors who did not own cars; and gray Cadillacs from the U.S.A.A.C. base in Allentown, which took officers of the Army Medical Corps around to the emergency hospitals. At night the officers would use the cars for their fun, and there were a few scandals. One of my friends, a Boy Scout who was acting as errand boy—"courier," he called himself—at one of the hospitals, swore he witnessed an entire assignation between an Army major and a local girl who was a clerk in the hospital office. One officer was rumored to be psychopathic and had to be sent elsewhere. Opinion among us boys was divided: some said he was taken away and shot, some said he was sent to Leavenworth, others said he was dishonorably discharged. The ambulances were being driven by members of the militia, who wore uniforms resembling those of the marine corps. The militia was made up of young men who were exempt from active service. They had to make one ambulance driver give up his job, because he would drive as fast as the ambulance would go even when he was only going to a drugstore for a carton of soap. Another volunteer driver made so much noise with the ambulance bell that the sick persons inside would be worse off than if they had walked. The women of wealth who could drive their own cars drove them, fetching and carrying blankets and cots, towels and cotton, but their husbands made some of the women stop because of the dangers of influenza and Army medical officers. Mrs. Barlow, the leader of society, did not stop, and her husband knew better than to try to insist. She was charming and stylish and looked very English in her Red Cross canteen division uniform. She assumed charge of the emergency hospital in the armory and bossed the Catholic sisters and the graduate nurses around and made them like it. Her husband gave money and continued to ride a sorrel hunter about the countryside. The rector of the Second Presbyterian Church appeared before the Board of Health and demanded that the nuns be taken out of the hospitals on the ground that they were baptizing men and women who were about to die, without ascertaining whether they were Catholics or Protestants. The *Standard* had a story on the front page which accused unnamed undertakers of profiteering on "rough boxes," charging as much for

pine board boxes as they had for mahogany caskets before the epidemic.

Doctor Myers at first wore a mask over his nose and mouth when
making calls, and so did I, but the gauze stuck to my lips and I
stopped wearing it and so did the doctor. It was too much of a nuisance to put them on and take them off every time we would go to
a place like Kelly's, and also it was rather insulting to walk in on a
group of people with a mask on your face when nobody in the
group was wearing one. I was very healthy and was always glad to
go in with the doctor because it gave me something to do. Of
course I could have cleaned spark plugs or shot some air into the
tires while waiting for the doctor, but I hated to monkey around the
car almost as much as I liked to drive it.

In a few days Doctor Myers had begun to acquire some standing
among the patients, and he became more confident. One time after
coming from my father's bedroom he got in the car with some prescriptions and we started out. To himself he said, looking up from
a prescription: "Digitalis . . . now I wonder?" I turned suddenly, because it was the first time in my life I had heard anyone criticize a
prescription of my father's. "Oh, I'm sorry, Jimmy," he said.

"You better not ever let him hear you say anything about his prescriptions."

"Yes, I know. He doesn't want anyone to argue with him. He
doesn't think I'm seeing as many people as I should."

"What does he expect?" I said.

"Oh, he isn't unreasonable, but he doesn't want his patients to
think he's neglecting them. By the way, he wants us to stop in at the
Evanses in Collieryville. The David Evanses. Mrs. Evans phoned
and said their maid is sick."

"That's O.K. with me," I said.

"I thought it would be," he said.

Collieryville seemed strange with the streets so deserted as on
some new kind of holiday. The mines did not work on holy days of
obligation, and the miners would get dressed and stand around in

front of poolrooms and saloons, but now they were not standing around, and there was none of the activity of a working day, when coal wagons and trucks rumble through the town, and ten-horse teams, guided by the shouted "gee" and "haw" of the driver, would pull loads of timber through the streets on the way to the mines. Collieryville, a town of about four thousand persons, was quiet as though the people were afraid to come out in the cold November gray.

We were driving along the main street when I saw Edith. She was coming out of the P.O.S. of A. Hall, which was a poolroom on the first floor and had lodge rooms on the two upper stories. It was being used as an emergency hospital. I pulled up at the curb and called to Edith. "Come on, I'll give you a ride home," I said.

"Can't. I have to get some things at the drugstore," she said.

"Well, we're going to your house anyway. I'll see you there," I said.

We drove to the Evans house and I told the doctor I would wait outside until Edith came. She appeared in about five minutes and I told her to sit in the car and talk to me. She said she would.

"Well, I'm a nurse, Jimmy," she said.

"Yes, you are," I said scornfully. "That's probably how your maid got sick."

"What!"

"Why, you hanging around at the P.O.S. of A. Hall is probably the way your maid got sick. You probably brought home the flu—"

"Oh, my God!" she said. She was nervous and pale. She suddenly jumped out of the car and I followed her. She swung open the front door and ran toward the kitchen, and I was glad she did; for although I followed her to the kitchen, I caught a glimpse of Mrs. Evans and Doctor Myers in Mr. Evans' den. Through the half-closed doors I could see they were kissing.

I didn't stop, I know, although I felt that I had slowed up. I followed Edith into the kitchen and saw that she was half crying, shaking her hands up and down. I couldn't tell whether she had seen what I had seen, but something was wrong that she knew about. I blurted out, "Don't go in your father's den," and was immediately sorry I had said it; but then I saw that she had guessed. She looked weak and took hold of my arms; not looking at me, not even speaking to me, she said: "Oh, my God, now it's him. Oh, why didn't I come home with you? Sarah isn't sick at all. That was just an excuse to get that Myers to come here." She bit her lip and squeezed my arms. "Jimmy, you mustn't ever let on. Promise me."

"I give you my word of honor," I said. "God can strike me dead if I ever say anything."

Edith kissed me, then she called out: "Hey, where is everybody?" She whispered to me: "Pretend you're chasing me like as if I pulled your necktie."

"Let go!" I yelled, as loud as I could. Then we left the kitchen, and Edith would pull my necktie at every step.

Mrs. Evans came out of the den. "Here, what's going on here?"

"I'm after your daughter for pulling my tie," I said.

"Now, Edith, be a good girl and don't fight with James. I don't understand what's the matter with you two. You usedn't to ever fight, and now you fight like cats and dogs. You oughtn't to. It's not nice."

"Oh—" Edith said, and then she burst into tears and went upstairs.

I was genuinely surprised, and said: "I'm sorry, Mrs. Evans, we were only fooling."

"Oh, it's not your fault, James. She feels nervous anyhow and I guess the running was too much for her." She looked at the doctor as if to imply that it was something he would understand.

"I guess I'll go out and sit in the car," I said.

"I'll be right out," said the doctor.

I sat in the car and smoked, now and then looking at the second floor window where I knew Edith's room was, but Edith did not come to the window and in about twenty minutes the doctor came out.

"The maid wasn't sick after all," he said. "It was Mrs. Evans. She had a slight cold but she didn't want to worry your father. I guess she thought if she said she was sick, your father'd come out himself."

"Uh-huh," I said. "Where to now?"

"Oh, that Polish saloon out near the big coal banks."

"You mean Wisniewski's," I said.

———

Doctor Myers must have known I suspected him, and he might even have suspected that I had seen him kissing Mrs. Evans. I was not very good at hiding my likes and dislikes, and I began to dislike him, but I tried not to show it. I didn't care, for he might have told my father I was unsatisfactory, and my father would have given me hell. Or if I had told my father what I'd seen, he'd have given Doctor Myers a terrible beating. My father never drank or smoked, and he was a good, savage amateur boxer, with no scruples against punching anyone smaller than himself. Less than a year before all this took place my father had been stopped by a traffic policeman while he was hurrying to an "OBS." The policeman knew my father's car, and could have guessed why he was in a hurry, but he stopped him. My father got out of the car, walked to the front of it, and in the middle of a fairly busy intersection he took a crack at the policeman and broke his jaw. Then he got back and drove around the unconscious policeman and on to the confinement case. It cost my father nearly a thousand dollars, and the policeman's friends and my father's enemies said: "God damn Mike Malloy, he ought to be put in jail." But my father was a staunch Republican and he got away with it.

I thought of this now and I thought of what my father would have done to Doctor Myers if he found out. Not only would he have beaten him up, but I am sure he would have used his influence at the University to keep Myers from getting his degree.

So I hid, as well as I could, my dislike for Doctor Myers, and the next day, when we stopped at my home, I was glad I did. My father had invented a signal system to save time. Whenever there was a white slip stuck in the window at home or at the office, that meant he was to stop and pick up a message. This day the message in the window read: "Mrs. David Evans, Collieryville."

Doctor Myers looked at it and showed it to me. "Well, on to Collieryville," he said.

"O.K., but would you mind waiting a second? I want to see my mother."

He was slightly suspicious. "You don't need any money, do you? I have some."

"No, I just wanted to see if she would get my father to let me have the car tonight." So I went in and telephoned to the Evanses. I got Edith on the phone and told her that her mother had sent for Doctor Myers.

"I know," she said. "I knew she would. She didn't get up this morning, and she's faking sick."

"Well, when we get there you go upstairs with the doctor, and if he wants you to leave the bedroom, you'll have to leave, but tell your mother you'll be right outside, see?"

"O.K.," said Edith.

I returned to the car. "How'd you make out?" said Doctor Myers.

"She thinks she can get him to let me have it," I said, meaning that my father would let me have the car.

When we arrived at the Evans house I had an inspiration. I didn't want him to suspect that we had any plan in regard to him, so I told him I was going in with him to apologize to Edith for our fight of the day before. There was the chance that Edith would fail to follow my advice and would come downstairs, but there was the equally good chance that she would stay upstairs.

The plan worked. In some respects Edith was dumb, but not in this. Doctor Myers stayed upstairs scarcely five minutes, but it was another five before Edith came down. Doctor Myers had gone out to wait in the Ford.

Edith appeared. "Oh, Jimmy, you're so nice to me, and I'm often mean to you. Why is that?"

"Because I love you." I kissed her and she kissed me.

"Listen, if my dad ever finds this out he'll kill her. It's funny, you and me. I mean if you ever told me a dirty story, like about you know—people—"

"I did once."

"Did you? I mustn't have been listening. Anyhow it's funny to think of you and me, and I'm older than you, but we know something that fellows and girls our age, they only guess at."

"Oh, I've known about it a long time, ever since I went to sisters' school."

"And I guess from your father's doctor books. But this isn't the same when it's your own mother, and I bet this isn't the first time. My dad must have suspicions, because why didn't he send me away to boarding school this year? I graduated from high last year. I bet he wanted me to be here to keep an eye on her."

"Who was the other man?"

"Oh, I can't tell you. Nobody you know. Anyhow, I'm not sure, so I wouldn't tell you. Listen, Jimmy, promise to telephone me every time before he comes here. If I'm not here I'll be at the Bordelmans' or at the Haltensteins', or if not there, the Callaways'. I'll stay home as much as I can, though. How long is he going to be around here, that doctor?"

"Lord knows," I said.

"Oh, I hope he goes. Now give me a good-bye kiss, Jimmy, and then you have to go." I kissed her. "I'm worse than she is," she said.

"No, you're not," I said. "You're the most darling girl there is. Good-bye, Ede," I said.

Doctor Myers was rubbing the skin in front of his ear when I came out. "Well, did you kiss and make up?"

"Oh, we don't go in for that mushy stuff," I said.

"Well, you will," he said. "Well . . . on to Wizziski's."

"It's a good thing you're not going to be around here long," I said.

"Why? Why do you say that?"

"Because you couldn't be in business or practice medicine without learning Hunkie names. If you stayed around here you'd have to be able to pronounce them and spell them." I started the car. I was glad to talk. "But I tell you where you'd have trouble. That's in the patches where they're all Irish with twenty or thirty cousins living in the same patch and all with the same name."

"Oh, come on."

"Well, it isn't as bad as it used to be," I said. "But my father told me about one time he went to Mass at Forganville, about fifteen miles from here, where they used to be all Irish. Now it's half Polack. Anyhow my father said the priest read the list of those that gave to the monthly collection, and the list was like this: John J. Coyle, $5; Jack Coyle, $2; Johnny Coyle, $2; J. J. Coyle, $5; Big John Coyle, $5; Mrs. John Coyle the saloonkeeper's widow, $10; the Widow Coyle, $2. And then a lot of other Coyles."

He did not quite believe this, but he thought it was a good story, and we talked about college—my father had told me I could go to Oxford or Trinity College, Dublin, if I promised to study medicine— until we reached Wisniewski's.

This was a saloon in a newer patch than Kelly's. It was entirely surrounded by mine shafts and breakers and railroads and mule yards, a flat area broken only by culm banks until half a mile away there was a steep, partly wooded hill which was not safe to walk on because it was all undermined and cave-ins occurred so frequently that they did not bother to build fences around them. The houses were the same height as in Kelly's patch, but they were built in blocks of four and six houses each. Technically Wisniewski's saloon was not in the patch; that is, it was not on company ground, but at a crossroad at one end of the rows of houses. It was an old stone house which had been a tavern in the days of the King's Highway. Now it was a beery-smelling place with a tall bar and no tables or chairs. It was crowded, but still it had a deserted appearance. The reason was that there was no one behind the bar, and no cigars or cartons of chewing tobacco on the back bar. The only decorations were a calendar from which the October leaf had not been torn, depicting a voluptuous woman stretched out on a divan, and an Old Overholt sign, hanging askew on the toilet door.

The men and women recognized Doctor Myers and me, and made a lane for us to pass through. Wisniewski himself was sick in bed, and everybody understood that the doctor would see him first, before prescribing for the mob in the barroom.

Doctor Myers and I went to Wisniewski's room, which was on the first floor. Wisniewski was an affable man, between forty and fifty, with a Teutonic haircut that never needed brushing. His body under the covers made big lumps. He was shaking hands with another Polack whose name was Stiney. He said to us: "Oh, hyuh, Cheem, hyuh, Cheem. Hyuh, Doc."

"Hyuh, Steve," I said. "Yoksheemosh?"

"Oh, fine dandy. How's yaself? How's Poppa? You tell Poppa what he needs is lay off this here booze." He roared at this joke. "Ya, you tell him I said so, lay off this booze." He looked around at the others in the room, and they all laughed, because my father used to pretend that he was going to have Steve's saloon closed by the County. "You wanna drink, Cheem?" he asked, and reached under the bed and pulled out a bottle. I reached for it, and he pulled the bottle away. "Na na na na na. Poppa close up my place wit' the County, I give you a drink. Ya know, miners drink here, but no minors under eighteen, hey?" He passed the bottle around, and all the other men in the room took swigs.

Doctor Myers was horrified. "You oughtn't to do that. You'll give the others the flu."

"Too late now, Doc," he said. "T'ree bottle now already."

"You'll lose all your customers, Steve," I said.

"How ya figure dat out?" said Steve. "Dis flu make me die, dis bottle make dem die. Fwit! Me and my customers all together in hell, so I open a place in hell. Fwit!"

"Well, anyhow, how are you feeling?" said the doctor. He placed a thermometer under Steve's arm. The others and Steve were silent until the temperature had been taken. "Hm," said Doctor Myers. He frowned at the thermometer.

"'M gonna die, huh, Doc?" said Steve.

"Well, maybe not, but you—" he stopped talking. The door opened and there was a blast of sweaty air from the barroom, and Mr. Evans stood in the doorway, his hand on the knob. I felt weak.

"Doctor Myers, I'd like to see you a minute please," said Mr. Evans.

"Hyuh, Meester Ivvins," called Steve. Evans is one name which is consistently pronounced the same by the Irish, Slavs, Germans, and even the Portuguese and Negroes in the anthracite.

"Hello, Steve, I see you're drunk," said Mr. Evans.

"Not yet, Meester Ivvins. Wanna drink?"

"No, thanks. Doctor, will you step outside with me?"

Doctor Myers stalled. "I haven't prescribed for this man, Mr. Evans. If you'll wait?"

"My God, man! I can't wait. It's about my wife. I want to know about her."

"What about her?" asked the doctor.

"For God's sake," cried Mr. Evans. "She's sick, isn't she? Aren't you attending her, or don't you remember your patients?"

I sighed, and Doctor Myers sighed louder. "Oh," he said. "You certainly—frightened me, Mr. Evans. I was afraid something had happened. Why, you have no need to worry, sir. She has hardly any temperature. A very slight cold, and she did just the sensible thing by going to bed. Probably be up in a day or two."

"Well, why didn't you say so?" Mr. Evans sat down. "Go ahead, then, finish with Steve. I'll wait till you get through. I'm sorry if I seemed rude, but I was worried. You see I just heard from my timber boss that he saw Doctor Malloy's car in front of my house, and I called up and found out that Mrs. Evans was sick in bed, and my daughter sounded so excited I thought it must be serious. I'll take a drink now, Steve."

"Better not drink out of that bottle, Mr. Evans," said the doctor, who was sitting on the edge of the bed, writing a prescription.

"Oh, hell, it won't hurt me. So anyhow, where was I? Oh, yes. Well, I went home and found Mrs. Evans in bed and she seemed very pale, so I wanted to be sure it wasn't flu. I found out you were headed this way so I came right out to ask you if you wouldn't come back and take another look. That's good liquor, Steve. I'll buy a case of that." He raised the bottle to his lips again.

"I give you a case, Meester Ivvins. Glad to give you a case any time," said Steve.

"All right, we'll call it a Christmas present," said Mr. Evans. "Thanks very much." He was sweating, and he opened his raccoon coat. He took another drink, then he handed the bottle to Stiney. "Well, James, I hear you and Edith were at it again."

"Oh, it was just in fun. You know. Pulling my tie," I said.

"Well, don't let her get fresh with you," he said. "You have to keep these women in their place." He punched me playfully. "Doctor, I wonder if you could come to the house now and make sure everything's all right."

"I would gladly, Mr. Evans, but there's all that crowd in the barroom, and frankly, Mrs. Evans isn't what you'd call a sick woman, so my duty as a—physician is right here. I'll be only too glad to come if you'd like to wait."

The Hunkies, hearing the Super talked to in this manner, probably expected Meester Ivvins to get up and belt the doctor across the face, but he only said: "Well, if you're sure an hour couldn't make any difference."

"Couldn't possibly, Mr. Evans," said Doctor Myers.

He finished with Steve and told him to stop drinking and take his medicine, then he turned to leave. Steve reached under the pillow and drew out a bundle of money. He peeled off a fifty-dollar bill and handed it to the doctor.

"Oh, no, thanks," said Doctor Myers. "Doctor Malloy will send you a bill."

"Aw, don't worry about him, eh, Cheem? I always pay him firs' the mont', eh, Cheem? Naw, Doc, dis for you. Go have a good time. Get twenty-five woman, maybe get drunk wit' boilo." I could imagine Doctor Myers drinking boilo, which is hot moonshine. I nudged him, and he took the money and we went to the barroom.

I carried the chair and table and set them in place, and the Hunkies lined up docilely. Mr. Evans waited in Steve's room, taking a swig out of the bottle now and then until Doctor Myers had finished with the crowd. It was the same as usual. It was impractical to get detailed descriptions from each patient, so the flu doctor would ask each person three or four questions and then pretend to prescribe for each case individually. Actually they gave the same prescription to almost all of the patients, not only to save time, but because drug supplies in the village and city pharmacies were inadequate, and it was physically impossible for druggists to meet the demand. They would make up large batches of each doctor's standard prescription and dole out boxes and bottles as the patrons presented the prescriptions.

It took about two hours to dispose of the crowd at Steve's. Mr. Evans told Doctor Myers to come in the Cadillac because it was faster than the Ford—which I denied. I followed in the Ford and got to the Evans house about three minutes after the Cadillac. Edith met me at the door. "Oh, what a scare!" she said.

"If you think you were scared, what about me?" I said. I told her how I had felt when her father appeared at Steve's.

"Your father phoned and wants you to take that Myers home," she said, when I had finished.

"Did he say why?" I asked.

"No, he just said you weren't to make any more calls this afternoon."

"I wonder why."

"I hope it hasn't anything to do with him and my mother," she said.

"How could it? Only four people know about it. He couldn't guess it, and nobody would tell him. Maybe he's got up and wants me to drive for him."

"Maybe . . . I can't think. I'm afraid of them up there. Oh, I hope he goes away." I kissed her, and she pushed me away. "You're a bad actor, James Malloy. You're bad enough now, but wait till you grow up."

"What do you mean grow up? I'm almost six feet."

"But you're only a kid. I'm seventeen, and you're only fifteen."

"I'll be in my seventeenth year soon." We heard footsteps on the stairs, and Doctor Myers' voice: ". . . absolutely nothing to worry about. I'll come in again tomorrow. Good-bye, Mr. Evans. Good-bye, Edith. Ready, Jim?"

I gave him my father's message and we drove home fast. When we got there one of the Buicks was in front of the house, and we went in the living room.

"Well, Doctor Myers," my father said. "Back in harness again. Fit as a fiddle, and I want to thank you for the splendid attention you've given my practice. I don't know what my patients would have done without you."

"Oh, it's been a privilege, Doctor. I'd like to be able to tell you how much I've appreciated working for you. I wouldn't have missed it for the world. I think I'd like to serve my interneship in a place like this."

"Well, I'm glad to hear it. I'm chief of staff at our hospital, and I'm sorry I can't offer you anything here, but you ought to try some place like Scranton General. Get the benefit of these mining cases. God-damn interesting fractures, by the way. I trephined a man, forty-eight years old—all right, James, I'll call you when I need you." I left the room and they talked for half an hour, and then my father called me. "Doctor Myers wants to say good-bye."

"I couldn't leave without saying good-bye to my partner," said the doctor. "And by the way, Doctor Malloy, I think I ought to give part of this cheque to James. He did half the work."

"If he did I'll see that he gets his share. James knows that. He wants one of these God-damn raccoon coats. When I was a boy the only people that wore them drove hearses. Well—" My father indicated that it was time for the doctor and me to shake hands.

"Quite a grip James has," said the doctor.

"Perfect hands for a surgeon. Wasted, though," my father said. "Probably send him to some God-damn agricultural school and make a farmer out of him. I want him to go to Dublin, then Vienna. That's where the surgeons are. Dublin and Vienna. Well, if you ever meet Doctor Deaver tell him I won't be able to come down for the Wednesday clinics till this damn thing is over. Good luck, Doctor."

"Thank you, many thanks, Doctor Malloy."

"James will drive you to the hotel."

I took him to the hotel and we shook hands. "If you ever want a place to stay in Philadelphia you're always welcome at my house." He gave me the address of a fraternity house. "Say good-bye to the Evanses for me, will you, Jim?"

"Sure," I said, and left.

My father was standing on the porch, waiting impatiently. "We'll use the Buick," he said. "That Ford probably isn't worth the powder to blow it to hell after you've been using it. Do you really want one of those livery stable coats?"

"Sure I do."

"All right. Now, ah, drive to Kelly's." We drove to Kelly's, where there was an ovation, not too loud, because there were one or two in the crowd on whom my father was liable to turn and say: "You, ya son of a bitch, you haven't paid me a cent since last February. What are you cheering for?" We paid a few personal visits in the patch. At one of them my father slapped a pretty Irish girl's bottom; at another he gave a little boy a dollar and told him to stop picking his nose; at another he sent me for the priest, and when I came back he had gone on foot to two other houses, and was waiting for me at the second. "What the hell kept you? Go to Terry Loughran's, unless the skunk got another doctor."

"He probably did," I said jovially. "He probably got Lucas."

"*Doctor* Lucas. Doctor Lucashinsky. Ivan the Terrible. Well, if he got Lucas it serves him right. Go to Haltenstein's."

We drove until one o'clock the next morning, taking coffee now and then, and once we stopped for a fried-egg sandwich. Twice I very nearly fell asleep while driving. The second time I awoke to hear my father saying: "... And my God! To think that a son of mine would rather rot in a dirty stinking newspaper office than do this. Why, I do more good and make more money in twenty minutes in the operating room than you'll be able to make the first three years you're out of college. If you go to college. Don't drive so fast!"

It was like this for the next two days. I slept when he allowed me to. We were out late at night and out again early in the morning. We drove fast, and a couple of times I bounded along corduroy roads with tanks of oxygen (my father was one of the first, if not the first, to use oxygen in pneumonia) ready to blow me to hell. I developed a fine cigarette cough, but my father kept quiet about it, because I was not taking quinine, and he was. We got on each other's nerves and had one terrible scene. He became angered by my driving and punched me on the shoulder. I stopped the car and took a tire iron from the floor of the car.

"Now just try that again," I said.

He did not move from the back seat. "Get back in this car." And I got back. But that night we got home fairly early and the next morning, when he had to go out at four o'clock, he drove the car himself and let me sleep. I was beginning to miss Doctor Myers. It was about eight o'clock when I came down for breakfast, and I saw my father sitting in the living room, looking very tired, staring straight ahead, his arms lying on the arms of the chair. I said hello, but he did not answer.

My mother brought me my breakfast. "Did you speak to your father?"

"Oh, I said hello, but he's in a stupor or something. I'm getting sick of all this."

"Hold your tongue. Your father has good reason to be unhappy this morning. He just lost one of the dearest friends he had in the world. Mr. Evans."

"Mr. Evans!" I said. "When'd he die?"

"At about four o'clock this morning. They called your father but he died before he got there. Poor Mrs. Evans—"

"What he die of? The flu?"

"Yes." I thought of the bottle that he had shared with Steve and the other Hunkies, and Mrs. Evans' illness, and Doctor Myers. It was all mixed up in my mind. "Now you be careful how you behave with your father today," my mother said.

I called up Edith, but she would not come to the phone. I wrote her a note, and drove to Collieryville with some flowers, but she would not see me.

Even after the epidemic died down and the schools were re-opened she would not see me. Then she went away to school and did not come home for the Easter holidays, and in May or June I fell in love with another girl and was surprised, but only surprised, when Edith eloped. Now I never can remember her married name.

Hotel Kid

My first encounter with Raymond was about a week after I had arrived in the strange city. I was going down in the elevator, thinking about death and love, when I felt my insides being pulled out as the car stopped at the eighth floor. The elevator operator pulled the door open, and a boy of seven or eight stood in the doorway and said: "Hey, Max, did you see my brother?"

"No," said the operator.

The boy stared at the floor, meditating, and then he said: "All right, Max. You can go. If you see him tell him I'm waitin' for him."

The operator closed the door and we dropped slowly, the more slowly so he could turn and explain to me that "That's Raymond. If you're gonna be here awhile you'll get to know him all right. He's the craziest kid!"

"Yeah?" I said. "Who is he?"

"Kid by the name of Raymond Miller. He lives here in the hotel. He's a little pest, and for a while there we use'n't to stop at the eighth floor sometimes, because we knew it was Raymond, but Joe, one of the other operators, got in Dutch, so we have to stop now, irregardless of whether we know it's Raymond or not."

I saw Raymond for the second time under somewhat similar circumstances. This time he stopped the elevator and asked for his brother, and then told Harry, the operator, that he could continue. "Is that kid always looking for his brother?" I said.

The operator laughed. "He ain't got a brother," said Harry. "That's a gag. You know. Like Gracie Allen on the radio, she's always talking about her lost brother, and this kid picked it up somewheres, I guess."

A few days later the elevator again stopped at the eighth floor, and this time a beautiful Jewess, about thirty years old, got on, and Max said: "Good morning, Mrs. Miller."

"Hello, Max," she said. The car began the descent. "Was Raymond pestering you again, or was it one of the other boys?" she said.

"It wasn't me," said Max. "I guess it must of been one of the others. Why?"

"Well, he was swearing at you this morning. Not you personally, but just the whole damn bunch of elevator boys, as he said. So naturally I thought he must have got a little too fresh and somebody gave him a talking to. Don't hesitate to when he gets too fresh, and especially if he wants to go down to the lobby. I won't have him hanging around down there. He has plenty of room to play . . ."

Late that same afternoon I had a date to meet someone in the lobby, and I was very early, so I was reading a paper, when I looked up, and there was Raymond, standing in front of me, apparently undecided between speaking to me and, I suspect, punching my paper.

"Hello, there," I said.

"Hello, Mr. Kelly," he said, and smiled very broadly.

I knew what was expected of me, so I said: "How'd you know my name?"

"Asked," he said. "Asked Miss McNulty. She's the room clerk Miss McNulty. The one over there." He pointed, and I looked over, and saw that Miss McNulty was looking our way and laughing. Raymond nodded at Miss McNulty, and then said to me: "Do you like this hotel?"

"Yes, it's all right," I said.

"Well, shake your head yes. Miss McNulty wants to know if you like it. She told me to ask you and if you said you did you were to shake your head yes." I thought it was strange, but I obliged with a pretty vigorous shake. Raymond smiled very broadly then and nodded again at Miss McNulty, then he looked at me and laughed, and then he ran away.

It was some time later that I discovered what it was all about: Raymond had told Miss McNulty that I wanted to kiss her, and when she wanted him to tell how he knew that, he said he'd prove it.

The next time I saw Raymond he stopped the elevator and when he saw me he started to run. "Hey, you," I said. "I want to talk to you."

He came back and got on the elevator. "My mother doesn't allow me to go down to the lobby," he said.

"That's all right," I said. "What was the idea of playing that trick on me the other day? I'm wise to you, Mr. Miller."

"Are you gonna tell my mother?"

"No," I said.

"Lemme off, Max," said Raymond. Max stopped the car at the third floor and Raymond got off.

I suppose Raymond dodged me after that, because I did not see him for a week or so, and then he came over and sat with me in the lobby. "Well," I said. "You're a stranger."

"Huh?"

"I said you're quite a stranger. Where've you been keeping yourself?"

"Upstairs. I wasn't allowed to leave the floor without permission. My mother wouldn't let me."

"Oh," I said. "What were you up to this time?"

"I didn't do anything," he said.

"Come on," I said.

"It wasn't me," he said. "It was another guy named Nathan Soskin. He comes up to play with me sometimes, and he put a pin in the elevator button and I got the blame for it. Somebody squealed and they said I did it. I get blamed for everything. He was going to turn on the fire hose if I wouldn't of stopped him."

"Well, you probably got away with a couple of things where nobody thought you did it."

"Not many," he said. "Not many. I bet if somebody did turn on the fire hose I'd be blamed."

"Well, you'd better not let any of your friends do it then."

"Oh, I don't mean Nathan or them. I mean the drunks. Were you ever here when there was a convention?"

"Yes," I said.

"Well, them. They do stuff like that. Boy! Some of the stuff they do! A man was killed here one time when I was seven. He got killed falling out the window but he was drunk."

"How do you know?"

"How do *I* know? Told. All the bellboys said so, and Max and Harry and Joe and Mr. Hurley and Mr. Dupree and Lollie, the chambermaid. They all said the man was drunk. Boy, they do crazy stuff. When we lived in Chicago they turned on the fire hose. I was only a little kid then."

"How old are you now? Eight?"

"Eight? Like fun. Nine, going on ten. You're from New York, aren't you?"

"Yes," I said.

"That's a sucker town," said Raymond. "That's what my mother said. We're going there soon, maybe next week. My mother said there isn't any big money in this town so we're going to New York. I guess I'll see you if you go back there. My mother said it was just a hick town like all the rest, but they have big money there."

"Well, I suppose that's true," I said.

"I'd like to see the New York Giants sometime," said Raymond. "A friend of my mother's took me to see them one time when they were here. Do you *know* my mother?"

"Not to speak to," I said. "We've never met."

"Oh," said Raymond. "Well, I guess I have to be going up. Mr. Hurley knows my mother to speak to. You can get him to make you acquainted. Well, so long."

"So long," I said.

THE PUBLIC CAREER OF
MR. SEYMOUR HARRISBURG

Seymour M. Harrisburg put away the breakfast dishes and took off his wife's apron and hung it in the kitchen closet. He frowned at the clock, the face of which was an imitation dinner plate, and the hands of which were a knife and fork. He tiptoed to the bedroom, put on his vest, coat and hat, and with one glance at the vast figure of his wife, he went to the door of the apartment. Opening the door he looked down and saw, lying on the floor, the half-clad body of Leatrice Devlin, the chorus girl who lived in the adjoining apartment. Thus began the public career of Seymour M. Harrisburg.

Miss Devlin was quite dead, a fact which Mr. Harrisburg determined by placing his hand above her heart. His hand roved so that no mistake was possible. The body was clad in a lacy negligee, and part of Miss Devlin's jaw had been torn away by a bullet or bullets, but she had not been disfigured beyond recognition.

Mr. Harrisburg, observing that there was some blood on his hand, wanted to run away, but it was five flights down to the street in the automatic elevator. Then his clear conscience gave him courage and he returned to his apartment and telephoned for the police. He readily agreed not to touch anything and not to leave, and sat down to smoke a cigarette. He became frightened when he thought of what was lying on the other side of the door, and in desperation he went to the bedroom and shook his wife.

"Get the hell out of here," said Mrs. Harrisburg.

"But, Ella," said Mr. Harrisburg. "The girl next door, the Devlin girl, she's been murdered."

"Get out of here, you little kike, and leave me sleep." Mrs. Harrisburg was a schicksa.

His repetition of the news finally convinced Mrs. Harrisburg, and she sat up and ordered him to fetch her bathrobe. He explained what he had come upon, and then, partly from his recollection of what he had seen, and partly from the complicated emotion which his wife's body aroused, he became ill. He was in the bathroom when the police arrived.

They questioned him at some length, frankly suspicious and openly skeptical until the officer in charge finally said: "Aw, puup, we can't get anything out of this mugg. He didn't do it anyhow." Then as an afterthought: "You sure you didn't hear anything like shots? Automobile back-firing. Nothing like that? Now think!"

"No, I swear honest to God, I didn't hear a thing."

Shortly after the officers completed the preliminary examination, the medical examiner arrived and announced that the Devlin woman had been dead at least four hours, placing her death at about three A.M.

Mr. Harrisburg was taken to the police station, and submitted to further questioning. He was permitted to telephone his place of employment, the accounting department of a cinema-producing corporation, to explain his absence. He was photographed by four casual young men from the press. At a late hour in the afternoon he was permitted to go home.

His wife, who also had been questioned by the police, had not missed the point of the early questions which had been put to Mr. Harrisburg. Obviously they had implied that there might have been a liaison between her husband and Miss Devlin. She looked at him again and again as he began to make dinner. To think that a hard-boiled man like that cop could have believed for one minute that a woman like Devlin would have anything to do with Seymour. . . . But he had thought it. Mrs. Harrisburg wondered about Seymour. She recalled that before their marriage he was one of the freshest little heels she ever had known. Could it be possible that he had not changed? "Aah, nuts," she finally said aloud. Devlin wouldn't have let him get to first base. She ate the meal in silence, and after dinner she busied herself with a bottle of gin, as was her post-prandial custom.

Mr. Harrisburg, too, had noticed the trend of the official questions, and during the preparation of the meal he gave much speculative thought to the late Miss Devlin. He wondered what would have happened if he had tried to get somewhere with her. He had seen two or three of the men she had entertained in her apartment, and he felt that he did not have to take a back seat for any of them. He deeply regretted the passing of Miss Devlin before he had had an opportunity to get around to her.

At the office next morning Mr. Harrisburg realized that the power of the press has not been exaggerated. J. M. Slotkin himself, vice president in charge of sales, spoke to Mr. Harrisburg in the elevator. "Quite a thing you had at your place yesterday," said Mr. Slotkin.

"Yes, it sure was," said Mr. Harrisburg.

Later, after he had seated himself at his desk, Mr. Harrisburg was informed that he was wanted in the office of Mr. Adams, head of the accounting department.

"Quite a thing you had at your place yesterday," said Mr. Adams.

"Yes, it sure was," said Mr. Harrisburg. "Geez, I'll never forget it, reaching down and feeling her heart not beating. Her skin was like ice. Honest, you don't know what it is to touch a woman's skin and she's dead." At Mr. Adams' request Mr. Harrisburg described in detail all that had taken place the preceding day.

"Well, you sure got in all the papers this morning, I noticed," said Mr. Adams. "Pictures in every one of them." This was inaccurate, but certainly Mr. Harrisburg's picture had been in five papers.

"Yes," said Mr. Harrisburg, not knowing whether the company applauded this type of publicity.

"Well, I guess it's only a question of time before they get the man that did it. So any time you want time off to testify, why, only say the word. I guess they'll want you down at headquarters, eh? And you'll have to appear at the trial. I'll be only too glad to let you have the time off. Just so you keep me posted," said Mr. Adams with a smile.

Throughout the day Mr. Harrisburg could not help noticing how frequently the stenographers found it necessary to go to the pencil sharpener near his desk. They had read the papers, too, and they had not missed the hints in two of the smaller-sized journals that Mr. Harrisburg knew more than he had told the police. Hardly a moment passed when Mr. Harrisburg could not have looked up from his work and caught the eye of a young woman on himself. At lunch time Mr. Harrisburg was permitted and urged to speak of his experiences. The five men with whom he lunched almost daily were respectfully attentive and curious. Mr. Harrisburg, inspired, gave many details which he had not told the police.

The only unpleasant feature of the day was his meeting with Miss Reba Gold. Miss Gold and Mr. Harrisburg for months had been meeting after business hours in a dark speakeasy near the office, and they met this day. After the drinks had been served and the waiter had departed, Mr. Harrisburg got up and moved to Miss Gold's side of the booth. He put his arm around her waist and took her chin in his hand and kissed her. She roughly moved away. "Take your hands off me," she said.

"Why, Reba, what's the matter?" said Mr. Harrisburg.

"What's the matter? You don't think I didn't get it what they said in the papers this morning. You and that Devitt or whatever her name is. Ain't I got eyes?"

"Geez, you don't mean to tell me you believe that stuff. You don't mean to tell me that?"

"I certainly do. The papers don't print stuff like that if it ain't true. You could sue them for liable if it wasn't true, and I don't hear you saying you're going to sue them."

"Aw, come on, don't be like that," said Mr. Harrisburg. He noticed that Miss Gold's heart was beating fast.

"Take your hands off me," she said. "I and you are all washed up. It's bad enough you having a wife, without you should be mixed up with a chorus girl. What am I, a dummy, I should let you get away with that?"

"Aw, don't be like that," said Mr. Harrisburg. "Let's have a drink and then go to your place."

"Not me. Now cut it out and leave me go. I and you are all washed up, see?"

Miss Gold refused to be placated, and Mr. Harrisburg permitted her, after a short struggle, to depart. When she had gone he ordered another drink and sat alone with his thoughts of Miss Devlin, with whose memory he rapidly was falling in love.

The next day he purchased a new suit of clothes. He had been considering the purchase, but it now had become too important a matter for further postponement. What with being photographed and interviewed, and the likelihood of further appearances in the press, he felt he owed it to himself to look his best. He agreed with his wife that she likewise was entitled to sartorial protection against the cruelty of the camera, and he permitted her to draw two hundred dollars out of their joint savings account.

In the week that followed, Mr. Harrisburg made several public or semi-public appearances at police headquarters and other official haunts. He was photographed each time, for the Devlin Mystery had few enough characters who could pose. The publicity increased Mr. Harrisburg's prestige at the office, Mr. Adams being especially kind and highly attentive each time Mr. Harrisburg returned to tell what line of questioning the authorities were pursuing. Miss Gold alone was not favorably impressed. She remained obdurate. But Mr. Harrisburg had found that Mr. Adams' secretary, who was blonde and a Gentile, was pleased to accompany Mr. Harrisburg to the speakeasy, and was not at all the upstage person she seemed to be in the office.

Then one day the police investigation began to have results. A Miss Curley, who had been one of the late Miss Devlin's intimates, admitted to the police that Miss Devlin had telephoned her the night of the murder. Miss Devlin had been annoyed by her former husband, one Scatelli, who had made threats against her life, according to Miss Curley. The night of the murder Miss Devlin had said over the telephone to Miss Curley: "Joe's around again, damn him, and he wants me to go back and I told him nuts. He's coming up tonight." Miss Curley explained that she had not spoken earlier in the case because Scatelli was a gangster and she was afraid of him. Scatelli was arrested in Bridgeport, Connecticut.

Mr. Harrisburg appeared before the Grand Jury, and it was after his appearance, when he was leaving the Grand Jury room with an assistant district attorney, that he first suspected that his news value had suffered as a result of Miss Curley's disclosures. For when he read the next day's newspapers he found only the barest mention of his name in one lone newspaper. Miss Curley, on the other hand, was all over the papers. Not only were there photographs of the young lady as she appeared after giving testimony, but the drama departments had resurrected several pictures which showed Miss Curley holding a piece of black velvet in front of her fair white form, and several others in which she was draped in feathers. Scatelli's rogues' gallery likenesses received some space.

The baseball season had become interesting, and Mr. Harrisburg could not help noticing that at luncheon the following day his colleagues' sole comment on the Devlin murder was that they saw where the police got that guy that did it. The remainder of the conversation was devoted to satirical remarks about the Brooklyns. In the afternoon, after hours, Mr. Harrisburg waited for Mr. Adams' secretary, but she left with Mr. Adams. Miss Gold walked past him without so much as a how-do-you-do, the little slut. Passed him up cold.

Mr. Harrisburg did not feel that this state of affairs could continue, and when the case came to trial he was smartly clad and nodded a friendly nod to the cameramen. Their faces were blank in response, but Mr. Harrisburg knew that they would come around at the proper time. However, when he gave his testimony the attorney for the defendant caused mild laughter with his tripping up Mr. Harrisburg. Mr. Harrisburg, describing the finding of the body, declared that Miss Devlin's chest was like marble, it was so cold; and that he had taken away his hand and found warm sticky blood on his fingers. The defense attorney suggested that Mr. Harrisburg was of more importance as a poet than as a witness, a suggestion with which the assistant district attorney secretly concurred. Getting down from the witness stand Mr. Harrisburg looked hesitantly at the photographers, but they did not ask him to remain.

Mr. Harrisburg's press the following morning did not total more than forty agate lines, and of pictures of him there were none. There was something wrong, surely, and he was lost in pondering this phenomenon when he was summoned to Mr. Adams' office.

"Now listen, Harrisburg," said Mr. Adams. "I think we've been pretty generous about time off, considering the depression and all that. So I just wanted to remind you, this murder case is all through as far as you're concerned, and the less we hear about it from now on, why, the better. We have to get some work done around here, and I understand the men are getting pretty tired of hearing you talk and talk and talk about this all the time. I've even had complaints from some of the stenographers, so a word to the wise."

Mr. Harrisburg was stunned. He stopped to talk to Mr. Adams' secretary, but all she had to say was: "I'm busy, Seymour. But I want to tell you this: You want to watch your step." She refused to meet him that afternoon, and by her tone she seemed to imply "any other afternoon." At luncheon Mr. Harrisburg was still so amazed that one of his colleagues said: "What's the matter, can't you talk about anything but that murder, Seymour? You ain't said a word."

Nor was there an improvement in the days that followed. Even one impertinent office boy told Mr. Harrisburg pointedly that he was glad Scatelli was going to get the chair, because he was sick of hearing about the case. Mr. Harrisburg began to feel that the whole office staff was against him, and this so upset him that he made a mistake which cost the company two thousand dollars. "I'm sorry, Harrisburg," said Mr. Adams. "I know it's tough to get another job in times like these, but you're just no good to us since that murder, so you'll have to go."

It was the next day, after he had passed the morning looking for another job, and the afternoon at a Broadway burlesque show, that Mr. Harrisburg came home and found a note tucked in his bankbook. The bankbook indicated that Mrs. Harrisburg had withdrawn all but ten dollars from their account, and the note told him that she had departed with a man whom she frequently entertained of an afternoon. "I should of done this four years ago," wrote Mrs. Harrisburg. Mr. Harrisburg went to the kitchen, and found that she had not even left him any gin.

IN THE MORNING SUN

The door between the kitchen and the dining room swung back and forth, wung-wung, wung-wung, behind Mrs. Demarest. She stopped, without seeming to stop, to straighten the centerpiece on the dining room table, and continued through the dining room to the side porch, which ran along that side of the house. Dining room and library opened onto the side porch, and the porch itself opened, through screen doors, to the garden. The porch was cool, almost as cool as the interior of the house, but she went out through the screen door to where her son was sitting under the tree.

"My, but it's going to be warm," she said. "You can tell it already."

"Mm," said Sam. He did not take his eyes off his book. Sam was very clean in a clean white shirt and white-flannel trousers. He wore no socks, and on his feet were rope-soled espadrilles, tied with strings around his ankles. Sam's face was brown, except for a small white line just in front of the ears, where he had not tanned. His ankles were white and sick, with just enough hair on the instep to make the white skin stand out. Mrs. Demarest would have known from the hair on his head that he had been reading quite a while, because he always ran his hand through his hair when he got interested in a book. Even as a boy he had done that.

Mrs. Demarest sat down and put on her spectacles. She knew she needed new ones; it took her eyes so long to get focused on newsprint. But new glasses were a nuisance. All the trouble of it, and the doctor in the village, Dr. Fleischer, would talk your head off. She would wait until she got back to New York. In the short time it took her to focus her eyes on the newsprint, she decided to suggest to Sam that he ought not to go without socks, and then she decided not to say anything. A lot of harm could be done by letting him think she coddled him; besides, it was warm, very warm. She wondered how hot it was in New York. Nobody—hardly anybody could catch cold from not wearing socks on a day like this. It was going to be a scorcher. But better than being in New York.

There was nothing on the front page to interest Mrs. Demarest, and her stocks were all right, considering. She was glad that she had enough of this world's goods. Sam, sitting across the little table from her, did not have to work. He could live forever without working. Well, forever if the country did not have a revolution and turn Communistic. Sam would not have to work so long as she had money. And that was something to be thankful for. There he was, getting better now. The doctor said he was taking on weight in a healthy way and was in the best shape he'd been in in years, literally years. He was only twenty-seven, but his health had not been good since college. And then the mess about the divorce. Not as bad a mess as some divorces, but still any divorce is a mess. You can't get around that. Mrs. Demarest wondered if Sam ever thought of Christine. Oh, he must think of her; but she wondered if Sam ever—if he still loved her. He never said so. He never spoke of her. He didn't, as a matter of fact, ever say much about anything.

She laid her paper in her lap and tried to think back over conversations she had had with Sam in the last six months. She thought a long time and she discovered that since he had come back from Albuquerque he hardly ever said anything. He would say he was going some place for dinner, or had a letter from someone in New

York, or was going to take the Ford instead of the Packard. He never talked about himself, his inner self, or of anyone or anything that concerned his inner self. He would be irritated by what he called people's stupidity, or he would praise this or that person or thing, but it never got deep. She wondered if he had any depth. Depth.

She watched him turning the page of his book, and something else struck her: she discovered that Sam was through. Oh, that was ridiculous. He was not through. He was only a young man. It would be almost three years before he was thirty, and his best years were ahead of him. But were they? Mrs. Demarest could not quite let herself say that in all honesty she believed that Sam's best years were ahead of him. The truth, she was beginning to suspect, was that Sam had lived a life.

A life lived at twenty-seven? Surely not. Yet there, sitting across the little wicker table from her, was—aside from her own relationship—a person, a citizen, a young man who had lived a life. If something happened to him—if he should die, he would die having lived a life, and who was to say it was not a complete life? He had been born, nursed, vaccinated, educated. He had fallen in love, married, been divorced, been very ill. That was enough life for anybody, more than many had. There you are, she thought, sitting in your flannel trousers and your nice white shirt, and you have been so many places—Russia, Egypt, New Mexico, California, the Panama Canal—and now you are back here with me, with no labels on you to show that you have seen so much of the world; and you are just a young man, twenty-seven years of age, who is wearing hardly any clothes and reading a book and smoking a cigarette. You have nothing on your arm or chest like a tattoo mark to show that you have been in love or that you have been married. At this moment, looking so tanned, you would have a hard time making anyone believe that you almost died six months ago. What are you? she wondered.

But she knew. He was her son, her own flesh and blood, and she loved him because he was her own flesh and blood, and also because he was anybody, because he was alive and handsome and breathing and able to spit out bits of tobacco that stuck on his lips. But she also knew that he had lived his life, enough life for anyone. He had been wild and bad, but now he was through. She knew this not sadly, but logically and sensibly. Later, she guessed, she would get this all mixed up with the mother-and-only-son feeling and she would not be able to think about it, but for the present she could think about it. She knew that Sam's life, the real living part of his life, was over, because she did not think of him as young or old or anything. If he were going to go on living a life, something inside her would have told her so and she would act differently toward him. As it was, she did not even think of him as a sick boy, someone to nurse and give your warmth to. Her instinct, she knew, was only to make him comfortable.

Ah, you, she thought. I am sturdy. And because I am sturdy I am young, so much younger than you. I am fifty years old and younger than you. I will go on and you are through. I wish it could be some other way, that you could have the years ahead, but you have no years ahead. You have lived too much, abused your body and done strange things to your mind, and done things to other people. I wonder what you did to your wife, she thought.

That was it, partly. Everyone who came in contact with him was affected by him. It never failed. People always remembered him, even people who had met him only once a long time ago. Even now he was always getting things like wedding invitations from people he had a hard time remembering. And now he was sitting in a chair, reading a book.

He looked up, resting his eyes for a minute, and he saw she was looking at him. She had to say something. "Have you any plans for today?"

"No, I guess not," he said. "I was thinking I'd play some golf, but I guess I'll wait till late this afternoon and see how the weather is."

"Too hot to play now," she said.

"Are you doing anything?" he said.

"No. Mrs. Curtis is coming over after lunch. She said something about going up to the Mountain House, but I guess I won't. Too much trouble."

"It'd be cool," he said.

"Oh, the heat doesn't bother me much. I hardly ever mind the weather one way or another. When it's cold, I'm usually bundled up, and right now the house is just about perfect." He wasn't paying much attention to her. She stood up. "I think I'll go inside."

"You just said you didn't mind the heat," he said.

"Oh, it isn't the heat," she said.

"It's the humidity?" he said.

"Oh, no," she said. She walked slowly to the side porch.

She sat on the porch and tried to figure out what suddenly had made her leave him. She had not even given any reason for leaving, and when she was walking away she had felt his eyes on her, like the feeling you have when you leave a room and know people are talking about you. Oh, she had not dared stay there with him, thinking about his life. He was keen, and she was a little afraid of him. He might have looked at her again and discovered what she was thinking about.

She crossed her legs, almost gripping the arms of the chair, and saying to herself: "My boy." But it did not thrill her to say it. It did not move her, want to make her laugh or shed a few tears, the kind you can swallow and want more of. And she did not feel the vague anger and satisfaction that you can derive from having classified a person, the superiority. She was angry with herself for saying "My boy," because it sounded insincere and sentimental. To think of Sam sitting there doing nothing made her nervous; she was hitting the heel of her right shoe on the grass mat, and her nerves were on edge. She stood up again and looked out at Sam. He was not reading, and he did not look as though he cared or knew whether there was anyone else in the world. When she first looked, he was leaning forward and his hands covered his forehead and temples and eyes, and then his head went back and his tired face faced the sky, and she could almost hear him saying: "Oh. Oh." And his mother shivered, for there was nothing she could do.

War Aims

The wardroom was quiet, next to the quietest it ever got. Radio Tokio was playing the Fred Astaire record of "Beginner's Luck." A Torpecker pilot was playing acey-deucey with the skipper of the Torpecker squadron, and about the only sound they made was when they would put a new man on the board, snapping it very deliberately on the hardwood. From the wardroom mess next door could be heard the murmurs of a bridge game—four fighter pilots who had been playing among themselves, the same four, since the carrier had left Pearl Harbor. One of the officers from Damage Control was reading *The Autobiography of Lincoln Steffens* and he had gas on his stomach. A Negro steward was pushing a long-handled dust brush across the deck, bumping the legs of the heavy chairs, which he obviously had no intention of moving. At infrequent intervals some unimportant announcement would come over the squawk box: "Now, hea' this . . ." Most officers had either hit the sack or were in their rooms writing letters. It had been a good day; three deckloads had taken off and all had returned, mission accomplished. There was the usual after-supper rumor that a Betty had turned up on the radar screen but this rumor had first made its appearance the night after the ship had left Eniwetok, and that was many, many days ago, and even if a Betty did turn up, that was another, and smaller, carrier's problem. That is to say, it was up to another carrier to take care of the Betty; it was, of course, this carrier's problem if the Betty *hit* this carrier.

Delaney, the middle-aged correspondent, came in the wardroom and searched the bookcase for a book he had been reading. The Damage Control officer made a rude noise and Delaney saw that the officer had the book, and Delaney went over to one of the davenports and sat down with Forrest, a fighter pilot. Delaney nodded and said hello, and Forrest took his cigar out of his mouth. "Hi, Mr. Delaney," he said. "Getting enough to write?"

"Oh, yes. Not so easy to get it back, though."

"I guess that is tough. How *do* you get it back?" Forrest was a friendly kid. He offered Delaney a cigar, which Delaney declined.

"Like regular mail. When a can comes alongside, we put our stuff in a special pouch, but it has to be censored at Pearl. If you write a letter, it gets to wherever you write it before our stuff gets to New York."

"You'd think they'd make some arrangements about that."

"They're always talking about it," said Delaney. "You want to play some gin?"

"Thank you, sir, but I never learned it. Only games I play are acey-deucey and, of course, poker. There's a poker game in the ready room if you'd like to play that. I didn't feel like it tonight, so I just came down here to commune with nature."

Delaney laughed. "They don't like transients in the poker game."

"Sometimes they do, if the transients are steady losers."

"Oh, sure, in that case," said Delaney.

"Sure you won't have a cigar, sir?"

"Yes, I think I'll change my mind. How about a cup of coffee? I'll get it."

"Oh, no. I'll get it."

"No, I was going to anyway. You sit still." Delaney went to the wardroom mess and brought back two cups of coffee and two pieces of rhubarb pie.

"Say, thanks. Not bad, not bad."

They ate the pie and drank the coffee in silence, and when they had finished, Delaney said, "Now I'll have that cigar you threatened me with."

"Sorry, I forgot. Here." Forrest handed Delaney the cigar, a brand that would have cost sixty cents straight at home.

"Good cigar," said Delaney.

"I guess so. I never smoked cigars before I joined the Navy. A lot of things I never did before I joined the Navy. A lot of things I do in the Navy I won't do when I get out."

"I'll bet," said Delaney.

"That's something I always wanted to ask somebody, Mr. Delaney. You were in the last war. Just how tough is it, getting readjusted and all that, when you go back to civil life?"

Delaney hesitated. "I don't think I'm the right one to ask that question, Forrest. I wasn't in the real Army. I was in a thing called the S.A.T.C."

"S.A.T.C.?"

"Students' Army Training Corps. Also known as the Saturday Afternoon Tea Club. One day I was just an ordinary student in college, the next day I was technically in the Army, getting paid, wearing a uniform. Then again, one day I was wearing a uniform, technically in the Army—next day, a student. Living on the same campus all the time. Not much of a reconversion problem there, so I don't know. You worried about it? I guess everybody is."

"Not worried, exactly. But I think about it. I wonder about it."

"Most of the fellows I knew that saw action in the last one— practically none of them would talk about it for two or three years. Quite a few of them were sore at guys that weren't in it."

"About the same now, I guess," said Forrest. He appeared to be looking into the far distance. "I'll be better off than most of these jokers. Most of them don't know a thing but how to fly an airplane.

I'm better off because I have a year of law school behind me. My old gent was a lawyer. Still is."

"You going to practice law?"

"I sure am. I have the spot all picked out—not with my old gent. It's a place where we go for the summer, in New England. It's the county seat. I have it all planned. I'll finish law school—first get married and *then* finish law school. Then I'm going to build a house. Not a summer house. I'm going to build one right in the town. Probably brick. I'll leave most of that to my wife, because she'll be the one that spends most of her time there. But I'm going to build my office to suit myself. It won't be on the main drag, but right around the corner from the courthouse. One story, see? Two rooms. One sort of outer office, reception-room kind of thing, behind a fence. I always liked those fences—you know, those fences they have in small-town lawyers' offices. Desks, chairs, tables, my diploma hanging on the wall, filing cases. All that will be in the outer office, where the public can see it. Very respectable, very official-looking. But my own office—the inner sanctum, so to speak—that's going to be completely unconventional. I'm going to have a head and a tub and a phone extension in there. And a radio. In my office I'm going to have all the junk I've collected all my life. For instance, when I was fifteen, I shot a deer. Deer head's going to be in there. Cups and stuff I won playing tennis. Pictures. All my favorite pictures. Reproductions of Grant Wood and van Gogh and some my girl painted at a place where she goes on Lake Michigan.

"Let's see what else. Oh, Christ, this is going to be the god-damnedest lawyer's office you ever saw, but anybody that doesn't like it can get another boy. I'll have a television set by that time. In my office. All the books I like. Oh, and a bar. A special closet that I'll keep my liquor in, with a Frigidaire and glasses and some ale tankards that my old man bought in England, but I can wangle them out of him. I think I may put them on a shelf on the wall of my office."

"You didn't say 'bulkhead,' " said Delaney.

"Intentionally," said Forrest. "Not that I'm going to forget all about the Navy. For instance, I imagine I'll join the Coast Guard Reserve, or whatever they call themselves. I'm going to have two boats. One about a thirty-three-footer that'll sleep four comfortably. There'll be a lot of those, good ones, after this little caper is over. Cheap, too, I'll bet. The other, I haven't made up my mind. My wife likes to sail. She's had boats all her life. I call her my wife, but you know what I mean. My future wife. A *very* elegant woman, absolutely four-O, as the Trade School boys say. Well, she can pick her own boat. I haven't made up my mind about a car. They'll be bringing out some wonderful stuff when this thing is over, so I'm not even planning about a car. I *would* like to have a motorcycle. We can get along with one car and the motorcycle, because I won't need the car much, having my office right around the corner from the courthouse, so my wife can use the car most of the time. You know McNamara, in our squadron? He comes from a little town about forty miles from this place, so I imagine we'll be seeing a lot of Mac and his wife."

"What about a plane?"

"Oh, the hell with that. Not right away, anyway." Forrest paused to relight his cigar, and as Delaney waited for him to go on, the squawk box became alive for that second before any message comes over. Then it came; they only needed to hear two notes on the bugle and they were on their feet. The acey-deucey game stopped; the Damage Control officer dropped his book; the bridge players' chairs scraped the deck.

"Taw-pedo defense, taw-pedo defense. Awl han's man yaw battle stations. Taw-pedo defense."

Forrest and Delaney looked at each other as they began to jogtrot. Forrest smiled. "You come and visit us, sir," he said, and smiled again. Then he began to run, and Delaney wearily trotted after him.

Secret Meeting

Eben Townsend was sitting on the screened-in porch smoking his after-dinner cigar when he heard the telephone ring. His wife answered it. She called to him, "For you. Joe Travers."

"Oh, hell," said Eben as he went to the phone. "What does *he* want?" He knew what Joe Travers wanted.

"Eben? . . . Joe. Not coming to the meeting?" Travers' voice was brisk.

"What meeting was that, Joe?"

"Board meeting about Doc Bushmill and you-know. Everybody here but you, Eben." Travers waited.

"Oh, yes, that's right. I'll put on a coat and be right over."

"We won't start till you get here," said Travers.

"Won't be five minutes," said Eben, and hung up. "Special School Board meeting. I forgot about it," he explained to his wife.

"*Forgot* about it. Hmph," said his wife. "I'll bet a dollar it's the secret meeting and you're trying to duck it. The one about—"

"If it's secret, *keep* it secret," said Eben. He went upstairs and changed from his bedroom slippers to shoes and put on a necktie and a tropical worsted coat. He got his straw hat from the porch table and started the short walk to the high-school building, where the Board had its meeting room.

The parked station wagons and convertibles near the movie house were more numerous than usual for so early in the season, and a lot of summer people were taking in the first show, which went on around seven. In the block ahead, a group of boys and girls—high-school students—whom Eben knew were standing in front of the drugstore, and Eben changed his course to avoid passing them. They couldn't possibly know that this was the night for the meeting, although they all surely knew a meeting was soon to be held. He turned the next corner and went down the back street to the high-school building.

As soon as he saw the building, he almost lost his temper; it looked as though half of the entire first floor was lit up. That was certainly a beautiful way to conduct a secret meeting. Someone must have turned on the lights on his way to the Board meeting room in the rear of the building and left them on. Eben went to the back door. It was open, as was the door of the meeting room.

—

The six other members of the Board were sitting around one end of the long conference table, the too-long conference table. The room was used for faculty meetings, but the table was still too long—an extravagance that Eben, as cashier of the bank, had been the first to point out. The other members exchanged hellos with Eben, and Joe Travers immediately took charge, by nodding to those on one side of the table and nodding to those on the other side, clearing his throat, and placing the tips of his fingers on the table.

"Just a minute, Joe," said Eben. "If this was supposed to be a secret meeting, I don't see why you had to advertise it, lighting up the entire building."

"You're right, Eben, but the harm's done, so we'll leave 'em on. May be a good thing after all. Cammyflodge. A lot of people most likely expect this meeting to take place in one of our private houses, if you see what I mean. Having it here with the place all lit up, a lot of people won't expect that. However . . ." He moved his mouth as though chewing something, and after the pause he began again. "There would have been a good reason to hold this particular meeting in a private house instead of school property. This is an unofficial meeting, and having it here may give it sort of the aspect of official. It is nothing of the kind. Notice I am not calling the meeting to order. Notice we are not going to have any minutes or any other regular proceedings. My gavel's in the drawer, and that's where it'll stay. In fact, I ain't even going to stand up. What I'll do, I'll try to get the discussion started, and we won't have anybody presiding. We'll keep it informal and unofficial."

"Well, let's get it started and let's get it over with," said Eben.

"Suits me right down to the ground," said Joe. "Luckily, our only lady member is a married woman and, the fact is, a grandmother, so we can speak more freely than otherwise. Mizz Drayton, Lucy, you came prepared for a frank discussion, I hope."

Lucy Drayton nodded. She was prepared, but reluctant—Eben could see that.

"We have a very nasty situation," said Joe. "I'm not going to mention any names, but I think we all know the situation. The situation is where a member of our faculty is accused of two crimes, or at least offenses. One, on Commencement Night, getting publicly intoxicated. Two, of forcing his attentions on a young female student while intoxicated and on school property. These offenses took place at the end of the school term, a little over two weeks ago, and we're not supposed to have a regular official meeting till August, but all of us received a number of anonymous letters calling our attention to the—uh—actions of this member of our faculty, and whereas anonymous letters should usually be thrown in the wastebasket, not when it's a matter of the morals of the children in our public schools. Here you have a particular kind of a situation.

"Now then. I called this informal, unofficial get-together to find out what we ought to do about the situation. Whether we ought to have a special official meeting or just go on ignoring the situation till it's called to our attention officially. Personally, what I would do with a drunken bum that goes around molesting our high-school girls, I would hand him his hat and give him a good, swift kick and see to it he never gets another job in the public-school system in the whole United States."

Joe Travers finished, and there was a long silence. The other members kept looking at Joe and he looked at each one individually, but no one accepted the implied invitation to take up where he had left off. Finally, Joe said, "Eben, what about you? I started the discussion, and we're not getting anywhere just sitting here cooped up on a pleasant summer's evening."

"Amen to that," said Eben. "Only thing I was wondering, where do we expect to get? There weren't any charges filed against the member of the faculty."

"You said yourself, Joe, anonymous letters . . ." said Mrs. Drayton.

"What do we know? What facts have we got?" said Sam Locke, the oldest member. "Oh, I *heard* things about the—gentleman being intoxicated. The rest of it, nobody said anything to me about it except the anonymous letters, which I threw away."

"Now, wait a minute," said Joe. "I'm as much against anonymous letters as anybody, only when it comes to—well, where there's smoke, there's fire."

Ed Wales, the druggist, spoke up: "It's understood this talk is all unofficial—right? Well, unofficially, I saw the party in question Commencement Night. After all the exercises were over. And unofficially I'd say he had a few too many. I took the night off, of course, but I went back to the store just when Frank, my new assistant, was locking up, and when we got through locking up, the party in question was standing out in front of my store. He was heeling and toeing, feeling pretty good, humming to himself. I said good night and he said good night, and I went home. But he wasn't *with* anybody, girl or man. I'd think if he had a . . ." He stopped and glanced embarrassedly at Mrs. Drayton.

"Go on, Ed," she said.

"Well, I don't know," said Ed.

"I know what you're thinking," said Joe. "You're thinking if he'd been molesting girls, he wouldn't be alone when you saw him. That don't follow."

"The letter I got—I only got one—" said John Eltringham, the Chevrolet dealer, "the funny business was supposed to be in a car parked somewheres near here. Well, sir, there wasn't a hell of a lot of chance—pardon me, Lucy—but there wasn't much chance for any funny business with both cops riding around seeing nothing was stolen out of the cars. Another thing I'd like to know, not because this faculty member bought a car from me, but why didn't the girl let out a yell? You could hear a good yell from one end of the village to the other. I know you could when I was a young fellow."

"Maybe nowadays the young girls don't yell," said Sam Locke. Everybody laughed but Joe Travers.

"That's right," said Eben. "They save their yelling till they have a couple of days to think it over."

"And then write anonymous letters," said Ed Wales.

"Yeah," said John Eltringham, "or else maybe she didn't yell because she thought it was somebody else."

"There's a lady present," said Joe.

"That's all right," said Mrs. Drayton. "John may be right. Why *didn't* she yell?"

"Well, I didn't think *you'd* make a joke out of it," said Joe.

"I'm not, Joe, but if she had yelled, the policemen would surely have heard her," said Mrs. Drayton. "Or somebody. And the faculty member was on the stage with us, right down in the auditorium, till the exercises were over, and then Ed saw him a little later in front of his drugstore. Mind you, I don't favor letting our faculty make overtures to the girls, but I don't know . . ."

After a long and thorough clearing of his throat, Morton Atherton, the watchmaker, spoke up: "*I* brought *my* letter with me. I bet I'm the only one."

"No, I did, too, Morton," said Joe.

"Well, let's see if yours checks with mine. I'll read it. 'Dear Sir: How much longer are you going to permit a member of the faculty to remain there if he becomes intoxicated and is a menace to the girl students by attempting to prey upon them as in an automobile on Commencement Night? He is also a disgrace to the faculty and is very inefficient as a teacher. Signed: Disgusted Taxpayer.' Yours check, Joe?"

"Yes. Word for word," said Joe.

Eben placed a hand on Mrs. Drayton's shoulder. "Now, don't you take offense at this, Lucy, but that letter sounds like a female to me."

"I think you're right," said Mrs. Drayton.

"Another hunch I have, if we want to go into this seriously, we could ask for the records and find out who he flunked among the girls. Or shall we just forget about it? How about a vote? Joe?"

Joe looked around and knew what the vote would be. "No, no vote. This is informal, unofficial."

Sam Locke stood up. "In that case, I informally and unofficially move we informally and unofficially go home. These chairs are hard sitting." The others rose.

"Right," said Ed Wales.

"Mm-hmm," said Morton Atherton.

"All the goddam foolish wastes of time," said John Eltringham.

"Well, there might of been something in it," said Joe Travers.

"Uh-huh," said Eben. "Lucy, just to be on the safe side, I think I better walk you home."

"A pleasure," said Mrs. Drayton.

OTHER WOMEN'S HOUSEHOLDS

It was Friday evening, the day the weekly paper was delivered, and Phyllis Richardson was going through it for mentions of herself. She had no trouble. On the front page she found three items of Page-One importance to the village and environs: Mrs. Valentine Richardson presided at the piano at the Eastern Star supper, which was given for the new members; Mrs. Valentine Richardson substituted for Miss Marianne Post, art instructor at the high school, during Miss Post's recent illness; Mrs. Valentine Richardson was among those present at the Norton-Williams wedding. Three items on Page One alone. Phyllis hummed as she turned to the third page. She was accompanied by the vast Cities Service Orchestra under the leadership of Paul Lavalle, since she possessed, like the modern child, the ability to concentrate while the radio was on full blast.

"Phyl, will you turn that down a little bit?"

"Hmm? What dear?"

"I'm trying to get some work done. Will you turn down the radio, not all the way, but we don't have to—"

"*I* know, *Val, dear*. We don't have to blow the side of the house out." She decreased the volume of the radio. The cabinet was closer to him than to her, but if he had turned it down to as low as he wanted it, he would not have reason to complain later, as he surely would do. She returned to her chair, the pleasure now gone from the three mentions on the front page; the pleasure of anticipation gone from the inside Personal Notes column. She sighed and lit a cigarette, humming no longer, leaving the singing to Miss Vivian della Chiesa, who was in a radio studio, appreciated, probably wearing a beautiful evening gown, earning two thousand dollars a week, soon going to a champagne supper on Park Avenue, where she would mingle with others who were famed on stage, screen, and radio.

Phyllis glanced about her, seeing nothing new, and nothing very old that she considered very good. The pictures of her class and Val's class at high school; her own class at the state teachers' college; the high-school football teams that Val had played on; the ship models that had been built by Val's great-grandfather; the brass bed warmer and candlesticks that had belonged to her own antecedents; the portrait-type photographs of her grandmother and grandfather; the small loving cups that Val had won in the 440 and 220; the furniture she had inherited, and the portable bar, resembling a barrel, which her friends and Val's had chipped together and bought for their wooden anniversary six years ago. Their last good party. She looked at Val and his fat back, hunched over his papers, with a dead cigar in his fat left hand and a thin yellow pencil in his fat right hand. That was a party, all right. At three-thirty nearly everybody had gone home but Bob and Edith Conforth, and Val and Edith went out to the kitchen to get some more ice, and when they came back, Val was wearing Edith's bra and panties and Edith was wearing Val's shorts and shirt. And Phyl and Bob stopped necking long enough to effect the same change. Only the four of them were left at the party, but Bob or Edith must have talked, or maybe it was Val, although he always denied he had. Anyhow, it got whispered around. Within a week the men who had left before three-thirty were stopping Phyllis on the street and saying, "Hey, Stingy, why didn't you ask *me* to stay the other night?" and some of the women, including two who had done some heavy necking of their own, stared at Phyllis as though she had burned down the orphanage. Val informed all who asked that the whole thing was exaggerated; he said he had put on Edith's hat and Bob had put on Phyl's hat. That was the story he had given at the bank when Ward Singer spoke to him. Phyl and Val never were sure whether Ward believed them or not. All Ward said was, "O.K., but if that story ever got to Old Lady Booth, your name is mud around here. I'd have to fire you, you know that." Yes, they knew that, all right, and it was what they had chiefly worried about. Old Lady Booth was the bank's principal stockholder. Fear of Old Lady Booth had made it certain that there had been no more parties like that one—hardly any parties at all. Six years of church suppers, ladies' auxiliaries, school activities, Val and his Scout Troop and air-raid-wardening, Phyl and her nurse's aid, Phyl and Val and their blood-doning, watching their step, saving pennies, getting no younger. She looked again at his fat back; you'd think he'd have lost some weight, all the blood he gave.

She picked up the paper again and turned to the third page and read the first item. "Huh," she said.

"What?"

"Mrs. Booth is back."

"Oh, God, yes. Good Lord!" He stood up as though his chair were electrically charged.

"What's the matter?"

"I forgot all about her," said Val. He took out his watch from one of the upper vest pockets. "I was supposed to go up and see her. Well, she usually eats pretty late."

"What do you have to see *her* about?"

"The usual stuff. Whenever she comes back from a trip, I always have to go and tell her how poor she's getting. Poor, my pratt." He started to button his vest and string the watch chain across his chest.

"I'm going with you," said Phyllis.

"No, I'll only be about a half an hour tonight. No use you driving up there twice for that short a visit. I'll just leave the car out in front of her house."

"I didn't mean that," said Phyllis. "I'm going with you and I'm going in the house with you."

"What are you talking about? You've never been in her house in your whole life."

"Well, I'm going tonight."

"You can't! What the hell's got over you all of a sudden? She won't let you in."

"Why won't she?"

"She just won't, that's all. There aren't five people in the whole township that can just drop in and pay a sociable call on that old battle-axe. When *I* go there, she doesn't even offer me a cup of coffee. You're coo-coo." He hesitated. "What do you want to go there for?"

"I want to see something. I want to find out something." She raised her voice. "I have my own reasons."

"Tell *me*. I'll find out for you. I'll introduce it in the conversation."

"I've made up my mind," she said. "You don't know where the keys of the car are."

"I'll walk," he said. He studied her. "What is it, Phyl? You're acting like a crazy woman."

"Are you going to take me?"

"Oh—all right," he said. "I don't know what I'll tell her. It's gonna be goddam embarrassing, I'll tell *you*. They'll hear about it at the bank tomorrow."

"*What* will they hear about? That you took your devoted wife with you when you called on Mrs. Booth. Is that awful? I always thought the bank—"

"All right, all right, all right," he said.

Mrs. Booth's butler was mildly astonished to see Phyllis. He had known her all her life and her father, the village veterinary, before her, but the question in his eyes was like that of a churchman seeing a staunch member of another faith going up the aisle. "Ho, good ebenin'," he said.

"Hello, Frank," said Val.

"Frank," said Phyllis.

"Yes, ma'am. You just come right in sit down. I'll tell Missus ya here." There was a cold little room on the left of the door, to which Frank led the Richardsons without seeming to lead them. He accomplished this by not turning his back on them and not letting them walk past him. He saw them seated and went out to speak to Mrs. Booth.

"That's a surprised coon," said Val.

"All right. What if he is?" said Phyllis.

"She's not gonna see you, and I don't even know what you wanted to come here for. What shall I ask her?"

"Nothing," said Phyllis.

"Don't start lighting a cigarette."

"I will if I want to."

"Where are you going to put the ashes? What about the butt?"

"I'll swallow it. Oh, all right." There were no ashtrays in the room and no fireplace or other possible place for the disposal of ashes and butt. Phyllis put her cigarettes back in her bag.

"Who?" They heard Mrs. Booth's querulous voice from somewhere deep in the house, and Val nodded at his wife, as much as to say, "You see?" They sat silent until Frank reappeared. He grinned first at Phyllis and then turned away to speak to Val. She could not tell whether Frank was being arrogant under his friendliness, or friendly and nothing more. "You come back in the libr'y?" he said to Val, plainly excluding Phyl from the summons.

They left her alone in the cold little room, a room ideally suited to its present use, which was to receive the unwelcome. The lady of the house had left nothing in the room that would have added warmth or charm or beauty to any other room in the house. The two rugs were threadbare, the warped flooring rose and sank, the chairs were plush-covered and straight-backed, and the only picture was a representation of a mess of fish spilling out of an open creel. Across and down the hall a little way Phyllis could see a living room. The sliding double doors were open, and through them she could see a grand piano, comfortable chairs, and a large, comfortable sofa in front of a large fireplace. The library probably was to the rear of the living room, according to her guess, and the dining room probably adjoined the reception room in which she now stood, wondering what to do next. She was of half a mind to go to the living room, but changed her mind. She went back to her chair, and before she could sit down, she was startled by Frank's voice.

"Brought you the New York paper," he said. "They'll be a while, I guess."

"Thanks," she said. She took the wrinkled *Sun* and sat down.

"Guess you never been here before," said Frank.

"Never inside," said Phyllis. "Of course, I used to come to the strawberry festivals."

"Oh, yes, I remember. Yes, that was a good many years ago. You was just a little girl. Yes, they was a lot of work for me, them festibles. People messin' up the lawn with papers and trash. I didn't have old Tom Zarnicki gardenin' then. Had to do it all myself. I finally said to the Missus, I said, 'Send 'em a check and be done with it and don't have 'em messin' up my lawn with their trash and papers.' Tramplin' all over my flower beds. Cigar butts. I tell you, I was glad when the Missus put a stop to all that."

"Did you tell—does Mrs. Booth know I'm here?"

"No," said Frank. "Well, maybe your husband told her. I didn't. Did you want to see her about anything special?"

"No." She knew he was lying and that he had made known her presence.

"I didn't think so, so I didn't bother tellin' her you was here."

"Here, I don't want the paper," she said.

"Go ahead and read it. It'll help you while away the time."

"I don't *want* to read it," said Phyllis.

"We're all done with it. You ain't keepin' it away from anybody." He did not put out his hand for the paper. "Maybe I *better* tell the Missus you're here, in case your husband don't. In case she come out here and find you sittin' here, she don't know you by sight. I don't *think* she does. No, I *know* she don't."

"How do you know?"

"Because I remember her tellin' me she didn't know you by sight. She said she wouldn't reccanize you if she saw you."

"When did she say that? She wasn't expecting me or anything. Why would she say she wouldn't recognize me?"

"Oh, I'm speakin' of some years ago. When all that talk was."

"*What* talk?"

"Huh?"

"*What* talk? What talk some years ago?"

"Oh, you know. Four, five years ago. I'll tell her you're here."

"Never mind," said Phyllis.

He smiled. "Oh, yes. She'd be a mighty vexed woman if I didn't. I should of told her when you came."

"Well, why didn't you, then?"

"Why didn't I? Why, because we wasn't expectin' you, that's why."

"I never heard of that before," said Phyllis. "When two people come to a house, I never heard of a butler that announced one and not the other."

"No? Well, I'll tell you why. It's because I thought she wouldn't like it. I didn't want to say anything, but you didn't have to go ahead and accuse me of being a bad butler, so I'll tell you this much, Mrs. Richardson. I didn't say anything to the Missus because I didn't think she'd like you bein' here. Ixcuse me."

He left, and she waited, hardly breathing, trying to hear what would be said, but no words came to her. Ten minutes passed and a clock struck, and ten minutes more and the silence of the house was unbroken until she heard footsteps. She opened the paper as though she had been reading it, just as Val appeared in the doorway.

"Oh, that's good," he said. "You had something to read."

"Mm-hmm." She looked up and saw he was alone.

"O.K., let's go," he said.

On their way to the car, he half turned around and then said, "Well, you find out what you wanted to know?"

"What happened to the old lady?" Phyllis demanded. "Didn't she say anything about me?"

"Just said to say good night to you."

"*How* did she say it?"

"How? What do you mean how? She said good night, and for me to say good night to you. 'Good night, and good night to your wife.' That's all. Went up to bed. Why? What was this all about? Did you see what you came to see?"

"I found out what I wanted to know," said Phyllis.

He started the car. "Women's curiosity about other women's households," he said. "What *did* you want to know?"

"Women's curiosity about other women's households," she said. It was the truth, all right, only it wasn't the whole truth. *That* she had been deprived of for six years, and she began to wonder whether she wouldn't have been better off deprived of it for the rest of her life.

Val let her out at the front of their house, and when he came from the garage, she was standing in the middle of the living room. "I'm getting awfully sick of that barrel," she said.

Val laughed. "Oh-ho. One look at Old Lady Booth's place and you start doing our joint all over."

Over the River and Through the Wood

Mr. Winfield's hat and coat and bag were in the hall of his flat, and when the man downstairs phoned to tell him the car was waiting, he was all ready. He went downstairs and said hello to Robert, the giant Negro chauffeur, and handed Robert the bag, and followed him out to the car. For the first time he knew that he and his granddaughter were not to make the trip alone, for there were two girls with Sheila, and she introduced them: "Grandfather, I'd like to have you meet my friends. This is Helen Wales, and this is Kay Farnsworth. My grandfather, Mr. Winfield." The names meant nothing to Mr. Winfield. What did mean something was that he was going to have to sit on the strapontin, or else sit outside with Robert, which was no good. Not that Robert wasn't all right, as chauffeurs go, but Robert was wearing a raccoon coat, and Mr. Winfield had no raccoon coat. So it was sit outside and freeze or sit on the little seat inside.

Apparently it made no difference to Sheila. He got inside, and when he closed the door behind him, she said, "I wonder what's keeping Robert?"

"He's strapping my bag on that thing in the back," said Mr. Winfield. Sheila obviously was not pleased by the delay, but in a minute or two they got under way, and Mr. Winfield rather admired the way Sheila carried on her conversation with her two friends and at the same time routed and rerouted Robert so that they were out of the city in no time. To Mr. Winfield it was pleasant and a little like old times to have the direction and the driving done for you. Not that he ever drove himself any more, but when he hired a car, he always had to tell the driver just where to turn and where to go straight. Sheila knew.

The girls were of an age, and the people they talked about were referred to by first names only. Ted, Bob, Gwen, Jean, Mary, Liz. Listening with some care, Mr. Winfield discovered that school acquaintances and boys whom they knew slightly were mentioned by their last names.

Sitting where he was, he could not watch the girls' faces, but he formed his opinions of the Misses Wales and Farnsworth. Miss Wales supplied every other word when Sheila was talking. She was smallest of the three girls, and the peppy kind. Miss Farnsworth looked out of the window most of the time, and said hardly anything. Mr. Winfield could see more of her face, and he found himself asking, "I wonder if that child really likes anybody." Well, that was one way to be. Make the world show *you*. You could get away with it, too, if you were as attractive as Miss Farnsworth. The miles streamed by and the weather got colder, and Mr. Winfield listened and soon understood that he was not expected to contribute to the conversation.

"We stop here," said Sheila. It was Danbury, and they came to a halt in front of the old hotel. "Wouldn't you like to stop here, Grandfather?" He understood then that his daughter had told Sheila to stop here; obediently and with no dignity he got out. When he returned to the car, the three girls were finishing their cigarettes, and as he climbed back in the car, he noticed how Miss Farnsworth had been looking at him and continued to look at him, almost as though she were making a point of not helping him—although he wanted no help. He wasn't really an *old* man, an *old* man. Sixty-five.

The interior of the car was filled with cigarette smoke, and Miss Farnsworth asked Mr. Winfield if he'd mind opening a window. He opened it. Then Sheila said one window didn't make any difference; open both windows, just long enough to let the smoke get out. "My! That air feels good," said Miss Wales. Then: "But what about you, Mr. Winfield? You're in a terrible draught there." He replied, for the first use of his voice thus far, that he did not mind. And at that moment the girls thought they saw a car belonging to a boy they knew, and they were in Sheffield, just over the Massachusetts line, before Miss Farnsworth realized that the windows were open and creating a terrible draught. She realized it when the robe slipped off her leg, and she asked Mr. Winfield if he would mind closing the window. But he was unable to get the crank started; his hands were so cold there was no strength in them. "We'll be there soon," said Sheila. Nevertheless, she closed the windows, not even acknowledging Mr. Winfield's shamed apologies.

He had to be first out of the car when they arrived at the house in Lenox, and it was then that he regretted having chosen the strapontin. He started to get out of the car, but when his feet touched the ground, the hard-packed frozen cinders of the driveway flew up at him. His knees had no strength in them, and he stayed there on the ground for a second or two, trying to smile it off. Helpful Robert—almost too helpful; Mr. Winfield wasn't that old—jumped out of the car and put his hands in Mr. Winfield's armpits. The girls were frightened, but it seemed to Mr. Winfield that they kept looking toward the library window, as though they were afraid Sheila's mother would be there and blaming them for his fall. If they only knew . . .

"You go on in, Grandfather, if you're sure you're all right," said Sheila. "I have to tell Robert about the bags."

"I'm all right," said Mr. Winfield. He went in, and hung up his coat and hat in the clothes closet under the stairs. A telephone was there, and in front of the telephone a yellow card of numbers frequently called. Mr. Winfield recognized only a few of the names, but he guessed there was an altogether different crowd of people coming up here these days. Fifteen years make a difference, even in a place like Lenox. Yes, it was fifteen years since he had been up here in the summertime. These trips, these annual trips for Thanksgiving, you couldn't tell anything about the character of the place from these trips. You never saw anybody but your own family and, like today, their guests.

He went out to the darkened hall and Ula, the maid, jumped in fright. "Ugh. Oh. It's you, Mr. Winfield. You like to scare me."

"Hello, Ula. Glad to see you're still holding the fort. Where's Mrs. Day?"

"Upstairs, I think ... Here she is now," said Ula.

His daughter came down the steps; her hand on the banister was all he could see at first. "Is that you, Father? I thought I heard the car."

"Hello, Mary," he said. At the foot of the stairs they went through the travesty of a kiss that both knew so well. He leaned forward so that his head was above her shoulder. To Ula, a good Catholic, it must have looked like the kiss of peace. *"Pax tibi,"* Mr. Winfield felt like saying, but he said, "Where have you—"

"Father! You're freezing!" Mrs. Day tried very hard to keep the vexation out of her tone.

"It was a cold ride," he said. "This time of year. We had snow flurries between Danbury and Sheffield, but the girls enjoyed it."

"You go right upstairs and have a bath, and I'll send up—what would you like? Tea? Chocolate? Coffee?"

He was amused. The obvious thing would be to offer him a drink, and it was so apparent that she was talking fast to avoid that. "I think cocoa would be fine, but you'd better have a real drink for Sheila and her friends."

"Now, why do you take that tone, Father? You could have a drink if you wanted it, but you're on the wagon, aren't you?"

"Still on it. Up there with the driver."

"Well, and besides, liquor doesn't warm you up the same way something hot does. I'll send up some chocolate. I've put you in your old room, of course. You'll have to share the bathroom with one of Sheila's friends, but that's the best I could do. Sheila wasn't even sure she was coming till the very last minute."

"I'll be all right. It sounds like—I didn't bring evening clothes."

"We're not dressing."

He went upstairs. His room, the room itself, was just about the same; but the furniture was rearranged, his favorite chair not where he liked it best, but it was a good house; you could tell it was being lived in, *this year,* today, tomorrow. Little touches, ashtrays, flowers. It seemed young and white, cool with a warm breath, comfortable— and absolutely strange to him and, more especially, he to it. What- ever of the past this house had held, it was gone now. He sat in the chair and lit a cigarette. In a wave, in a lump, in a gust, the old thoughts came to him. Most of the year they were in the back of his mind, but up here Mr. Winfield held a sort of annual review of far- off, but never-out-of-sight regrets. This house, it used to be his until Mary's husband bought it. A good price, and in 1921 he cer- tainly needed the money. He needed everything, and today he had an income from the money he got for this house, and that was about all. He remembered the day Mary's husband came to him and said, "Mr. Winfield, I hate to have to be the one to do this, but Mary— Mary doesn't—well, she thinks you weren't very nice to Mrs. Win- field. I don't know anything about it myself, of course, but that's what Mary thinks. I expected, naturally, I thought you'd come and live with us now that Mrs. Winfield has died, but—well, the point is, I know you've lost a lot of money, and also I happen to know about Mrs. Winfield's will. So I'm prepared to make you a pretty good offer, strictly legitimate based on current values, for the house in Lenox. I'll pay the delinquent taxes myself and give you a hun- dred and fifty thousand dollars for the house and grounds. That ought to be enough to pay off your debts and give you a fairly de- cent income. And, uh, I happen to have a friend who knows Mr. Harding quite well. Fact, he sees the President informally one night a week, and I know he'd be only too glad, if you were interested ..."

He remembered how that had tempted him. Harding might have fixed it so he could go to London, where Enid Walter was. But

even then it was too late. Enid had gone back to London because he
didn't have the guts to divorce his wife, and the reason he wouldn't
divorce his wife was that he wanted to "protect" Mary, and Mary's
standing, and Mary's husband's standing, and Mary's little daughter's standing; and now he was "protecting" them all over again, by
selling his house so that he would not become a family charge—
protecting the very same people from the embarrassment of a poor
relation. "You can have the house," he told Day. "It's worth that
much, but no more, and I'm grateful to you for not offering me
more. About a political job, I think I might like to go to California
this winter. I have some friends out there I haven't seen in years."
He had known that that was exactly what Mary and her husband
wanted, so he'd gone.

There was a knock on the door. It was Ula with a tray. "Why two
cups, Ula?" he said.

"Oh. Di put two cups? So I did. I'm just so used to putting two
cups." She had left the door open behind her, and as she arranged
the things on the marble-topped table he saw Sheila and the two
girls, standing and moving in the hall.

"This is your room, Farnie," said Sheila. "You're down this way,
Helen. Remember what I told you, Farnie. Come on, Helen."

"Thank you, Ula," he said. She went out and closed the door, and
he stood for a moment, contemplating the chocolate, then poured
out a cup and drank it. It made him a little thirsty, but it was good
and warming, and Mary was right; it was better than a drink. He
poured out another cup and nibbled on a biscuit. He had an idea:
Miss Farnsworth might like some. He admired that girl. She had
spunk. He bet she knew what she wanted, or seemed to, and no
matter how unimportant were the things she wanted, they were
the things she wanted, and not someone else. She could damn well
thank the Lord, too, that she was young enough to have a whack at
whatever she wanted, and not have to wait the way he had. That girl
would make up her mind about a man or a fortune or a career, and
by God she would attain whatever it was. If she found, as she surely
would find, that nothing ever was enough, she'd at least find it out

in time; and early disillusionment carried a compensatory philosophical attitude, which in a hard girl like this one would take nothing from her charm. Mr. Winfield felt her charm, and began regarding her as the most interesting person he had met in many dull years. It would be fun to talk to her, to sound her out and see how far she had progressed toward, say, ambition or disillusionment. It would be fun to do, and it would be just plain nice of him, as former master of this house, to invite her to have a cup of cocoa with him. Good cocoa.

He made his choice between going out in the hall and knocking on her door, and knocking on her door to the bathroom. He decided on the second procedure because he didn't want anyone to see him knocking on her door. So he entered the bathroom and tapped on the door that led to her room. "In a minute," he thought he heard her say. But then he knew he must have been wrong. It sounded more like "Come in." He hated people who knocked on doors and had to be told two or three times to come in, and it would make a bad impression if he started the friendship that way.

He opened the door, and immediately he saw how right he had been in thinking she had said "In a minute." For Miss Farnsworth was standing in the middle of the room, standing there all but nude. Mr. Winfield instantly knew that this was the end of any worthwhile life he had left. There was cold murder in the girl's eyes, and loathing and contempt and the promise of the thought his name forever would evoke. She spoke to him: "Get out of here, you dirty old man."

He returned to his room and his chair. Slowly he took a cigarette out of his case, and did not light it. He did everything slowly. There was all the time in the world, too much of it, for him. He knew it would be hours before he would begin to hate himself. For a while he would just sit there and plan his own terror.

I COULD HAVE HAD A YACHT

"What do you do?" I said to him. "Do you just sit around and drink coffee all night long till daylight?" He looked at me kind of funny, the most amazing look, and I thought he didn't understand me. "Is that all you do?" I said, and repeated my question, "Don't you ever do anything but sit around and drink coffee all night?" I said. I said, "I should think the waiters'd get sick and tired of looking at you, drinking coffee. What *is* it?" I said.

"Darling," he said, looking at me just as dead-pan as I don't know what. "Darling, you mustn't worry so about me," he said. Well, I told him, I said I wasn't worrying about him. God forbid. Me worry about just some ordinary piano-player? I guess he is like Terry said. He has to put everything on a personal basis, right away. There I'd only been with him, I mean been in his *company*, just that one night, and I asked him a casual question and he wants to build up a great big love affair out of it or something. At least that's the impression I gathered by his remark, otherwise why would he say like that, "Darling, don't worry so about me"? I wasn't worrying about him, I was only trying to make casual repartee so's the both of us wouldn't sit there like two mummies. I wasn't worrying about him. I wasn't even thinking about him when I said it, if he wanted to know the truth, but naturally when you're with a man like that, sitting in Dave's or any place, and he doesn't carry on a conversation, naturally you try to make conversation by finding out if you have interests in common that the two of you can talk about, because otherwise you just *sit* there and it looks terrible to see two people sitting in a restunt the man drinking one cup of coffee after the other and smoking these cigars and not saying anything. Right away he wants to put everything on a personal basis and I practically had to tell him I just wasn't innarested.

Like he said to me on the way home in the taxi. He was sitting there with the cigar in his mouth and not even condescending to hold up his end of the conversation except yes or no once in a while, and then this all of a sudden he said, "Say, Toots, you have a nice pair of gams." "Oh," I said. "I have a nice pair of gams." I said to him, "Aren't you old eagle eye, though? You been to the show three nights in succession, if one is to believe your story," I said, "and," I said, "just now you notice I have nice legs. Where were you looking if you're just finding that out?" I said. I said, "Mr. Carroll thinks so, too, and so do a lot of other people that I'd take their word for it sooner than I would yours. Where were you looking all the time?" "Not at your legs," he said.

You know I asked a lot of other musicians about him. I asked them if they knew this fellow, and they all did. As a rule I wouldn't even spit on a musician. You know what they did to a friend of mine, don't you? Priscilla Wortman. She was with a unit that played, you know, the movie houses around. Boston, Chicago, Baltimore. You know. One of those units. So Priscilla, every town she went to— first of all I ought to tell you. The show opened in Pittsburgh, the unit did, and played there a week, and Priscilla had a great big mad love affair with a trumpet-player there. But gave! Then the unit played I think Boston, and so on. Well, every town they went to, always one of the musicians would make a big play for Priscilla, and after they were on the road a month or so, Priscilla began to notice that it was always a trumpet-player that made a play for her. Always a trumpet-player. Well, so when they played Chicago they were held over a couple weeks in the same theatre, and Priscilla went out with this trumpet-player in the theatre, and she kind of fell for him, about this much. And one night he got a little drunkie and he told her plenty. He got sore at her for something and he told her plenty, right before a room full of people. Explained why trumpet-players always took her out. You know what? This guy in Pittsburgh, or wherever it was, he wrote on the music: "For a good time get the brunette third from the right in the military number." And of course every town the unit went to the trumpet-player in that town would see this note on the music, and he'd make a play for Priscilla. And by the time the unit reached Chicago the trumpet-players in all the towns had put okay and the name of the town on the music, to show that they all agreed with the original one. So when they went to Detroit and the trumpet-player there asked her to go out with him you bet Priscilla told him what she thought of him and all trumpet-players in general. If it'd of been me I'd have made them get new music, but Priscilla isn't equipped with much up here.

So ever since I heard that story I wouldn't even spit on a musician, but I had to find out about this Jack. I wanted to know if they ever heard of him, *and*, they all did. Some of them even stuck up for him. He wrote "Blue Moon." . . . No? Well, it had Blue in the title. I guess it wasn't "Blue Moon." Blue something. Who wrote the "Rhapsody in Blue"? I know it wasn't this Jack, but the one he wrote is *like* the "Rhapsody in Blue," so he must be very well known in those circles. Not that that impresses me. You have to be more than a musician to impress me. I could have had a yacht, so it takes more than a musician to impress me, but I must admit I like his attitude. He said to me the other night—oh, I see him. I see him two or three times a week. I didn't see him Tuesday of this week, so it isn't every night. But I was gunna say, the other night he said to me, "Darling," he said, "don't talk. Just don't talk," he said, "just be beautiful." And that's a nice compliment, you know. We have things in common, I can see that, but if he only wouldn't make these crypty remarks all the time.

A RESPECTABLE PLACE

Matty Wall was getting a little old, and for that reason if for no other he preferred to keep a respectable place. Promptly at eleven o'clock every night except Saturday he came from behind the bar and hung the out-of-order sign on the nickel piano and disconnected the plug. Matty did more of a beer business. Husbands, with their own wives, dropped in after the movies, especially on Thursday night. Saturday afternoon there were quite a few men getting their load on, and then the calls were for a shot of rye and water for a chaser. That was about the way it was at Matty's. He could spot a lush or a hustler a block away, and he saw to it that neither was made comfortable in his place. He didn't throw them out, because he couldn't without help, and he was alone most of the time. He just took his own good time waiting on them.

He was alone that Monday night, a dull night, and he was more or less watching the clock as he read the New Haven paper, wishing the handful of customers would go home, so he could close up. When Roy Morley came in, his heart did not exactly sink, but he didn't feel any too good about it either. Roy Morley's trips to Matty

Wall's place were infrequent, and Matty's was only a way station, one of many stops that Roy would make on such a night.

Morley was a really big man, all big and all man. He was a town boy who had played high-school football and then gone to a prep school that had a high record for good football players, who in turn did not help the school's record for sending home its boys the same pure, healthy youths they had been when they came away. Morley played football at Detroit U. for a while in the early twenties, then at Fordham and at Lafayette. He had six years of college but did not get a degree. He tried out for the Pottsville Maroons and the Frankford Yellowjackets, but the going was too tough when those teams began to have daily practice, and so Morley would play with smaller teams, arriving at the town for which he was to play on Sunday morning, getting the signals over a couple of cups of coffee at the restaurant nearest the railroad station. Along about that time he started coming home for longer and longer periods, and when people wanted to know what he was doing—friends of his father and mother—he said he was an automobile salesman. It was true that he was, on a commission basis, selling Hudson and Essex. He was also bootlegging.

Then one day Roy Morley was standing at the corner of Main and Elm. Cap, blouse, breeches, puttees, revolver, twisters, notebook, and shield. He was a cop. That, of course, was the doing of his uncle, Roy Durant, vice-chairman of the State Republican Committee. The new job naturally made some changes in Morley. He had fewer friends and he put on weight.

Occasionally, like that Monday night, he would go out and get drunk all over the town. Usually he missed Matty Wall's, but on that particular Monday night there he was, in a brown suit that was too tight for him. He did not seem to be very drunk, but Matty knew he was the kind of drunk that is the same way from the very first drink to the last. "Rye, and water for a chaser," he told Matty. Matty put the bottle up on the bar, and a pitcher of water. There it was, and so Roy did not immediately pour himself a drink. He stood with both hands pressed on the edge of the bar, and then, as though he had some pleasant surprise for Matty, he smiled and took out his revolver. He put the barrel in his mouth and pulled the trigger. Nothing, of course, happened, except that a woman in one of the booths fainted. Matty knew it for an old cop's trick. Bartenders, too, usually keep one chamber empty in their revolvers, just in case someone else grabs the gun first. When Roy pulled the trigger and Matty merely made a little face, Roy did not like it. "Oh," he said. "Wise guy. You thought it was empty. This is how empty it was." He fired five shots. Two of them ruined the mirrors on the back bar and Matty did not know what happened with the other slugs; he was on the floor, hoping and waiting. Roy called out, "Ya son of a bitch, ya," and threw the rye bottle at the rows of bottles on the back bar and went out.

Mrs. Dore, the woman who had fainted, came to when the shots went off. Her husband called across the room, "Put it on the tab, Matty, we're getting outa here."

"He won't come back here, but go ahead," said Matty. "He'll be everywhere in town but this place, but go ahead." They left, and Matty was temporarily free to look over the damage and see how much it was going to cost him. He decided that it was going to cost him enough so the Dores' tab wasn't going to help, and he tore up the tab and waited for the cops in the radio car, who were sure to come.

When they arrived, Lawrence, the one he knew, said, "We're sorry about this, Matty. We got him locked up. The Chief or somebody'll be down to see you in the morning."

The next morning it was not the Chief but Fredericks, a lieutenant, who came to see Matty. "We squared it with the papers, Matty. How much d'you think it's gunna take all told?"

"What about Johnny Dore and his wife?"

"Johnny Dore's on the city payroll. He'll keep quiet. We're loaning Morley the money out of the benevolent fund."

"O.K. I don't want to make any stink if somebody'll foot the bill for the wreckage and damage. A hundred and seventy-five dollars'll cover it."

"And call it square?"

"And call it square," said Matty.

They shook hands, Fredericks thanked Matty, and that seemed to end it. But it didn't.

When, in a couple of weeks, no cop had come in to try to sell Matty a book of tickets for the Police Benefit he thought it was just a little strange, but then he put it down to good nature. They were laying off because he had been on the square with them as regards the Roy Morley matter. The first hint Matty had of any kind of trouble was when his daughter got a parking ticket. He called up Fredericks to try and square it, but Fredericks said he couldn't do anything; a parking drive had been ordered by the Mayor, and that was that. Then Matty began to notice that every cop he knew avoided speaking to him. "A man'd think I deliberately went into police headquarters and shot up the place," Matty told his wife. The first actual act against Matty was a summons for violating a city ordinance against obstructing traffic—a beer truck unloading at his place. The same trucks had been unloading there in the same way three times a week for five years, but now all of a sudden it was a violation. Matty protested that after all the trucks did belong to the brewery, why not give the brewery the summons. "The ordinance reads either way," he was told. He paid the fine. When he spoke to the brewery salesman about it the salesman said, "So what shall I do?," and when Matty hinted that he would try another beer the salesman said, "And so what? It ain't worth our while to have a truck go out of its way to unload here. And anyway, what I hear, my guess is our boys in blue over at headquarters are about ready to put the slug on you when renewal time comes up. What the hell did you do to those coppers?"

He decided to see Fredericks. He went to headquarters and got into Fredericks' office. A civilian was sitting there, chatting with him. "Well, Wall?" said Fredericks. The words sounded funny, but Matty did not smile.

"Could I see you alone?"

"No. What do you want?"

"Well, Lieutenant, I been thinking it over and I decided to make a present to the Police Benevolent Fund. A hundred and seventy-five *dollars*?"

"What is this, a bribe? You heard him, Mr. George, in case I need a witness."

"It's no bribe, for Christ's sake," said Matty.

"I thought you were a member of the Holy Name Society. Get outa here."

Matty put on his hat and went out.

The following Saturday night all drinks were on the house. This was strictly against the law, but Matty knew he wasn't going to open up again.

A Note on the Type

The principal text of this Modern Library edition
was set in a digitized version of Janson, a typeface that
dates from about 1690 and was cut by Nicholas Kis,
a Hungarian working in Amsterdam. The original matrices have
survived and are held by the Stempel foundry in Germany.
Hermann Zapf redesigned some of the weights and sizes for
Stempel, basing his revisions on the original design.

MODERN LIBRARY IS ONLINE AT
WWW.MODERNLIBRARY.COM

MODERN LIBRARY ONLINE IS YOUR GUIDE
TO CLASSIC LITERATURE ON THE WEB

THE MODERN LIBRARY E-NEWSLETTER

Our free e-mail newsletter is sent to subscribers, and features sample chapters, interviews with and essays by our authors, upcoming books, special promotions, announcements, and news.

To subscribe to the Modern Library e-newsletter, send a blank e-mail to: **join-modernlibrary@list.randomhouse.com** or visit **www.modernlibrary.com**

THE MODERN LIBRARY WEBSITE

Check out the Modern Library website at
www.modernlibrary.com for:

- The Modern Library e-newsletter
- A list of our current and upcoming titles and series
- Reading Group Guides and exclusive author spotlights
- Special features with information on the classics and other paperback series
- Excerpts from new releases and other titles
- A list of our e-books and information on where to buy them
- The Modern Library Editorial Board's 100 Best Novels and 100 Best Nonfiction Books of the Twentieth Century written in the English language
- News and announcements

Questions? E-mail us at **modernlibrary@randomhouse.com**
For questions about examination or desk copies, please visit
the Random House Academic Resources site at
www.randomhouse.com/academic

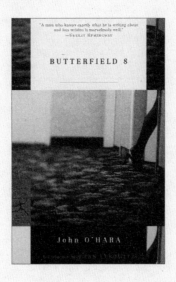